Sounds Like a Plan

Sounds Like a Plan

A NOVEL

Pamela Samuels Young &
Dwayne Alexander Smith

ATRIA PAPERBACK

New York London Toronto Sydney New Delhi

ATRIA
PAPERBACK

An Imprint of Simon & Schuster, LLC
1230 Avenue of the Americas
New York, NY 10020

First Atria Paperback edition July 2024

ATRIA PAPERBACK and colophon are trademarks of
Simon & Schuster, LLC

Simon & Schuster: Celebrating 100 Years of Publishing in 2024

For information about special discounts for bulk purchases,
please contact Simon & Schuster Special Sales at 1-866-506-1949 or
business@simonandschuster.com.

The Simon & Schuster Speakers Bureau can bring authors to your live event.
For more information or to book an event, contact the Simon & Schuster
Speakers Bureau at 1-866-248-3049 or visit our website at
www.simonspeakers.com.

Interior design by Dana Sloan

Manufactured in the United States of America

1   3   5   7   9   10   8   6   4   2

Library of Congress Cataloging-in-Publication Data has been applied for.

ISBN 978-1-6680-2429-4
ISBN 978-1-6680-2430-0 (ebook)

For Edwin Vaultz,
Who always encourages me to reach for the stars.

For Albert "Snake" Strother,
Not just a great dad, also the coolest man I ever met.

Sounds Like a Plan

Chapter 1

JACKSON

I'm not accustomed to leaving a woman unsatisfied, especially an attractive woman who'd already shown me a great deal of generosity. Still, it couldn't be helped. No matter how hard I tried, I couldn't catch Mrs. Green's cheating husband in the act.

My name is Jackson Jones. I make my living sticking my nose in other people's business. In other words, I'm a private investigator. I work out of a respectable-sized office suite twenty-seven stories above Century City. My picture-window view of Beverly Hills is pricey, but never fails to impress my well-heeled clientele.

J. Jones Investigations, Incorporated, specializes in servicing everyone from the well-off to those wealthy enough to have POTUS on speed dial. Truth be told, it's been a while since a substantial case crossed my threshold. I try to pass on the routine gigs, so I'll be available for the high-dollar cases. But if I'm going to keep the lights on, I may have to rethink that strategy.

Mrs. Allison Green, my latest client, fell squarely in the comfortably rich category. She was brunette and fortyish, but with a twentyish face and body that were miracles of modern science. She always dressed stylishly, yet strategically to display her goods.

A former wannabe actress, Mrs. Green had shelved her dreams of stardom eighteen years ago when a loaded producer slid a diamond onto her finger. Now, a mansion and a yacht later, Mrs. Green suspected said producer of stepping out on her and scheming to trade up. Shrewdly, Mrs. Green wanted to get the goods on her husband so she could, well, get her husband's goods.

It was for this reason Mrs. Green loomed over my desk, manicured hands planted on her hips, blue eyes drilling into me. She had the demeanor of a woman accustomed to getting what she wanted.

"Well?" she demanded. "Why is this taking so long?"

I ignored the heat of her stare and gestured casually to the chair facing my desk. "Mrs. Green, please. If you'd just have a seat, I can explain."

Except for the narrowing of her eyes, she did not budge. "I told you, Mr. Jones, I don't want to sit. Stop asking me to sit. I didn't come here to sit. I came to get answers."

I flashed a smile in an attempt to cool Mrs. Green down. "That's what I'm here for. To get you answers."

I'm tall. A fit thirty-five years old, and Denzel handsome—and I'm talking Denzel from back in the nineties. My smile's world-famous for its soothing effect on the fairer sex. But on this white lady hovering over me, flashing my pricey dental work evoked the opposite effect.

"Are you sure?" Mrs. Green snapped. "I've been standing in this office for five minutes and you still haven't answered a damn thing. Why is it taking you so long to get me the proof I need? You told me you'd have a photograph in two weeks at most. That was two months ago."

Knowing Mrs. Green wouldn't like what I had to tell her, I was trying to ease into it. Clearly that wasn't working.

"Okay," I said, raising my hands. "It's like this. Your husband is not a stupid man."

Her perfectly microbladed eyebrows clenched. "Excuse me?"

"I suspect he knows he's being shadowed so, of course, he's being extra careful. I must ask. Did you let anything slip about hiring a private investigator? Like maybe during an argument?"

"Mr. Jones, you're right. My husband isn't stupid. And neither am I. In fact, I'm smarter than he is. So don't insult me. Of course I didn't *let anything slip*. Maybe he spotted you following him because you're incompetent. That would explain your failure to meet your guaranteed deadline."

Although I still wore a pleasant smile, I was quickly losing my patience. I'd come to expect a certain level of superior snarkiness from these high-net-worth types, but a brother can only take so much.

Maintaining my cool, I said, "I assure you, I'm the best at what I do. Also, I never guaranteed anything. I gave you an estimate and nothing more."

"Then what's your explanation?" she said. "How does he know you're following him?"

"Like I said, he's smart. If he *is* having an affair, he's being extremely cautious. Behaving as if he's being followed. That makes my job much more difficult."

"Meaning?"

"Meaning, catching him in the act could take a few more months."

"*Months*? Not at the rates I'm paying you."

"I think my rates are more than fair."

"I want a discount."

"As I said, my rates are fair."

"You're a crook! I want my money back. Every last dime."

I shouldn't have laughed, but I couldn't help myself. I was done with Mrs. Big Mouth. I stood, forcing her to look up at me. "I'm terminating our agreement. Go find someone else to yell at. Goodbye."

For a moment she just glared, trembling, as if she were about to blow. Finally she took a deep breath and said, "You'll be hearing from my attorney."

With that, Mrs. Green was gone. The fact that she didn't slam the door told me she'd probably never call her lawyer. It's been my experience that rich folks love to brandish lawyers, but seldom pull the trigger.

I sank back into my seat feeling a twinge of regret. Customers who paid well and on time, like Mrs. Green, were hard to come by lately. On top of that there was a notice on my desk from the landlord informing me that my million-dollar view was about to get even pricier. I was seriously considering intercepting Mrs. Green at the elevator when my assistant poked her head into my office.

"Whoa," Nadine said, a smirk on her face. "Mrs. Green sure looked pissed."

"She's no longer a client. And, oh yeah, she's suing us."

"Us? I just get coffee and answer phones. Don't get it twisted."

We traded smiles.

Nadine's my cousin. She's a few years younger than me, "put-together plump" as she likes to say, and funny as hell. We were crazy close as kids, then lost touch for a bunch of years. When we reconnected as adults she was fresh out of rehab and needed a break. For years I worked without an assistant, but decided to give Nadine a shot. Now I don't know how I ever managed without her.

"Guess what." Nadine gestured to the reception area behind her. "You have a walk-in."

"Okay. Just give me a couple of minutes. I need to make a few quick calls."

"Are you sure? This is a new client. Very nice suit. Slick shoes too. Oh yeah, and a briefcase that probably costs more than my car."

I put down the phone. "Briefcase, huh?"

She nodded.

"Lawyer?"

She nodded again. "Big-time from the looks of him."

"Wait. Are you trying to tell me Mrs. Green came with her lawyer?"

Nadine laughed. "No. He's someone else's lawyer. Should I send him in?"

"No. Send him on a sandwich run to Subway."

"Ha-ha. Fix your tie."

Yes, I wear a tie. Suit too. Sure, I'd be more comfortable in jeans and a T-shirt like the PIs on TV, but this is real life. The type of clients I cater to don't do business with black men in T-shirts.

I straightened my tie as Nadine disappeared, then reappeared moments later ushering in a man in a finely tailored suit. He looked to be in his sixties, maybe even early seventies. His polished appearance, refined posture, and air of confidence brought the word *dashing* to mind. And Nadine wasn't kidding about his briefcase. My visitor clutched a black Dunhill Heritage, definitely pricier than Nadine's eight-year-old Corolla.

I rounded my desk and greeted him with a handshake.

"My name is Raymond Patterson," he said. "I'd like to discuss engaging your services. The matter is quite urgent and will require your immediate and exclusive attention. Of course, your compensation would be commensurate with the level of dedication I'm requesting. Are you interested, Mr. Jones?"

"You definitely have my attention." I gestured to the visitor's chair and returned to my seat. "Please, tell me what I can do for you."

Chapter 2

MACKENZIE

Are you Mackenzie Cunningham?"

The first thing I noticed about the white guy standing in the doorway of my office was his suit. It was an Italian cut. Blue-gray fresco mouline wool. I knew men's clothing. My dad is a lawyer who never buys off the rack. Although my father was too busy working to spend a lot of quality time with me as a kid, hugs were never in short supply. The soft feel of his pricey suits was practically imprinted on my cheeks. I almost wanted to leap across my desk and brush my face against this guy's lapel.

So far, my day had been a complete crapshoot. I'd gotten burned earlier that morning and my screwup might cost me the first decent client I've had in a while. And by *decent*, I mean a client whose check wouldn't bounce its way back to my office the moment I deposited it.

I'm a PI, and I'm good at my job. That's why today's mishap stung so much.

A target I'd been surveilling for several hours—a gambler with a very unhappy bookie—rushed up to my Jeep Grand Cherokee and started banging on the window. My trusty old Jeep was more old than trusty and didn't need the battering. He drunkenly demanded to know why I was following him. It took me a few tries to crank up my engine, as usual, and speed off.

And for the record, I've never been made on a stakeout before today. Being a woman in this business, I can't afford to let that happen. It's frustrating that most guys don't take me seriously. At least not at first. My capabilities are repeatedly questioned because of my mellow mocha skin and unstatuesque height—I'm five-four in heels. A few knuckleheads have learned the hard way, though, that my quick wit, lightning speed, and black belt in Krav Maga render me far more dangerous than a man twice my size.

My company is called MC Investigative Services. I run my business out of a shared office space above a Chinese takeout restaurant in a strip mall in Inglewood. My office mates—a workers' comp attorney and a chiropractor—are model candidates for a future FBI raid. In the five years that we'd been cohabitating, I'd only accepted one job from them. I'm bright enough to know a fraud ring when I see one.

When I'm feeling stressed, I like to gaze out onto Manchester Boulevard. Watching traffic soothes me. Go figure. I was engaged in this form of self-therapy when the uninvited visitor showed up at my office.

Normally I'd be annoyed that Joy, the receptionist I shared with my two suite mates, had allowed this guy in without buzzing me first. It was her job to keep out the riffraff, aka angry clients, cheating spouses, and process servers. At least he wasn't setting off any red flags. Yet.

"Yes, I'm Mackenzie Cunningham," I replied to the distinguished-looking older gentleman. I found it odd that he was carrying a leather briefcase. Most people stored all their essentials on an iPhone or iPad. I certainly did. "How can I help you?"

"I have a case I'd like you to handle," he announced, closing the door behind him. Somehow my trespasser looked at me without actually *looking* at me. He set his briefcase on the floor and took a seat in front of my desk before I could invite him to do so. "And it's quite urgent."

All clients acted as if their cases were fires that needed to be snuffed out yesterday. I grabbed a notepad and pen from the corner of my desk. "Let's start with your name and the nature of your case."

The man held up a masculine but manicured hand. "My name is Raymond Patterson. Before we proceed, I'll need your agreement to a couple of stipulations."

I've never been one to let a client take control of the conversation or define the parameters of my engagement. But as Mr. Well-Dressed White Guy spoke, I found myself rocking back in my leather chair and giving him the floor.

"First, this case will require your immediate and exclusive attention," he said in a commanding voice. "That means you'll be prohibited from handling any other cases for the duration of our engagement."

I raised an eyebrow. Yeah, right. As if I could just drop everything I was working on. Anyway, how would he even know? But instead of arguing the point, I tilted my head and locked my arms across my chest. "And the second stipulation?"

"There's a very urgent deadline that you'll need to meet."

I didn't accept or reject his stipulations. I simply let him keep talking.

"I need you to find someone," he said, placing a five-by-seven photograph on my desk. "Her name is Ashley Cross. She's been estranged from her family for the past four months. Her mother—my client and her only real family—is terminally ill and is desperate to reunite with her only child. I need you to find Ashley before her mother dies."

As I stared at the photograph, I tried to keep my face emotionless as my brain registered the first shocker: the missing girl was black. Perhaps that explained why he had chosen me for the job. Did he think a black female PI would have a better shot at tracking down another black woman?

"How much time does the mother have?" I asked, still mulling over why this guy wanted me for the job.

"A couple of weeks at best. Maybe even days."

"Is there an inheritance involved?"

Patterson nodded. "I'm the executor of her mother's estate. Ashley will soon be a very wealthy young woman. Here's some background information I was able to gather."

He handed me a folder with several pages inside. The first page included many of the PI essentials: Ashley's Social Security number, last three addresses, high school, college, best friend, last known boyfriend, and a few other tidbits.

"And, oh yes, Ashley is Mrs. Cross's adopted daughter. Her adoptive father is deceased."

I found a photograph of the happy threesome inside the folder. Yet another shocker: Ashley's adoptive parents were white.

"Do you have any information about her biological parents?" I asked.

Patterson shook his head. "Those records are sealed. Ashley never knew them and never expressed a desire to know them."

I continued to peruse the folder. "I don't see any information about the Crosses."

He shrugged. "There's no reason you should need any background information on them. As I said, her father is deceased, and her mother is extremely ill. So it's imperative that you refrain from contacting Mrs. Cross for any reason. She's in a very fragile state and I don't want to put any additional stress on her. Whatever you find out about Ashley should only be reported to me."

Ding, ding, ding, ding, ding. Alarm bells started clanging in my head. There was likely more to this story than the scant facts Patterson had just revealed.

I stared into Ashley Cross's wide brown eyes. She was petite, almost doll-like, with a long mass of thick, kinky hair. According to the background sheet, she was just twenty-four years old, a decade my junior.

Her most recent address was Rancho Palos Verdes, about thirty miles south of here. But in economic terms, a galaxy away.

I wasn't in the habit of turning down gift horses, but I couldn't help wondering what Raymond Patterson wasn't telling me and why he'd descended from his tower of power to go slumming in Inglewood. Even if he wanted a black PI, I wasn't in the top echelon of that list. Not yet.

"Does Ms. Cross have some connection to this area?" I asked.

"Not that I'm aware of."

"Then why hire me for the job?"

"You came highly recommended."

"By whom?" I pressed.

"I'd rather not say. But I've done my homework. You're very good at what you do. You have superior internet tracking skills and extensive expertise in finding missing people."

All true. Perhaps I shouldn't have played the race card so quickly. It was nice to know my rep traveled far beyond my limited sphere. But what was the real deal? Why was Patterson so insistent that I shouldn't contact Ashley's dying mother? Was there a reason other than her health for the stay-away order?

Neither of us spoke for a long beat. I'm good with silence. Most people aren't.

The man crossed his legs in that self-assured, manly way—ankle resting on opposite knee—and made extended eye contact for the first time.

"So, Ms. Cunningham, is this case something you'd like to take on?"

Although he was requesting my consent, his assertive tone conveyed that he assumed he already had it.

I've learned to trust my intuition and there was something not quite right about Raymond Patterson or his urgent matter. I briefly glanced at the parking lot below. The burgundy Jaguar taking up two spaces no doubt belonged to him. He obviously didn't understand that hogging two spots in an overcrowded urban strip mall was an invitation to have your car keyed.

I turned back to him. "If I'm required to put my existing clients on the back burner, I'll have to ask for a lot more than my normal retainer."

"I don't think you'll have an issue with the retainer I'm offering." He retrieved a thick, rectangular envelope from his briefcase and slapped it on my desk. "I hope this will be sufficient. It's twenty grand. Cash."

Despite the rush of exhilaration I felt, I displayed no outward emotion. That was more than six times my regular retainer. Enough to put a dent in my credit card bills and cover the mortgage on my town house for a few months. My attempt at emotional restraint wasn't quite strong enough to keep a smile off my face.

And just like that, my day had gone from downright miserable to absolutely marvelous.

Chapter 3

JACKSON

I sped down the 405 freeway with the intention of poking around Ashley Cross's apartment in Rancho Palos Verdes.

I had the top down on my AMG E-Class Mercedes and my favorite crime podcast on my Bose sound system. The air was unusually clear and the late afternoon sunlight seemed to have an almost magical quality.

My elated mood could be directly attributed to the thick stack of crisp one-hundred-dollar bills I'd received from my new favorite client. Twenty grand, to be exact. The influx of cash would allow me to treat myself to a couple of new suits and make some upgrades to my loft and my Mercedes. My expensive ride was a huge but necessary cost of doing business. In Los Angeles, you are what you drive. Although my car has zero correlation to my investigative skills, I'd much prefer that my clients see me pull up in my leased Benz, not my old but fully paid-for Toyota 4Runner.

With my all-cash retainer in hand, I was more than happy to get right to work. It didn't surprise me that Ashley's disappearance hadn't been picked up by the media since there had been no indication of foul play. But even when there is, missing black girls don't get the same press. Patterson, however, had made it sound like Ashley wanted to be off the grid.

She had a habit of becoming entangled with questionable men. Not dangerous types, Mr. Patterson had made clear, just good-for-nothings. Men whom Ashley's mother never approved of. Often Ashley would go off with these men, vanishing from the family radar for weeks at a time. In fact, it was one of these sordid adventures that had led to Ashley's estrangement from her mother. Mr. Patterson now assumed Ashley was simply off on another romp, unaware of her mother's recent downturn. Therefore, involving the police was unnecessary.

While I was anxious to track down her past boyfriends, first I wanted to see what I might find at Ashley's apartment.

Rancho Palos Verdes is an affluent coastal community of mansions, condominiums, and overpriced apartments perched upon lush cliffs overlooking the Pacific Ocean.

Ashley's address led me to a Spanish-style apartment complex called Ocean Estates. Like all gated communities, visitors had to be vetted to get past the guardhouse.

I had no definitive plan when I drove up to the booth, but I've always been quick on my feet. When the guard approached, I told him I was driving by, liked the looks of the place, and wanted to check out any available apartments. Ten minutes later I was in the property manager's office, seated across from a blonde with a perma-smile who introduced herself as Sharon Miles. When I revealed the true intent of my visit to Miss Miles and offered to slip her some cash, she didn't seem at all surprised.

That was odd.

Although I sometimes used cash to leverage information and access, most folks were not accustomed to having their palms greased. For them, a bribe was something that only happened in movies. So the property manager's muted reaction—a stiff smile and a shake of her head—caught me off guard.

"No. I'm sorry. I can't help you."

Thinking I'd miscalculated and offered too little, I doubled the amount. "What if I made it two hundred? Just for a quick look around. In and out. Ten minutes tops."

Once again, that stiff smile, then: "Someone else was just here, also asking to see Ms. Cross's apartment. I let her in, but then I got a bad feeling, so I quickly cut the visit short."

My mind did a loop.

"Hold on. Someone else offered you money to get into Ms. Cross's apartment? Today?"

"Just a half hour ago. But the woman didn't offer me any money. Claimed she was a building inspector and needed to check three of my units, including Ms. Cross's. I thought she was legit until we stepped inside Ashley's place. She was way too interested in examining Ashley's electronics equipment. I realize now that she probably asked to inspect the other two apartments first just to throw me off."

With an upturn of her perfect nose she went on, "I don't know what's going on, but here at Ocean Estates our residents are of a certain stature. We take pride in protecting their property as well as their privacy. Is there anything else I can help you with?"

My next stop was an upscale lounge in Manhattan Beach called Shadows. Raymond Patterson mentioned that he had received information that Ashley had been spotted there. Although this supposed sighting had occurred two weeks ago, I figured I'd pop in and flash her picture to the staff. Maybe I'd get lucky and someone would recognize her.

During the twenty-minute drive from Palos Verdes to Manhattan Beach I couldn't stop thinking about what the property manager had told me. Who else was searching for Ashley? Was it possible the bogus building inspector was connected to Ashley's disappearance? I was tempted to call Patterson and ask his opinion about the mystery woman, but stopped myself. Why bring up something that might cause him to end such a lucrative gig? Besides, I was certain the man was hiding something. His insistence that I not contact Ashley's mother felt off.

For that reason, I'd spent some time earlier digging into both the attorney and his dying client. Patterson had a significant digital footprint as a lawyer and even checked out on the state bar website. As for Mrs. Cross, my online search found nothing inconsistent with the information Patterson had provided. For the past three months, Mrs. Cross had been a patient at a hospice facility in Manhattan Beach, and she was indeed a very wealthy woman, mostly from commercial real estate investments. Still, I planned to use the services of an old friend to take a deeper dive into Patterson, Mrs. Cross, her wayward daughter, and any bad boy that she might have slipped off with.

As the sun dipped below the horizon, I wheeled into a cozy parking lot adjacent to Shadows. Occupying a coveted corner lot on Ocean Drive, the lounge's exterior was minimalist bordering on arrogant. There was no signage that I could see, and I was a trained observer. Just an unmarked black door with a muscular dude in a black sport coat stationed out front. A buff scarecrow to discourage a flock of the younger, T-shirt crowd.

As I approached the doorman, I made the split-second decision to save my questions about Ashley for the inside staff. If I let on that I was a PI, the dude might get the crazy idea my presence would be bad for business. I didn't want to strike out twice in one day. I would show him Ashley's photo on the way out.

I stepped through the door into a dimly lit space of plush booths, chandeliers, and mellow music. It was a nice-sized crowd. Lots of good-looking people in great-looking clothing nursing delicious-looking cocktails. All white, but this being Manhattan Beach, that wasn't a surprise. Not really my kind of scene, but I'm a chameleon of sorts. Able to fit in anywhere. An essential skill for any decent PI.

The sleek bar was a luminous work of art, causing the endless bottles of booze to glow. Shadows was the kind of place where the drinks came to you, so I found an empty booth and slipped into it. There was a near-empty wineglass on the table that I promptly handed off to a passing busboy. An instant later, a waitress appeared. Young, shapely, blond in a clingy short skirt. I'd bet anything she had a stack of headshots in the glove compartment of her Prius in case a producer wandered in.

She flashed an impeccable smile. "Welcome. What can I get for you?"

After ordering a top-shelf gin and tonic, I whipped out Ashley's photo. "Could I ask you a question? Have you ever seen this woman in here?"

To her credit the waitress didn't get all weird. She gave the photo the once-over, then shook her head. "Not that I can remember. Are you a cop?"

"No. Investigator. Private. Her mother's trying to find her."

"Oh. Cool."

"She was in here two weeks ago," I said, "right about this time. Were you working?"

"Probably."

"Take another look, please."

She did and drew a blank. "No. Sorry. I don't remember her."

"Thanks. Hey, could you do me a favor? Could you show this photo to the bartender? I'm trying to lie low."

"Who, Josh? He's only worked here a week." She glanced at her watch. "The bartender who worked this shift two weeks ago will be here in about an hour if you want to wait. I'll get your drink."

As I tucked the photo back into my jacket, I watched the waitress walk away. She was good at it. More confirmation of my theory that white girls' butts were evolving faster than normal. I couldn't help noticing the way she'd perked up when she learned I was a PI. Some women find what I do exciting, even titillating. I was weighing whether or not to explore my chances with her when a voice interrupted my thoughts.

"Exactly what do you think you're doing?"

Somehow I was no longer the only customer of color in Shadows. I wasn't quite sure where she came from, but there was a black woman standing over me. She was hands-down gorgeous. Tight, petite figure. The works.

She also looked as if she wanted to strangle me.

Chapter 4

MACKENZIE

Excuse me?" the man said.

The flashy lawyer type who had commandeered my booth was playing dumb. I didn't appreciate having to repeat myself.

"I said, what do you think you're doing?" I gestured to the plush circular booth. "This is *my* booth. A few seconds ago, *my* drink was sitting right there."

The hint of a snicker grazed his lips, only pissing me off more.

"Sorry about that," he said. "No one was sitting here. I did see a wineglass when I sat down, but it was almost empty so—"

"It wasn't almost empty. It was half-full."

"Half-full. Almost empty." He shrugged his broad shoulders. "I guess it depends on your worldview."

I didn't have the energy or the patience to deal with this wise-cracking jerk. "So are you going to move or what?"

He laughed. "Bad day, huh?"

"You might say that."

After Patterson left my office, I'd been riding high. I was also super hyped about picking up some clues at Ashley Cross's place.

Getting inside wasn't that hard. My building inspector ruse never failed. A simple flash of my fake badge and no questions asked.

Ashley's apartment had the kind of surveillance equipment reserved for the NSA. The equipment wasn't out in the open. You had to know what you were looking for. I guess I must've appeared too eager, because ten short minutes into my inspection, my visit was suddenly cut short. The woman had the nerve to demand that I call my main office so she could speak to someone who could confirm my identity. I blame TV crime dramas for this brazen lack of trust. They've exposed too many PI tricks of the trade, making it a lot harder to dupe people.

After that debacle, despite Patterson's orders, I tracked down the hospice facility where Ashley's mother was a patient. The nurse who answered my call seemed to believe my story about being an old friend, but told me Mrs. Patterson was too sedated to accept calls. At least Patterson's story about Ashley having a dying mother was legit.

So after striking out twice, the last thing I wanted to deal with was some entitled lawyer thinking he could hijack my booth.

"Could you just move?" I doused my tone with just a drop of sweetness. "Please."

"Tell you what," the guy said, grinning, "have a seat and you can tell me your troubles. I'm a way better listener than the average bartender. Who knows? I might be able to help. I'll even spring for another glass of wine."

He slid to his left to make room for me.

"No, thanks." My hands were now defiantly pinned to my hips. He didn't know it, but that wasn't a good sign. "I'd just like my booth back."

"Are you always this feisty?"

"Are you always this irritating?"

He laughed again, revealing a killer smile enhanced by teeth too straight to be God-given. Admittedly, I have a thing for guys with pretty teeth, but his smug air of superiority was a major turnoff. Besides, flirting isn't something I'm particularly good at.

"That couple over there is leaving." His gaze gravitated over my shoulder as he pointed. "Why don't you grab their booth before someone else does?"

My jaw tightened. "Why don't *you* go over there? If you were a gentleman, you'd move."

"Oh. So you want it both ways?"

"What does that mean?"

"You storm up to me like a dude anxious for a fight, yet you still want the benefit of privileges reserved for the weaker sex."

I took a breath. A long, deep one. This guy was deliberately trying to push my buttons.

"Anyway, you don't look like the kind of babe who'd appreciate chivalry."

Okay, consider my buttons officially pushed.

"*Babe*? Really? And exactly what kind of *babe* do I look like?" I leaned in closer. "You don't even know—"

"I'm not drunk," slurred a chubby man sitting at the bar. He slammed down his empty glass so hard I was surprised it didn't shatter. "I want another drink!"

The commotion drew everyone's attention to the back of the lounge where a bar ran the length of the wall. The man's garbled words, ruddy cheeks, and disheveled clothes confirmed that he was indeed sloshed.

A lanky man approached and tried to reason with the unruly patron. "Sir, I'm the manager. How about we call an Uber for you?"

"I have a two-hundred-thousand-dollar Bentley outside. I don't need a damn Uber. Give me another fucking drink."

The doorman, who apparently doubled as a bouncer, made his way inside and stalked over. He firmly placed a hand on the man's back. "Let's go. We don't allow—"

"Don't fucking touch me!"

The drunk jerked away, snatched his glass, and hurled it against the mirrored wall behind the bar. It splintered into a kaleidoscope of jagged cracks, firing off shards of glass in all directions.

A collective gasp ricocheted around the lounge. The dozen or so people who'd been sitting at the bar instantly scattered, drinks in hand.

The manager and the doorman flanked the guy from opposite sides, each grabbing a chunky arm.

"We're going to help you outside, sir."

"I don't need your help!" His volume shot up a few decibels.

They struggled to heave the much heavier man off the stool and had only walked a few steps when he jerked away and flopped across the bar, tumbled over to the other side, and disappeared from view. Seconds later, he staggered to his feet. Gripping the edge of the bar with both hands, he glared at the stunned crowd.

"I'm not leaving until I'm ready to leave!"

As the manager and doorman pushed through the swinging gate leading behind the bar, the man grabbed bottles of booze and started torpedoing them around the lounge. Customers screamed and ducked as bottles crashed at their feet, spraying them with alcohol.

The manager jumped on the man's back while the bouncer helped to wrestle him to the floor. When the three of them resurfaced, blood gushed from a cut over the man's eye.

"This is police brutality! I want a lawyer!"

"Sir, we aren't the police," the manager said. "But they're on the way."

By now, most of the customers had sprinted for the door.

"Everybody out!" the manager yelled, breathless from the work-out. "We're closing early."

When I turned back to the booth, Mr. Wise Guy was on his feet. I had to admit, he had a sexy swagger about him.

He peeled off a twenty from his bill clip and slapped it on the table. "Normally, in a situation like this, I'd escort a lady safely to her car. But I guess you—"

"Yeah, you guessed right. I'll be fine."

He snorted. "I bet you will. Enjoy the rest of your day."

Chapter 5

JACKSON

As I sped home, I tried to calculate my next move in the investigation, but Miss Half-Full kept intruding upon my thoughts.

She was beautiful for sure, but tigers are good-looking man-eaters too. I chuckled. Perhaps I was being too harsh—but then again, maybe not. It suddenly occurred to me that she'd probably caught me eyeballing that waitress. That could've been what caused her claws to come out. Some sisters spew steam when they catch a brother ogling a white girl. Especially a blonde. Still, there was something intriguing about Half-Full's spirit. I couldn't help wondering what she'd be like if she dialed it down to a scintillating simmer. But wondering was good enough for me. I was more than happy to leave the mystery of Miss Hotness unsolved. I felt sorry for the poor sucker who became entangled with her. I'd escaped from another hellcat two years earlier and vowed never to dip into that well of dysfunction again.

I parked in my underground garage, grabbed my mail, then rode the elevator up to the top floor. My Venice Beach loft, with its twenty-foot vaulted ceilings, was just a Frisbee fling away from the Pacific Ocean. From my leather couch, I had a fantastic view of an overpriced beachfront motel. If I dynamited that neon tourist trap, the value of my place would shoot up half a million, easy.

Good thing I'm a law-abiding citizen.

An eighty-five-inch wall-mounted plasma TV with surround sound did a good job of making up for my shitty view. After a long day of making zero progress and being berated by not one but two women, I treated myself to a cigar and a glass of Glenfarclas 25 while *The Real Housewives of Atlanta* did battle in 4K resolution. Watching beautiful women go at each other was a bit of a turn-on. I dig sports, too, but I'm no TV snob.

After a couple hours of decompression I was ready to get my head back in the game. I needed a plan for tomorrow. For now, returning to Shadows was out of the question. Considering the damage done by drunk King Kong, that place would be shuttered for at least a day or two. Shadows was a long shot anyway. I needed something more solid.

I was about to abandon my couch in favor of my desk when my phone rang. A glance at the caller ID told me it was my ex-wife, Robin. As usual, the muscles in my neck instantly tightened. I muttered a silent prayer that it was my daughter, Nicole, calling instead of her mother. Nicole was only thirteen. Robin and I had agreed she wouldn't get her own phone for another three years.

As my phone continued to ring, I glanced at the clock. I brightened when I realized it was just a little past eight. Nicole was definitely still up. *Let it be Nicky.*

When I heard my baby say, "Hey, Dad," I felt light enough to float.

"Nicky, how you doing, baby?"

Nicole was doing great. She updated me on school, relayed the latest drama with her BFFs, and hit me up for money for a new outfit. All music to my ears. Some parents say their children are their heart. Nicole was more than that to me. She was my everything.

"You're still coming to my belt test, right, Dad?"

"Of course," I said, opening my calendar app to search for the date. "It's next Saturday, right? I'll be there with bells on."

"Bells on? What for?"

"Sweetie, that's just a saying. Means I'm excited."

"Sounds kinda weird."

I chuckled. "I can't believe you're already getting your orange belt."

"It's not a sure thing, Dad. These moves are hard."

"Don't worry about it. You're going to kill it."

She grunted. "If you say so."

"I do say so."

I heard Robin's voice in the background but couldn't make out what she was saying.

"Dad, Mom wants to talk to you."

In an instant, my mood darkened in anticipation of impending friction.

"You promised to split the cost of Nicky's classes," Robin said. She always cuts to the chase. A simple "How you doing?" would be way too much to ask.

"I'm well aware of that."

"Then why haven't you sent the money?"

I inhaled, unwilling to intensify the drama. "I'll Cash App you three hundred right now."

"Four hundred would be better."

"Fine."

"Thank you."

"You're welcome."

The line went dead.

I wished Robin had put Nicky back on the phone so I didn't have to end the call with her attitude resonating in my ear. It was sad that our love had turned so ugly. At least something great came out of it.

To relax my throbbing temples, I poured another neat glass of scotch, then walked over to my desk and turned on my iMac. I signed on to an exclusive people finder site called Target ID that had provided me with amazingly accurate information in the past. Tonight I planned to see what more I could uncover about Ashley and her past boyfriends.

I started by entering Ashley's name and birth date, hoping to score some info on her adoption, most importantly the names and location of her birth parents. I knew it was a long shot, but maybe Ashley had decided to seek them out and kept it a secret because she feared her mother wouldn't approve. Even better, maybe Ashley had actually found her birth parents, there were lots of tears and hugs, and she had decided to stay with them for a while.

Yeah, right. It's never that easy. Target ID's search results turned up several Ashley Crosses, but all were the wrong age or race.

After another soothing sip of scotch, I decided to try something a little different. Something I'd been wanting to try for a while. You couldn't watch TV or surf the net without seeing articles about the AI program ChatGPT. Depending on who you listened to, the software was either working technological miracles or plotting the destruction of mankind. The demonstrations I'd witnessed online were truly impressive and I wondered if I could use ChatGPT to help with my investigations. The Ashley Cross case gave me a great opportunity to test this out.

Signing up to use the latest version of ChatGPT was just a matter of paying for a twenty-dollar-a-month subscription. After my debit payment was accepted I was presented with a surprisingly vacant screen featuring only a text window that read: *Send a message.* From the videos I had watched, I knew the quality of the prompt greatly affected the quality of the results. I also knew I could speak to the software as if speaking to a person. Deciding to keep it simple, I typed in Ashley's full name and birth date and asked ChatGPT to tell me everything it knew about her.

ChatGPT immediately typed back that it wasn't allowed to provide personal information on private individuals, but public information was fair game. For that reason, the software didn't provide me with much. A high school track achievement. She'd won an essay contest. Her name on a roster of political science majors at USC. Small stuff. But there was one item that immediately struck me as a damn good lead.

Suddenly I knew exactly where I'd be heading tomorrow morning and I had a good feeling I'd find some answers there as well.

Chapter 6

MACKENZIE

I'd always had a bad habit of beating up on myself when things didn't go my way. It was one of those personality quirks I knew I needed to fix but probably never would.

So, after the drama at Shadows, I decided to put Ashley Cross on the back burner and enjoy a little me time.

My two-bedroom town house was four blocks from my office in a cozy complex with lots of tall windows but rooms barely big enough to do a backflip in. A big contrast to the five-thousand-square-foot monstrosity I grew up in.

As I changed into sweatpants and a tank top, I couldn't stop thinking about the asshole with the sexy smile who'd stolen my booth at Shadows. He'd hit a sore spot when he said I came at him like a dude. My brash side has proved to be an asset on the job, but that wasn't how I wanted to come off to guys. Not that I was interested in *him*. He was way too cocky, though he wasn't at all bad on the eyes.

Generally speaking, men required too much attention and I didn't have time for that kind of distraction. Not now. Probably not ever.

I turned on the TV, which was usually tuned to a classical music channel. Other than *The Rachel Maddow Show* on Mondays, I rarely watched TV. I didn't have a Netflix account and I'd never binge-watched anything. My parents disapproved of make-believe worlds, so TV was all but forbidden in my childhood home. Quite ironic, considering that my upbringing was total fantasyland.

My entire childhood was a string of impossible expectations that, for the most part, I managed to achieve. *You know you can do better than this,* my mother would chide me the few times I brought home a B.

Donnell and Giselle Cunningham are seven-figure corporate lawyers. The two of them earned more *first-black* this or that titles than anybody I knew. I was well into adulthood before I finally understood the motivation behind their near-psychotic ambition. If they were the best—at everything—they would have to be accepted. But racism had wounded them so profoundly, they could never hide the scars, not even from themselves.

I can still remember the horror on my mother's face when, after graduating from Princeton, I announced that I was turning down an internship at the *LA Times.* Taking a cub reporter job in Rockford, Illinois, about ninety miles outside Chicago, was my first true act of parental defiance. While my mother sulked, my father quietly applauded my independence.

My stint at the *Rockford Register Star* had turned out just as I'd expected. I got the kinds of meaty assignments I would've never received at a major metropolitan newspaper. After spending three glorious years digging up dirt on local politicians, investigative reporting became my passion. After stints at two other newspapers, I'd moved on to PI work.

I made myself an all-veggie smoothie, sat on the balcony, and called my bestie.

"Hey, knucklehead."

"Whuz up, sister-girl?"

Most women had a girlfriend or two with whom they shared all. I had my brother, Winston. During my teenage years, I had never really bonded with the equally well-to-do white girls I grew up with. I always hated being the only black girl and grew increasingly uncomfortable with their attraction to anything black, from rap music to my kinky hair to their obsession with black men. To be honest, not all of them were that way. I just never gave their friendship a fair shot.

In college, I was initially excited to meet other black girls who'd grown up privileged like me. They'd spent their lives being the token black friend and understood the cultural isolation.

But over time, I didn't much like those girls either, especially the chameleons who easily navigated both worlds. They seemed to revel in their token status—partying every weekend with the white sorority types who professed to be color-blind. But in a group of black girls, they worked overtime at being down with the oppressed, hiding the fact that their parents earned seven figures and that even their great-grandparents had college degrees. In the end, they turned out to be just as fanatical about increasing their TikTok following as the shallowest white girls.

In truth, I had never enjoyed a close female friendship because I'd never learned how to be a friend. Iron Man couldn't have penetrated the force field I'd built around myself.

The bond I had with my baby brother, though, made up for that. Winston was a successful orthopedic surgeon who liked to talk to me in rapper speak. It was his only act of rebellion against our oppressive parentage.

"I'm glad you finally hollered back at me. What you gettin' into this weekend?"

"Same as every weekend. Work."

"Good. Alexis has a friend she wants to hook you up with."

My brother and his wife had a marriage so adorable you couldn't help but hug yourself when you were in their presence. But love was not in the cards for me. My first serious boyfriend broke my heart my sophomore year of college when he slept with my dorm supervisor. I flailed around in a few relationships after that, but never opened up to anybody else long enough to erase the pain of that initial heartbreak.

"What? What did you say? You're breaking up. I can't hear you."

"Girl, stop it. We'll invite him over for dinner. How about Saturday at seven?"

"I'll be out of town."

"You just said you'd be working."

"I know. Working out of town."

"C'mon, Mac, don't you even want to hear about the dude?"

"Nope."

"You know Mom is beginning to wonder if you're a lesbian, right?"

"Let her wonder."

Winston paused. "You need to call her, by the way. Something's going on with her."

"Something like what?"

"I don't know. She sounded a little down the last time I talked to her."

"Hmm. Probably means she only received two community service awards this month, not three."

"You need to stop being so hard on her. Just give her a call."

I sighed. "Fine. I will."

"Now, back to you. You don't have to stay for dinner. Just swing through Saturday to meet the guy, and if there's no connection, you can bounce."

"We'll see."

"I'm serious, sis. You better show up."

I let Winston lecture me on the importance of having a man in my life for two additional minutes, then hung up. After trying to read a novel that wasn't pulling me in, I did exactly what I'd promised myself I wouldn't.

Heading back inside, I grabbed my laptop and resumed my quest to find out everything I could about Ashley Cross.

Her social media presence was significant. Every couple of days, she shared a photograph or video on Instagram or TikTok, allowing the world a glimpse into her life—a life that stopped me cold.

Ashley Cross was a regular at pro-life protests and proudly publicized her conservative political leanings. How did a young black girl from Southern California find herself identifying with the far right? I'd grown up with girls exposed to Ashley's kind of wealth—black and white—but I couldn't think of a single one who shared her political ideology. Had Ashley been indoctrinated by her wealthy white parents or radicalized in some other way?

Opening a separate screen, I made a list of the people pictured most recently on Ashley's social media. Three of them were on the list of contacts Patterson had given me.

As I continued scrolling, something jumped out at me. Ashley had volunteered on multiple political campaigns, all staunch Republicans. There was one politician she posted about rather frequently.

I took a sip of my smoothie as a smile crept across my face. I was on to something. I could feel it in my gut. And nine times out of ten, my gut was spot-on.

Bright and early tomorrow morning, I knew where I needed to be.

The campaign headquarters of US Congressman Martin Vanderpool.

Chapter 7

JACKSON

Martin Vanderpool's campaign headquarters occupied the entire third floor of an office building in downtown Burbank. The real estate values in this part of town weren't nearly as exorbitant as my digs in Century City, but the swanky office building conveyed the same degree of opulence.

The instant I stepped off the elevator, I was ambushed by an enormous red-and-white banner that monopolized the wall. REELECT REPRESENTATIVE MARTIN VANDERPOOL FOR US CONGRESS. HIS VALUES ARE YOUR VALUES.

Although he was focused for the moment on getting reelected to his long-held congressional seat, it was common knowledge that Vanderpool had his sights on the White House. Many considered him the Republican Party's best shot.

A cute, fresh-faced receptionist politely finger-signaled me to wait as she wrapped up a phone call.

Behind the reception desk, a brightly lit, open workspace of cubicles and communal tables was abuzz with busy staffers and volunteers. It was impossible to look in any direction without seeing a wall plastered with Vanderpool's name and face. The images were classic politician. Fiftysomething, slightly graying white guy sporting a red tie and a forced smile. In one corner, stacks of lawn signs awaited their turn to contribute to the visual pollution of some suburban neighborhood. In the few minutes I stood there, the bombardment of political messaging almost sent me in search of the nearest voting booth. Vanderpool was fortunate that I didn't reside in his district. There was no way a dude that uptight would get my vote.

"Good morning. May I help you?" The receptionist smiled up at me.

"I'd like to speak to the congressman." I made a show of smiling back.

"What time is your appointment?" She began tapping her keyboard. "And what's your name?"

"It's Jones. But I don't have an appointment. I just need to ask the congressman a few quick questions."

"What is this concerning?"

"It's confidential. I'd prefer to discuss it with the congressman."

The woman frowned. "I'm sorry, but the congressman has a very tight schedule. He's always happy to meet with his constituents, but an appointment is required." She pecked a few more keys. "His first opening is in three weeks."

"Three weeks? I only need five minutes of his time," I lied. "I promise it won't take any longer than that. It's very important."

"I'm sorry. The congressman's schedule is packed."

Before I could continue to plead my case, a voice behind me cut in.

"We have over seven hundred thousand constituents. Could you imagine the chaos if we accepted walk-ins?"

I turned around to face a blonde in her late forties sporting a stylish shoulder-length bob with perfect highlights. She was particularly well dressed—almost too particular. Navy-blue double-breasted pantsuit, white silk blouse, red pumps, and tiny red, white, and blue earrings. Her demeanor was welcoming, but at the same time guarded. I recognized her instantly. His wife, Abigail Vanderpool. She had appeared in countless photos with the congressman, usually holding his hand.

"I'm not a constituent, Mrs. Vanderpool. I'm a private investigator. I'm working a missing person case."

"And what does your case have to do with the congressman?"

"The person I'm looking for is Ashley Cross. She was a volunteer here. Do you know her?"

She pressed a palm to her chest. "Of course I know Ashley. I know everyone working for the campaign. But I didn't know she was missing."

"Hopefully, not for long. If I could just ask your husband a few quick questions."

"I'm not sure he'll be able to help, but we'll assist you in any way we can."

Mrs. Vanderpool started down a narrow hallway. "Follow me."

I trailed after her through a maze of busy volunteers, then down a corridor lined with offices. A moment later, I found myself standing just outside a well-appointed corner office overlooking Olive Avenue.

Martin Vanderpool was seated on a sofa in the lounge area of his office, across from two much-younger men. Their jeans and sport jackets were a stark contrast to the congressman's suit and tie. I picked up snatches of their conversation. *Polling data could be better. . . . Need to hit her more aggressively. . . . No way she should be within eight points. . . .*

I assumed the *she* was his opponent, Tasha Rahmani. A twenty-eight-year-old progressive who made AOC look like a conservative.

Mrs. Vanderpool stepped inside and closed the door, leaving me outside.

Seconds later, the two men walked out and the congressman opened the door to greet me. "Please come in."

Vanderpool was more fit than I'd expect of a man who made his living shaking hands and leaning on podiums. I shook his extended hand. Damn firm grip. Must be all the practice.

"My wife just filled me in," he said, his face creasing with concern. "I'm glad that so much effort is being put into finding Ashley."

"Yes," Mrs. Vanderpool agreed, nodding. "My husband told me someone else was just here asking about her."

Once again I was slapped by déjà vu. This time I recovered much faster and decided to play along.

"Ashley's family is really worried, so we're really pulling out all the stops. Who else have you spoken to? We really should be coordinating our efforts a lot better."

"So far," the congressman explained, "just the family friend who was here asking us about Ashley's work on the campaign."

"What was her name?" I asked.

"I'm sorry, but I don't remember. There wasn't much we were able to share. Ashley hasn't volunteered with us for months."

My mind was racing. *Her* had to be the faux building inspector. Had this chick beaten me to the punch again?

"Could you describe the woman?"

He scratched his jaw. "Petite, attractive. She was also African American."

African American?

That didn't quite square with me. Maybe the *family friend* was someone from Ashley's biological family. I instantly got the sense that I was way behind the curve on this case.

"In fact"—the congressman glanced at his watch—"she just walked out. I'm surprised you didn't pass her on the way in. If you hurry, you might be able to catch her before she drives out of the garage."

My first instinct was to stay and press for more information.

But a greater need had me sprinting out of the office and hurling myself down the stairs to demand some answers from this impostor.

Chapter 8

MACKENZIE

Hey! Hold up!"

My hand was on the door of my Jeep when a thundering baritone jolted my internal menace meter out of sleep mode.

I glanced over my shoulder, bracing for something bad. A man was sprinting toward me like I'd stolen his wallet. My 9mm was in the glove compartment. I kept it there on outings where there was a low probability I'd need to brandish it. Or, God forbid, actually shoot somebody.

My mind cycled through possible Krav Maga strikes. De-escalation was the first rule of Krav. When that wasn't feasible, inflicting the maximum amount of pain as quickly and as efficiently as possible was the only goal.

The threat was about twenty feet away when my heightened anxiety deflated into disbelief. The man skidded to a stop as if a glass wall had dropped down from the heavens. His head hit the invisible wall at the same moment mine did.

What the hell? It was the Pretty Boy Lawyer from Shadows.

I charged up to him, but I didn't say a word. A holdover from my reporter days. I learned early on to shut up and listen. People tended to give up way more information when you weren't peppering them with questions.

Anyway, there was no need for me to speak. Pretty Boy needed some time. His broad chest heaved up and down as he gasped for air. He must owe his taut body to genes rather than gym time. He was breathing way too hard from that short sprint across the garage.

"Were you just in Congressman Vanderpool's office?" he finally panted.

Wait. This dude is stalking me?

"Why are you asking? Are you following me?"

"Just answer my question." His tone was more than impatient.

Men were such pricks. He was talking to me like he was my dad. Well, not actually *my* dad. Donnell Cunningham never lost his cool.

"Nope," I fired back. "*You* answer *my* question."

A nonverbal, eyeballing, heavy-breathing standoff followed. I hated having to look up at him.

After a few seconds, he threw up his hands and ditched his demeaning tone. "Look, just tell me what you're doing here."

His tempered voice conveyed calm. But I knew that technique. I wasn't about to let him play me.

I crossed my arms. "Okay, but you go first."

He rolled his eyes like I'd just asked him to take out the trash during the fourth quarter of the Super Bowl.

"No, I asked you first. Why were you asking Congressman Vanderpool about Ashley Cross?"

I blinked as my folded arms fell to my sides. "And exactly how would you know I was asking about her?"

"I know quite a bit." A sinister half-smile failed to hide the frustration in his eyes. "Enough to get you charged with impersonating a building inspector."

What the hell? "So you *are* following me."

"Better be glad I don't have you on tape 'cause that response would qualify as an admission of guilt in a court of law."

The same smug ladies'-man demeanor that had irked me so much last night resurfaced.

"C'mon, level with me," he pleaded. "I'd really like to know why you were asking about Ashley."

My first instinct was to see what I could get out of him. "Some personal family business that I'm not at liberty to discuss with you. So why are you looking for her?"

"I never said that I was."

"Then why did you nearly burst a blood vessel rushing down here to talk to me?"

He paused, as if weighing whether he could trust me. "Like you, I can't disclose that."

"Fine then." I started stalking back toward my Jeep as he followed. When I pulled the door open, he stretched out his long arm over my head and closed it.

For the second time, I seriously calculated which Krav Maga move would take him down the fastest. I turned back around and mentally prepared to pounce if I had to.

"Okay, I'll level with you," he said. Remorse filled his eyes, but I didn't trust them. "I'm a PI. I've been hired to find Ashley Cross."

Whoa.

I had not expected that. I would've bet my mother's Bulgari diamond necklace that he had a business card with *Esq.* next to his name. It wasn't just his lawyer-like arrogance. The PIs I knew didn't dress to impress. His paisley lime tie was the perfect complement to his pin-striped gray suit.

I hunched my shoulders. "I'm a PI too. And I've also been hired to find Cross."

"C'mon, stop playing around." He smiled that sexy smile again.

"I'm being straight with you. Just tell me why you're here."

My teeth clenched. Men always reacted to my choice of employment with instant incredulity.

"I just told you why I'm here. Were you hired by Raymond Patterson or someone else?"

This time *he* took a step back. "How do you know . . ." His voice trailed off.

His eyes suddenly glazed over with bewilderment. But not at the mention of Patterson's name.

"Damn. So you really *are* a PI." He smiled big. "The only females I know in this business are old, ugly white women who look like they've done time at San Quentin."

"Oh, so you think I'm cute."

He laughed and extended his hand. "I'm Jackson Jones."

"Okay," I said, not bothering to accept his overture. "I'm Mackenzie Cunningham. My friends call me Mac. You can call me Mackenzie."

"Damn," he marveled again, still beaming. "A sista PI. This right here is a unicorn moment."

"I don't know what you have to be smiling about," I taunted him. "Patterson obviously didn't think you could get the job done. So he hired me as backup."

He hesitated just long enough for me to know he was pondering my assertion. Then he grinned. "You wish."

I climbed into my Jeep and tried to shut the door, but Jackson Jones kept me from closing it.

"Where're you going?"

"Where do you think? To ask Patterson what the hell is going on."

Chapter 9

JACKSON

Miss Hotness and I reached Raymond Patterson's reception area about the same time. Located on Sunset Boulevard, his office suite reeked of wealth.

No surprise there.

The receptionist, an older woman with a robotic demeanor, played referee when Mackenzie and I demanded to see Patterson in stereo. A moment later we were both in the waiting area, seated side by side on the most comfortable leather sofa my ass had ever met.

If I had to be double-booked on a case, going up against Mackenzie Cunningham wasn't the worst thing in the world. The woman had more sass than a Cardi B video. But truthfully, her involvement in this case had me worried. If Mackenzie found Ashley Cross before I did, I could end up losing Raymond Patterson as a repeat customer. I needed to get into Mackenzie's head. To find out just how good she was at her job.

The way Mackenzie grabbed a magazine from the coffee table and began flipping pages gave me the impression she did not want to chitchat, much less compare notes. But my police academy training and years of playing poker had honed my body language reading skills to a fine point. The uptick of her head and the way she was slightly reclined revealed she was, in fact, very approachable. Her posture could even be interpreted as desirable of interaction. Wouldn't that be interesting.

I turned to Mackenzie. "You think it's just a coincidence?"

My vague question had the desired effect. With knitted brow, she lowered the magazine. "What's a coincidence?"

"Come on. There aren't a lot of *us* in Los Angeles."

She hunched a shoulder. "Ashley's black. We're black. Maybe he thought a black PI would have an edge."

"Then why hire both of us?" I asked.

"If the mother really is dying, he needed to pull out all the stops."

"You just said *if the mother is really dying*. You don't think she is?"

"My gut tells me there's more to this story."

"Care to share your theory?"

She smiled daintily. "Nope."

Gorgeous and shrewd.

During the forty-minute drive to Patterson's office, I had tossed the question around in my head but nothing had jelled.

"Well, Patterson has a lot of explaining to do."

Mackenzie rolled her eyes. "Ya think?"

She tossed her magazine onto the coffee table, a clear sign that her defenses were dropping. I decided to do a little fishing.

"Hey, did the congressman give you anything useful?"

Mackenzie fixed me with a stare and angled her head. I'm sure she didn't intend to come off as sexy, but damn.

"Really?" she said.

"Really what?"

"You think I'm going to share information with my competition?"

"Competition? We're working the same case."

"For now. Maybe Patterson wanted to see who'd get traction first before settling on one of us? Why else double-book?"

"Maybe he just wanted faster results. Two heads are better than one, right?"

She looked down her nose at me. "Depends on the heads."

Ouch.

Spicy was one thing, but I was beginning to consider a less flattering label for Ms. Cunningham. "You know what, maybe what you said in the garage was right. Maybe Patterson just wanted a backup in case *you* couldn't deliver."

"You got that backward, sport. I said that about you."

"I'm an ex-cop. Real investigative experience. What's your background? Trade school?"

She flashed a saccharine smile. "Princeton, then eight years as an investigative reporter."

Admittedly, I was impressed, but no way I was going to give her the satisfaction. "In other words, just *book* experience. Nothing that might cause you to break those pretty nails."

I could almost see steam coming out of her ears. *Something must be wrong with me for getting off on that.*

If the receptionist hadn't rounded her desk at that moment, I actually think Hot Chocolate would've taken a swing at me.

"Follow me, please."

Raymond Patterson's massive wood-paneled office had a goddamned fireplace. The law books lining the walls gave the place that earthy, academic smell. The lawyer was perched behind an ornately carved wooden desk cluttered with paperwork. If the opulent setting was intended to impress, mission accomplished.

He didn't appear bothered to see Mackenzie and me standing before him. It was almost as if he'd anticipated this moment.

Mackenzie, still perturbed from our exchange in the reception area, got straight to the point. "What's going on?" she said to Patterson. "Why'd you hire two PIs for the same case?"

"Actually, I didn't."

Mackenzie and I traded puzzled looks. Was he seriously going to deny the obvious?

Patterson gestured across the room to the lounge area. I'd been so focused on jamming up Patterson when we entered, I hadn't paid much attention to the rest of the room. I was stunned to see a man seated on a couch a few feet away with his legs comfortably crossed. From the look on Mackenzie's face, she was having the same reaction.

"I didn't hire two PIs to find Ms. Cross," Patterson said with the hint of a smile. "I hired three."

Right on cue the man stood and approached wearing a snide smirk.

I recognized him instantly. It was the drunk jerk from Shadows who'd wrecked the place.

What the hell?

"Mr. Jones, Ms. Cunningham, meet private investigator Lance Brooks."

Chapter 10

MACKENZIE

Before I could get my head around this fiasco, Pretty Boy lost it.

"Why'd you hire all three of us for the same job?" Jackson demanded. His arms were folded and his head was cocked, hip-hop style. "What kind of head games are you playing?"

"Why don't we all sit down?" Patterson walked over to his conference table and took a seat at the head. The still-smirking interloper sat to his right.

Jackson and I didn't follow. At least not immediately. We exchanged a glance, then hesitantly took seats next to each other, opposite Lance Brooks. We weren't on the same team, but neither of us wanted anything to do with Brooks. And for good reason.

Patterson propped his elbows on the table and steepled his fingers. "As I told each of you, my client's final wish is to reconnect with her daughter before she dies. I wanted multiple investigators on this case because time is of the essence."

"Well, you're wasting your client's money," I said. "I can handle the job. You don't need these two."

"Simmer down, little girl." Lance spoke in a slow growl. His sober voice wasn't all that different from the inebriated version.

"*Girl*? Who do you think you're talking to?" Two strikes and I'd have him sprawled on the floor, writhing in pain.

I could tell from the way Jackson flexed his fingers that he didn't appreciate the slight either, but he had his own battle to wage. "Give me a break," he said. "If anybody's going to solve this case, it's me. I'm—"

"You two are out of your league," Lance interrupted.

Patterson raised a refined finger. His restrained grin told me he was enjoying this forced competition. "Let's all settle down." He pinned his gaze on me. "Tell me why you think you're the best PI for this job."

I crossed my arms. None of this felt right. Patterson had told me I came highly recommended. So why hire two other PIs?

"You obviously know I've never had a missing person case I wasn't able to solve. And as a *girl*"—I glared at Lance—"I'm able to go places and get information in ways these two can't."

"Oh, so that's how you do it?" Lance chuckled. "Throw in a little skirt action?"

Before I could strike back, Jackson did it for me. "Watch yourself, dude."

Wow. Defending my honor. Nice.

I stood up. "In fact, I'm so good at what I do, I don't need to be involved in this shady situation. You can count me out."

Jackson stared up at me with an odd combination of relief and regret.

"Well, if she's out, I'm your best bet." He pointed a finger across the table at Lance. "You apparently didn't do much homework on this guy. I've never met him before, but his name is notorious in PI circles. The word on the street is that he's usually too busy hitting the bottle and flying off into drunken rages to do much work. In fact, I smell liquor on his breath from all the way across this table.

How much did it cost you to bail out of jail after your little tirade at Shadows last night?"

Splotches of red dotted Lance's chubby cheeks. "If I were you, I wouldn't go there," he growled at Jackson.

Patterson dismissively waved his hand. "I know all about Mr. Brooks's penchant for the bottle. Regardless, he gets results."

I'd had enough and started making my way toward the door.

"Please wait, Ms. Cunningham," Patterson said, getting to his feet. "As I said, the reason I retained all three of you is because it's imperative that Ashley be found before her mother dies. And the more people on the job, the more likely that's going to happen. To emphasize how important this case is, I'm upping the ante. The first person to find Ashley will receive a very generous bonus. A cash payment of fifty thousand dollars."

His words stopped my forward motion as I imagined all the doors of possibility that whopper of a bonus would open.

"Are you still in?" Patterson asked me.

I nodded.

"Good." He glanced at his watch. "I have an important call I need to take, so I'll let you get to work."

We silently trudged out of the office and down a hallway, congregating at the elevators. I stabbed the button, intentionally turning my back to Jackson and Lance.

When the elevator doors opened, we shuffled inside, each retreating to a separate corner.

Lance, of course, was the first to extinguish the temporary peace accord. "You two might as well head home," he said, grinning, "because that bonus is mine."

"If you say so," Jackson replied, just as the doors opened onto the first floor.

I was done with all of this pettiness. I charged into the lobby as if one of them had given me a two-handed push.

Jackson called after me, "Hey, wait up."

"Sorry. I gotta go." My thoughts were spinning as fast as my footwork.

There was a $50,000 bonus with my name on it.

Chapter 11

JACKSON

I'm confused."

"About what?"

"When you say put all pending cases on hold, that baffles me because there are no pending cases. Hello?"

I was reclined in my Herman Miller Aeron chair, my fingers entwined behind my head. Nadine was seated across from me, staring as if I'd sprouted horns.

"That can't be right. What about that dognapping thing?"

Nadine made a face. "Really? Fluffy came back on his own. I put that in last Friday's memo. Remember?"

It took effort not to roll my eyes. In Nadine's attempt to run a *professional* operation, she'd adopted the habit of issuing a weekly update memo.

"What about that woman scheduled to come in about finding her father?"

"Mrs. Calfe?"

I leaned forward and snapped my fingers. "Yeah."

"Dead."

"She died?"

"Nope. Her father died."

"Oh."

"That was in Friday's memo too." Nadine cocked her head. "I get the feeling you're not reading my memos. That really hurts."

"Forget the memos. There's just two of us here. Your desk is right outside my door. You can just tell me stuff."

"Sure, if you want to run a janky business."

"Okay, forget canceling my clients—"

"Easy enough."

I shot her a glare. Sometimes I just wanted to toss my dear cousin out a window.

"What?" she snapped. "Don't give me that look. The last time I asked for a raise all I got was a speech about the ups and downs of the PI business. Right now we're in a down period. Live with it. I mentioned that in my memo too, by the way."

I deflated with a sigh. Nadine wasn't wrong. I was so caught up chasing that fifty grand payday and so intrigued by the curves of one of my competitors that I had forgotten about the anemic state of my client list. It was peculiar how PI work seemed to come in waves. Some months I'd have a waiting list of clients, and other months I'd spend my afternoons at my desk shaking my head at TikTok videos. But when the phone did ring, the upscale quality of my clients and the premium prices they paid more than made up for the dry spells. With this thought came a pang of guilt. The weekly memo thing might be a bit much, but Nadine did work hard at keeping my business running smoothly. Maybe it was time to give her a raise.

"Any other way I can help?" she asked.

"Call all the airlines. If Ashley got on a flight, I want to know about it. Check the trains and buses too. Work fast and be thorough. Remember, there's a huge bonus on the line."

"I know, I know. Fifty thousand bucks. How do you know Mr. Fancy Pants will even pay?"

I blinked. "What do you mean?"

"Did he give you some kind of guarantee? Did you sign something? How do you know he's not just dangling a candy bar?"

"You mean a carrot."

"No, I don't. Candy bars are better dangling material."

My cousin had a point, but I couldn't concern myself with that now. It's not like I could go back to Patterson and demand he put his offer in writing. I just had to trust that the lawyer was a man of his word.

"If you'd seen this guy's office, you'd know fifty thousand is no big deal to him. He'll pay it. Hopefully to us. Get moving."

Nadine didn't budge; instead she raised a finger as if struck by a brilliant idea. "You know, if you really want an advantage, you should let me work in the field with you."

This time I did roll my eyes. "We talked about this. I'll give you a shot when the time is right."

"I think that time has come. I mean, considering how good this Mackenzie woman is."

I sat up in my chair. "Who said anything about Mackenzie being good?"

Nadine ticked off each point on her fingers. "She beat you to Ashley's apartment in Rancho Palos Verdes, she was already at Shadows when you got there, and she beat you to the congressman's office. Sounds to me like she's always one step ahead of you."

"She's annoying. Like you're annoying."

"Threatened by smart, self-sufficient women, I see. Typical."

"I'm not threatened."

Nadine moved to the edge of her seat. "Come on, cuz. Take me with you. We can beat this beeyotch."

"Don't call her that."

Nadine chuckled. "Holy shit. You just met the woman. Are you sweet on her already?"

"What? Where are you getting *that* from?"

"Remember that book you gave me, *How to Read a Person Like a Book*? Your body language said it all."

"Well, you're wrong. You need to keep reading."

"I finished it."

"Then read it again. I'm not into Mackenzie, she's not better than me, and I don't need your help in the field. I need you here on the phones, doing what I asked. Can you handle that, *cuz*?"

"Okay, boss. Calm down. Guess I hit a nerve, huh?" Nadine rose from the chair and smirked her way out of my office.

How in the hell had Nadine picked up on my attraction to Mackenzie? Not that anything happening between us was even worth fantasizing about. The chick had made it abundantly clear that she had absolutely no interest in me. She was all about business. I couldn't believe it when she basically told Patterson to take his case and shove it. That was nothing short of ballsy, and I loved it.

Nadine stuck her head inside my office. "I forgot to tell you that hacker weirdo called."

"Roxanna?"

"That's what I said, the hacker weirdo. She said you can come by at three. Says she has something solid."

I felt a wave of elation. When it came to digging up info, Roxanna was the real deal. If she said she had something solid, she meant it. I could already see Patterson stacking fifty grand in one-hundred-dollar bills on my desk.

Checking my watch, I saw that it was close to two thirty. "Why didn't you tell me sooner?" I snapped at Nadine. "This could be just the edge I need."

"Relax. Weirdo's only twenty minutes away. That gives you another fifteen minutes to daydream about Mackenzie Cunningham before you have to leave."

"Out!"

Damn, she's good.

Chapter 12

MACKENZIE

Jab with the left. Cross with the right.

When I was stumped on a case, the most effective way to deal with my frustration was to take it out on a punching bag. I was in a ratty gym on Prairie Avenue near my office, indulging in a much-needed evening workout, Krav Maga style.

Jab, cross. Jab, cross. Jab, cross.

I assumed the position: slight crouch, feet apart, palms facing out, elbows down. My exposed palms might have looked as if I was raising my hands in surrender, but a strike to the head with the heel of the hand could do far more damage than a fist.

Jab, cross. Jab, cross. Jab, cross.

The mental and physical exertion demanded by Krav Maga always left me feeling replenished. I'd taken up the self-defense technique in college, a week after a guy I considered a friend refused to understand that no meant no. That night, on my dorm room floor, my *friend* stole far more than my sense of security. He stole my sense of self.

I didn't call the police. Never told a soul. Not even my brother. I just vowed that no one would ever violate me that way again. Krav Maga helped me keep that promise to myself.

After leaving the fiasco at Patterson's office, I'd spent a few hours bent over my laptop, risking serious eyestrain to find even a sliver of information that might lead me to Ashley Cross. I had to find her before Lance or Jackson did. I desperately needed that bonus.

I couldn't stop thinking about how Jackson had chastised Lance for making that sexist *skirt action* remark. I appreciated his chivalry. It was nice to know the guy had at least one other redeeming quality besides his captivating smile.

I'd googled his name and was stunned when a bunch of news stories popped up from his LAPD days. He'd actually turned in another cop who'd engaged in misconduct. That certainly took guts.

What was I doing thinking about Jackson? I needed to stay focused on my workout.

My Apple Watch rang, signaling a phone call. It was my brother. I hated talking on my watch, so I rushed to pull my iPhone from my duffel bag, but the call went to voicemail before I could pick up. Using cell phones on the gym floor was a no-no, so I grabbed my bag, stepped outside, and called him back.

"Hey, Winston, sorry I—"

"Mom wants to see us," he said. "Now."

"Now? About what?"

"I have no idea. I told you something was going on with her. Did you call her?"

"I was going to, but didn't get a chance yet."

An unsettled feeling began to swell in my stomach. My mother was a planner. Last-minute invites offended her sense of proper etiquette. If she needed to see us right away, it was important.

I eyed the clock on the wall of the locker room. It was almost five. It would take more than half an hour to make it to Beverly

Hills in rush-hour traffic. I wasn't all that sweaty from my work-out, but I still wanted to shower and change clothes before heading to my parents' place. The worry in Winston's voice caused me to reconsider.

"I'm on my way."

As I turned off Wilshire Boulevard onto Bedford Drive, the grandness of my parents' neighborhood left me feeling disoriented. So much wealth, so little happiness. My parents had bought this six-thousand-square-foot McMansion my freshman year of college. So it had never really been home for me. More like a showroom floor where my parents could display their wealth.

When I stepped inside the massive foyer with its too-big chandelier and too-shiny marble floors, my father greeted me with a familiar smile and a genuine hug.

"Hey, sweetheart."

I noticed more gray around his temples than the last time I'd seen him, which was just a month ago. Sadness dipped at the corners of his eyes.

"What's going on?" I asked.

"Your mother's in the living room," he said, ignoring my question.

This was my mother's show and he wasn't going to let me peek behind the curtains even a few seconds before showtime.

My mother was sitting in the middle of a white, eight-foot couch, dressed in a floor-length black silk robe. Her hair was slicked back into a bun, and she wore just a hint of makeup—a sheer lipstick and a light blush. She looked like royalty.

"How's the PI business?" she asked, a familiar hint of derision in her tone.

"Fine, Mom."

"I hope you're being safe. As pretty as you are and with all the money we spent on your education, I'll never understand why you'd want to spend your day tracking down criminals."

Before I could respond, Winston entered the room and did it for me. "It's not like she's a bounty hunter, Mom. She doesn't track down criminals. And she's good at what she does. And more importantly, she loves it."

"I love what I do too," my mother fired back. "And it doesn't require me to rub shoulders with unsavory characters."

My father chuckled. "I don't know about that. Those bankers you were telling me about last week sounded pretty unsavory to me."

I smiled inside. My dad and Winston always had my back.

As we settled into matching armchairs facing my parents on the couch, Winston took command.

"You've got us pretty worried, Mom. What's going on?"

"Thanks for coming," she began. "I know you both have incredibly busy lives so I'll make this quick. I just wanted you to know that I'm going to be having a minor procedure, but it's nothing to worry about." She glanced at my father, who squeezed her hand.

The one certainty I knew about my parents was that they loved each other immensely.

"Procedure for what, Mom?" Winston asked.

"Breast cancer. Well, not exactly. I found a lump in my breast. They've done an ultrasound, and now they want to do a biopsy to see if it's malignant. But I'm sure I'll be fine."

If that's the case, then why have us rush over here?

Winston said, "Mom, you should've told us when you first found the lump. I'm a doctor, in case you forgot." Winston never lapsed into his urban speak in front of my parents. If he ever did, it would send my mother to an early grave.

"I tried to tell her," my father said. "But she wouldn't listen."

My mother waved a hand in the air. "I didn't want to worry you."

"Well, I am worried," Winston said. "With our family's history of triple negative breast cancer, this isn't something to just brush off. "

I flinched as my brother's words reverberated in my ears.

Triple negative? I had no idea what he was talking about.

I knew that both my grandmother and my mother's first cousin had died of breast cancer, but I'd never heard the words *triple negative* before. The apprehension in Winston's voice made me uneasy. Despite our strained relationship, the thought of losing my mother hit me with a wave of unexpected terror. I loved her dearly. And I knew my mother loved me. Too bad neither one of us knew how to show it.

"If it is malignant, my doctors think we've caught it early." She turned to me. "Are you okay, Mackenzie?"

I nodded, unable to speak. I wanted to run to her, to hold her close. But Giselle Cunningham wasn't the touchy-feely type.

"When are you having the biopsy?" Winston pulled out his phone. "I'll clear my calendar so I can be there. Who's your doctor? I want to check him out."

"I don't have a date yet, but I'll get all of that to you," my mother said. "Right now, I'm extremely tired, so I'm going to my room to rest."

And with that she rose from the couch and floated out of the room.

Chapter 13

JACKSON

Roxanna Novakova answered her front door wearing a red silk robe and nothing more. Not even slippers. She lived alone in a stately Bel Air mansion hidden behind high hedges. Roxanna and I were close in age, but light-years apart when it came to tax brackets.

As always, my Czechoslovakian acquaintance greeted me with a warm smile and a perfumed kiss on each cheek, then led me inside.

I'd visited Roxanna's countless times, but was always struck by how empty her house felt. The pricey furnishings were sleek and minimal. The walls adorned with a few works of modern art, but conspicuously bare of anything personal, like family photographs.

My footsteps on the polished marble echoed as I trailed Roxanna down a wide hall. We passed the open door of her study, giving me a glimpse of a multiscreen computer setup reminiscent of a sci-fi movie. Her ergonomic, high-backed leather chair, with countless knobs and levers, looked like it belonged on the bridge of a starship. That's where the magic happened. The control center where Roxanna used her considerable hacking skills to amass her fortune. I didn't know on what side of the legal fence her online activities fell, and I never asked. All I knew was, even after dozens of visits, Roxanna never took me inside that room. Never.

Reaching the end of the hallway, we entered a custom-designed massage room. Wood-paneled walls, soft lighting, shelves of bottled oils, and fluffy white towels. At the center of it all a Magic Earth massage table. Costing over ten grand, it was the most expensive table on the market. A sound machine added the atmosphere of running water and a potpourri scent sweetened the air.

Without a hint of self-consciousness, Roxanna removed her robe and hung it on a wooden hook. Blond and built like a porn star, she would have been gorgeous if not for all those ridiculous tattoos. Her curvy body was covered with a collage of fanciful images. Unicorns, fairies, mermaids, even a Disney princess. They were beautifully done, probably by the best tattoo artist in town, but way over the top for my taste. For me, Roxanna's nude body was like a classic sculpture vandalized by graffiti.

Of course, I'd never revealed that view to my hostess.

Roxanna lay belly-down on the table and nestled into the cushioned face rest. After covering her lower half with a towel, I grabbed a bottle of vanilla-cream-scented oil, her favorite, and squirted some into my palm. I rubbed my hands briskly to bring the oil to body temperature, then began to knead Roxanna's shoulders.

She moaned with pleasure. "Harder. Please."

My fingers dug deeper and she melted in my hands.

I was eager to learn what Roxanna had found out about Ashley, of course, but I knew better than to interrogate her at the beginning of a rubdown. We both knew the routine. Roxanna would give me what I came for when she was good and ready.

For five years I'd proudly worn an LAPD uniform. I loved the work, but hated the culture. To advance through the ranks you had to be a loyal brick in the blue wall. That meant sometimes looking the other way from shit you didn't want to see in the first place. I stayed in line until Russ Dixon, my older partner, did something I couldn't keep quiet about.

During a traffic stop for a red light violation, the lone driver, an attractive young woman, spewed some ugly words at Russ. We're used to verbal abuse, trained to be thick-skinned, so I wasn't sure why Russ lost it that night. Before I knew what was happening Russ snatched the woman out of her car, slammed her against the cruiser, and frisked her in an inappropriate manner. Even when the woman began sobbing, Russ didn't let up. I had to physically pull him away. We let the woman go without ticketing her, but I wasn't surprised when she filed a complaint. We weren't equipped with body cams back then, so it came down to her word against ours. I told the truth because it was the only way I could think of to get that woman's crying face out of my head. Russ never spoke to me again. Neither did half the department.

Internal affairs transferred me to another precinct, but in policing, getting your partner fired is an indelible stain. My LAPD career was over. Wanting to pivot as far away from law enforcement as possible, I decided to try something completely different.

I became a massage therapist.

The choice surprised even me, but an old college buddy was in the massage game and killing it. In less than two years, he went from transporting his portable table in the back of a Camry to the rear of a Porsche Cayenne.

After getting my license, I began to build my client list through word of mouth. But business was never as lucrative as my buddy had made it out to be. He finally confessed that a majority of his work came from the *special services* he provided for male clients.

"You don't really have to do anything sexual," he assured me. "Just work with your shirt off. You're in great shape. I'm telling you, the tips will be huge."

Definitely not for me. Luckily, I had quite a few regulars, Roxanna being my best. But there weren't enough Roxannas on my client list to keep me from throwing in my massage towel.

She had not been happy to see me go.

Deciding to stick with what I knew, I'd landed a job at a top private investigations firm in Beverly Hills. And a few years after that, I'd parlayed what I'd learned into my own business.

My deal with Roxanna actually began while I was still working for the Beverly Hills firm. After hearing about her hacker skills, I realized she'd be an excellent resource. So we'd agreed to barter. Whenever I needed her unique skills, she'd manipulate the internet the way I manipulated her muscles.

Deal.

As my thumbs glided over Roxanna's spine and the tattoo of a flying Pegasus, she purred with pleasure.

"*Moje láska*, you are still the best."

"Glad you like it."

Roxanna had a thick Czech accent and always called me pet names in her native tongue. I'd started putting her words into a translation app. *Moje láska* meant *my love*.

As I continued to caress her shoulders, between moans and groans, Roxanna finally got down to business. The highlight was Ashley's dealings with a security company with a creepy name. This information had potential, but Nadine's message from Roxanna had me expecting more. When I told Roxanna as much, she politely shushed me, then rolled over and said, "But I do have more. Much more."

I'd seen Roxanna's full-frontal nakedness many times, but I could never resist staring in admiration. Despite all the ink, she was still a sight.

Roxanna chuckled. "*Miláček*, you are welcome to indulge. Yes?"

I laughed. "C'mon, Roxanna. You know the deal. We are strictly business." Then I covered her with the towel again.

Roxanna routinely tried to tempt me, but I was not about to ruin my best connection. Nothing screws up a perfectly fine relationship like screwing.

"You are so awful sometimes." She smiled and pouted at the same time. "Perhaps you change mind when you hear the rest."

Chapter 14

MACKENZIE

The minute I got home from my parents' place, I spent the next hour or so researching triple negative breast cancer. What I read stunned me.

Triple negative breast cancer disproportionately affects black women, spreads faster than other breast cancers, and tends to have a worse prognosis.

Then another sentence jumped out at me.

Having a mother with breast cancer almost doubles the risk of breast cancer.

Not only was my mother's risk doubled, but if she had breast cancer, *my* risk would be doubled too.

Despite my family history, I'd never given much thought to what it meant for me. In my mind, breast cancer *couldn't* happen to me. I lived a healthy lifestyle. I worked out. I ate a clean diet. I didn't have a lot of stress in my life. The realization that my genes could decide otherwise shook me up.

I closed my laptop. I was jumping the gun. My mother would be okay. I didn't have time to obsess over this. I needed to find Ashley Cross.

To give me an edge, I decided to turn to a friend with far savvier computer skills than my own to do a deep dive on Ashley.

Craig had been a low-level computer forensics type with the LAPD, but lost his job because he couldn't seem to get to work on time. I loved using him because he came cheap and was paranoid enough to never leave a trace. He was actually Mensa certified and liked digging around in the virtual lives of strangers. There was no way he should've been wasting his days playing Minecraft in his grandma's two-bedroom apartment, but intellect and ambition aren't necessarily qualities that come as a packaged set.

I gave Craig the specifics over the phone and enticed him to meet me an hour later at a late-night Thai restaurant in downtown Los Angeles. Craig would do almost anything for Thai food.

"So you wanna know what I got?" he asked excitedly when I arrived. He'd already ordered the usual: spring rolls, chicken satay, and shrimp pad Thai.

"Of course I do. So spill it."

Craig was a late twentysomething, extremely hairy Filipino guy who spent so much time in front of computers his people skills were severely stunted.

"I found nothing out of the ordinary regarding her credit cards," he mumbled between bites of a spring roll. "Frequent charges at a Whole Foods near her place, a couple of gas stations, and a boatload of Amazon purchases. But for almost a month now, she's been completely off the grid. Your girl Ashley may well be dead."

That wasn't what I wanted to hear. If I found Ashley's dead body, would I still get the bonus? Patterson had hired us to find her before her mother died. He hadn't expressly stipulated that she had to be alive. I'd never had a case where the person I was hired to find turned up dead. I prayed that I'd be able to reunite Ashley with her dying mother.

Craig drained half of his Thai iced tea in a single slurp and frowned across the table at me. "I don't understand why you never eat."

"I'm on a diet," I lied.

My crazy-smart friend had atrocious eating habits, which was why I always sprang for the meal but never indulged along with him.

I tried to ignore the rice noodle hanging from the left corner of his mouth.

"What about her phone records?" I asked, disappointed that the credit card search hadn't produced a lead.

He crunched on his third spring roll. "Nada."

I sighed loudly. "Please tell me you didn't have me drive all the way down here just to tell me you didn't find anything."

"I did find a couple of tidbits."

He loudly guzzled down the rest of his iced tea and raised his glass in the air. A mouse of a woman instantly refilled it.

"Okay," I said, perking up.

"Your missing woman contacted Tentacle."

"What's that?"

"A high-tech security company. They specialize in video surveillance systems. Think of Ring on steroids. She had two conversations with them over a six-day period. But that was almost three months ago."

That gave me pause. "That explains all the high-tech equipment I saw in her apartment. But why would she need that level of security?"

"Maybe it wasn't about security."

"What do you mean?"

He stuffed a forkful of pad Thai into his mouth, then smiled like he was dangling a carrot. Craig had a crush on me and liked to extend our time together for as long as I let him. I was just glad he was way too socially awkward to ever ask me out.

"So you found something else?" I could feel my pulse picking up.

"Yep." He grinned. "And it's going to blow your mind."

Chapter 15

JACKSON

Eager to get Roxanna talking again, I went to work on her long, firm legs, starting with her thighs.

Roxanna, still on her back and covered with a towel, shut her eyes and after a moment began to speak. "I found an offshore bank account in the Caymans with just the initials AC."

"Okay, but that seems thin. Why do you think it's Ashley's?"

"Number one. The date account created is exactly one day before she go dark. Coincidence? Perhaps. Number two. The account IP address belong to coffee shop two miles from Ashley's apartment. She used internet many times in the past. Also a coincidence? I think not."

"It has to be her."

"*Ano*. Correct. And one more very interesting thing. Account contain only one hundred US."

The importance of this eluded me; then I got it. "Is that the minimum to open the account?"

She nodded. "*Ano*."

"She is likely setting up the account for a much bigger deposit."

Roxanna opened her eyes. "That means this girl involved in something to hide. Something not good. Trust me. Your Ashley only looks like nice girl."

My eyes narrowed. Roxanna was all about facts. It was rare for her to editorialize. "Okay. What else did you find?"

She laughed. "*Múj Bože*, is that not enough?"

"I just get the feeling you're holding something back."

Roxanna laughed. "You know me well. Mind and body."

"Must be big, the way you're stalling."

"Yes. Pretty big, I think."

"Tell me."

She pulled away the towel, once again exposing her perfect body. I politely looked away. "Roxanna, please."

"Just one happy ending for good friend, no? Your hands like magic. This fair, yes?"

"Sorry, Roxanna."

Twenty minutes later, smelling of vanilla cream, I was staring at a video on Roxanna's iPad. For hidden camera footage recorded in a dimly lit bedroom, the quality was exceptional—4K, full color, and very sharp. The faces of the man and woman engaged in heated sex were clearly visible. The man I didn't recognize, but the woman, to my astonishment, was Ashley Cross. Even more surprising, at the start of the clip, before Ashley led the man into the bedroom, she could be seen surreptitiously turning on the hidden camera. Ashley had made the recording.

"Where'd you get this?" I asked Roxanna.

The Magic Earth massage table was now raised into a recliner position. Roxanna was seated there, wrapped in a towel, looking quite refreshed. "I found in Ashley's cloud."

"Were there any other videos?"

"Yes. But mostly political stuff. No more videos in Ashley's bedroom on cloud."

"How do you know it's her own bedroom?"

"All you see is sex. I see more." Roxanna chuckled. "Some detective."

The moment my eyes left the action on the bed, I spotted it immediately. A framed photo of Ashley on the night table.

"Do you know when this was recorded?"

"Yes, of course. Two months ago. But you're not asking right question."

My eyes widened. I knew what question Roxanna was hinting at, but I couldn't imagine she actually knew the answer. "Wait. You know the man's identity?"

A knowing smile bloomed on her beautiful face.

"But how?"

"Facial recognition. AI-enhanced. New software, actually. I just install few weeks ago."

"Okay, who is he?"

Roxanna took the iPad from me, swiped the screen a few times, then handed it back. A mug shot filled the screen: a pissed-off-looking fortysomething white male, with one of those well-groomed Viking beards. His suit was rumpled, but I knew a $5,000 Kiton when I saw one.

"Name Lucius Findley," Roxanna said. "Digital assets operations manager for Coin Gate International. A crypto specialist. Arrested one year ago. Domestic abuse and false imprisonment."

I stared at Roxanna as if she had just told me I hit the lottery. "You're kidding."

"I am not. The charges drop. Two more arrests for same. Charges always drop. Treat ladies like shit then get good lawyer to fix. I believe good chance your Ashley with this man."

Zeroing in on Lucius's mug shot, I chuckled. *Good chance* was an understatement. I was looking at a sure thing. That bonus was as good as mine.

I just had one more question for Roxanna. "Please tell me you know where I can find this asshole."

Chapter 16

MACKENZIE

My personal Geek Squad had come through before, but this time Craig had gone above and beyond.

As I drove my Jeep along the Pacific Coast Highway toward the Palisades, I couldn't resist daydreaming about expanding my bank account with that fifty grand.

The connection Craig had found between Ashley and a serial domestic abuser named Lucius Findley was money in the bank. The fact that he resided in the Palisades—the second-richest neighborhood in Los Angeles—explained why he'd never been convicted. He had enough money to hire formidable lawyers and could pay for his accusers' silence.

Did Lucius's past guarantee that he was mixed up in Ashley's disappearance? Absolutely not. Only a rookie investigator would believe that *any* lead was a sure thing. Still, the pattern made sense. The crypto broker's violent past increased the odds that Ashley Cross was with him, either willingly or by force.

Of course, there was another possibility. A grim one. Maybe this time the shithead had gone too far. Maybe Lucius had killed Ashley and used his considerable resources to get rid of her body.

But that scenario did not fit his MO. Lucius Findley wasn't a killer, he was just a cowardly batterer hiding behind a fat wallet.

So, yes, I liked my odds. Maybe she'd be frightened and bruised, but very much alive. In fact, I was so confident that I had to resist flooring the gas and zipping around all the Teslas and Porsches clogging up the highway.

Inevitably, thoughts of purchasing a new car invaded my cash-fueled daydream. My old Jeep had definitely seen better days. Of course, had I followed the path my mother had laid out for me, I wouldn't have to pay a mechanic with the regularity of a Netflix subscription. But my independence was far more important to me than driving a car that cost almost as much as my mortgage. It made much more sense to use the bonus on something practical, like zeroing out my credit card debt.

One thing I was really looking forward to was the look on Jackson's face when he found out I'd scored that bonus. It was going to feel great to beat Mr. Cocky. As I passed a highway sign telling me my exit was just one mile away, I had the urge to call my competition and tell him I was about to crack the case. But instead of reaching for my iPhone, I bit my lip. I wasn't one to count my chickens too early. Better to find Ashley first. I could dance on Jackson's ego later.

I took the next exit and drove north along Palisades Drive, a four-lane thoroughfare flanked by the rolling hills of Topanga State Park. A few minutes later, I was cruising up a private road into an exclusive neighborhood tucked into the surrounding wilderness. Every home I passed could have been featured on *Million Dollar Listing*. Lucius's house loomed at the very end of a cul-de-sac, a sleek and striking mix of natural stone, wood, and smooth stucco. I was so distracted by its beauty that I failed to notice a candy-apple-red Mercedes convertible coming up on my rear. As it cruised past me and parked in front of Lucius's house, I spotted Jackson behind the wheel.

I couldn't believe my eyes. Correction: I could believe that Jackson "Rooster" Jones drove a flashy, top-of-the-line German sports car. What I couldn't believe was that he was staking a claim to my lead. Gaping and squeezing my steering wheel, I parked behind him and practically leapt out of my Jeep. Jackson emerged from his car, looking as surprised and irritated as I was. At the foot of Lucius's driveway, we squared off, each blurting out the same question.

"What the hell are you doing here?"

We exchanged stories. Of course, Jackson had his own computer snoop. According to him, a world-class superhacker. And I believed him. Not only did he have all the pertinent information on Lucius's past crimes, Jackson's Czech connect had also given him a video. Jackson held up his iPhone and showed me a quick clip of Ashley and Lucius getting it on.

"Wow," I said. "She's good."

"Ashley?"

I rolled my eyes. "No. Your hacker girlfriend."

"Roxanna isn't my girlfriend."

"Whatever you say. Now what?"

"Now you jump back into your little Jeep and skedaddle off home to Inglewood."

"And why would I do that?"

"Because I was here first."

I laughed in his face. "Yeah, but only because you snuck past me."

"Technically, I was still first."

I knew Jackson was playing around, but I had to fight the urge to get upset. In my mind, I had just lost a major payday. At least half of it. I was about to tell Jackson where he could put his technicality when a voice interrupted.

"Excuse me. Something I can help you two with?"

Lucius Findley stood framed in his doorway. He was draped in a white terry-cloth robe that accentuated the gross, square-sculpted black mass of hair that covered half his face. The iced-gold bitcoin pendant around his neck and the fat smoldering cigar pinched between his fingers completed his look. I'd bet anything he wore a wifebeater under that robe.

Jackson and I traded looks. We needed to settle our little disagreement fast. I raised a *one moment please* finger to Lucius, then whispered to Jackson, "If Ashley's here, we split the bonus, fifty-fifty. Deal?"

Jackson nodded. "Sounds like a plan."

Chapter 17

JACKSON

Lucius, dragging on a Cuban Montecristo, watched with narrowed eyes as Mackenzie and I moved up his walkway.

Out of courtesy, I asked an obvious question. "Lucius Findley, right?"

Lucius blew a cloud of smoke as he looked us over. "Who's asking?"

"My name's Jackson Jones. She's Mackenzie Cunningham. We're private investigators."

"Good for you. What do you want?"

"We're working a missing person case. Ashley Cross. You once dated her, correct?"

Without missing a beat, he replied, "Incorrect. Never heard of her. Now, if you don't mind."

Lucius tried to retreat into the house, but Mackenzie stiff-armed the door. "Cut the crap. We have video of you and Ashley from just a couple of months ago."

"Bullshit, sweetheart."

"My name's Mackenzie, not sweetheart."

When I'd spotted Mackenzie's Jeep headed toward Lucius's

place, I felt gut-punched, fearing I might have to kiss that bonus goodbye. But seeing the way she made that asshole flinch just now was easily worth half the bounty. I held up my phone and showed Lucius a sample of Ashley's hidden-camera work.

Lucius watched the video wearing a slight smile. "That sneaky little bitch."

"Where is she?" I asked.

Lucius shrugged. "I have no idea."

Mackenzie nodded toward the house. "Is she in there?"

"You got a hearing problem, honey?"

"It's Mackenzie, not honey."

"Whatever. I'm through talking."

Lucius tried to shut his door again, but this time I grabbed it. "If you don't talk to us, you'll be downtown talking to the police. No one's seen Ashley for months, except for you, it seems." I waved my phone in Lucius's face to remind him of the video. "With your record of being heavy-handed with your girlfriends, the police will be quite interested in your connection to Ashley."

Mackenzie pressed him further. "If you've hurt her in any way—"

"Hurt her?" Lucius laughed. "Ashley comes off like a princess, but she's no delicate flower. Not even close. The bitch used me."

"And just how did she use you?" I asked.

Lucius took a puff of his cigar. "I met Ashley about three months ago at a crypto event in Irvine. I was the keynote. She came on real hard. That surprised me because I've never had much luck with the sistas." Lucius winked at a glaring Mackenzie, then continued. "I took Ashley for a crypto groupie. That's a thing, you know. We hooked up for a few weeks, but nothing serious. She kept bugging me about helping her set up an offshore account. Encrypted. Untraceable. Real fishy shit that I wanted no part of. I kept putting her off, but she kept screwing my brains out." He spread his palms.

"What's a guy to do? The moment Ashley got what she wanted, she ghosted me. End of story."

Mackenzie shot me a look that told me she was thinking exactly what I was thinking. This asshole sounded like he was telling the truth. Of course, he could just be a damn good liar.

As if reading my thoughts, Mackenzie pinned Lucius with suspicious eyes. "So, you're saying you have absolutely no idea where Ashley is?"

"Exactly. Now, if you both would—"

"Prove it," Mackenzie said. "Let us look around inside."

"What?"

It took balls for my fine colleague to make such a bold request, and I loved it. I also noticed that Lucius suddenly looked a little rattled.

"Yeah," I jumped in. "We just wanna make sure Ashley isn't handcuffed to your bed."

"Or worse," Mackenzie jabbed.

"Fuck off," Lucius said with a nervous laugh. He was definitely hiding something, and I could sense that Mackenzie had picked up on it as well.

"If you're telling us the truth," I said to Lucius, "what's the harm?"

"Come on," Mackenzie said. "Give us a quick tour, then we're gone."

Lucius's devil-may-care demeanor vanished scary fast. His voice boomed, "Listen, motherfuckers. Both of you get the fuck off my property before I call the neighborhood watch."

I thought it was odd that he threatened to call the local rent-a-cops and not the police.

He looked us up and down with seething contempt. "They're armed . . . and it's clear you two don't belong in this 'hood."

Mackenzie opened her mouth to lay into the prick, but before she could get a word out a female voice called out from inside the house: "Sir, is everything okay? Sir?"

There was recognition on Mackenzie's face. "Who's that?" she said to Lucius.

"None of your fucking business." Lucius tried to slam the door in our faces, but Mackenzie and I threw our shoulders against it. The door burst open and Lucius went crashing to the marble floor.

Mackenzie and I leapt over Lucius, like side-by-side hurdlers, and charged into the house.

Chapter 18

MACKENZIE

Can you hear me, sir?" the female voice continued to call out from upstairs.

Jackson and I sprinted across a garishly modern foyer, centered by a crystal chandelier, and ran up a sweeping stairway to the second floor. Looking past the ornate railing that lined the overlook, I could see a furious Lucius below, lifting himself from the floor.

"Get out of my fucking house," he shouted.

Jackson pointed to large double doors at the end of a long hall. "I bet she's in there."

Our footfalls resonated on intricate mosaic marble as we bolted past several closed doors and pushed through the double doors into the master bedroom. It was as if we had entered a stylish black void. Every piece of the angular decor was the color of dark charcoal trimmed with gold. Even the wood-paneled walls were black. A floor-to-ceiling blackout curtain concealed any hint of the sunny day outside. Instead, the room was barely lit by dim recessed lighting.

A woman, wearing only a bra and panties, lay in the center of a huge California king bed. She was young and pretty with curly red hair.

The woman was not Ashley.

Understandably, the woman recoiled when we charged into the room, panting. "Who are you?" she said in a trembling voice. "Please don't hurt me!"

Before Jackson or I could reply, Lucius barreled into the room gripping a .38. Jackson reached into his jacket, but Lucius took aim and hissed, "Don't you move another fucking inch."

Jackson froze.

Lucius and his Smith & Wesson stood between us and the exit. "Hands up," he barked. "Both of you."

"Look, clearly we made a mistake," Jackson said. "Just let us leave and—"

"I said hands in the air!"

Jackson raised his hands. Mine were already up. Having a gun pointed in my direction was a chilling experience.

The young redhead said to Lucius, "Sir, who are these people?"

"Just shut up and keep quiet," he snapped, then returned his glaring eyes to us. "This is a home invasion. I could shoot both your asses right now and get away with it."

"So do it, then," Jackson challenged him.

I glared over at Jackson, but his eyes were locked on Lucius, not me. I assumed Jackson knew the man was no killer. Still, I didn't think it was wise to taunt him.

"Don't tell me what to do in my own house, motherfucker."

"Okay," Jackson said. "So what now?"

Jackson appeared relatively cool. I probably looked the same, but I could feel my pounding heart in my neck. During my five years as a private detective, I'd never had a gun pointed at me. Now I was just a finger twitch away from death.

Remembering my Krav Maga training, I centered myself and steadied my breathing.

"You two think you're so fucking smart," Lucius said. "I told you the truth about that bitch Ashley. Instead of thanking me and going about your business, you run in here and scare my girlfriend."

"You're right," Jackson said. "And we apologize." Then he turned to me. "Right?"

I nodded. "Yes. Sorry."

Lucius stared at us for a tense beat, probably trying to decide how much humiliation he could milk from us. Finally he nodded toward the woman on the bed and said, "Her too. Apologize to her, then get the fuck out."

Without hesitation, Jackson pivoted to face the redhead. "Sorry we frightened you, ma'am."

Following Jackson's example, I turned and looked the young woman in the eye. "I'm really sorry. We didn't mean to scare you."

She nodded, then did something that made my heart stop. She extended the fingers of her right hand, then closed them around her thumb. I'd seen that hand signal before. I'd never admit it to anyone, but I'm a closeted TikTok watcher. I find the endless stream of homemade videos wildly entertaining. But TikTok isn't all stupid pranks and trendy dances. Occasionally I'd come across videos that were poignant, heart-wrenching, or educational. The hand gesture the redhead had just made was a way for domestic violence victims to secretly signal for help.

"All right," Lucius said. "Good enough." He stepped sideways and waved his gun toward the doorway. "Now get out."

Jackson was already moving past Lucius and through the bedroom door. I hadn't moved an inch and I had no intention of leaving without taking the young woman with me.

"Hey, sweetheart," Lucius said to me. "I said you're free to go. Get the fuck out."

"Mackenzie," Jackson called from beyond the door. "Come on. Let's get out of here."

I was no longer focused on the weapon in Lucius's hand. All I saw was a hairy human target who was about to reap the benefit of my years of Krav Maga training.

"Move it, honey," Lucius said. "Before I change my mind."

"Okay, okay." I took a few steps toward the exit. The instant I was in striking distance, my fist slammed into Lucius's throat. He made a gagging sound and the gun discharged into the floor. He tried to raise it, but my straight kick reached his groin first. A sickly cry escaped Lucius's gaping mouth. I grabbed the hand holding the gun and twisted it with every ounce of upper body strength I could muster. The snap of bone was followed by the thud of the gun hitting the floor.

"Owww! You broke my wrist!" Lucius yelled.

He stumbled forward just as I yanked on his stupid beard, pulling his face down to meet my rising knee. Another snap, and blood gushed from his broken nose. I took a step back and let Lucius crumple to the floor, out cold.

A shocked Jackson rushed to grab Lucius's gun. "Whoa," he said to me with a nervous laugh. "I will never call you honey. Never."

I turned to the young woman. Tears rolled down her face.

"Get dressed," I told her. "We're getting you out of here."

Chapter 19

JACKSON

No fewer than six LAPD emergency vehicles, lights flashing, crowded the cul-de-sac outside Lucius Findley's house. I stood nearby, listening as Mackenzie briefed a huddle of uniforms and detectives.

The redhead, who'd told us her name was Jessica Sutton, waited apprehensively in the back seat of an unmarked police car. A few yards away, a handcuffed Lucius was being treated by paramedics under the watchful eyes of several officers.

I had to give Mackenzie her props. Even if I had noticed Jessica's hand signal, I wouldn't have known what it meant. As it turned out, Jessica was not Lucius's girlfriend. She'd met the bearded crypto expert at a nightclub and decided to go home with him, only to find herself trapped in his bedroom for the last three weeks. Lucius had used a combination of threats, psychological abuse, restraints, drugs, and even beatings to keep her captive. While he insisted it was all consensual role-playing, Jessica said she'd made it clear that she had wanted to leave from day one.

Given Lucius's history of violence, the detectives seemed to get a real kick from the beatdown he'd taken from Mackenzie. We were asked to accompany them to the precinct for further questioning.

After telling us we'd probably be subpoenaed to testify against the shithead if he didn't plead out, we were finally free to leave.

In the chaotic aftermath of Jessica's rescue and Lucius's arrest, there'd been little opportunity for Mac and me to exchange more than a few words about what went down. We decided to leave our vehicles in the precinct's parking lot and walk down the block to a corner diner with a classic Hollywood theme. We slid into a booth beneath a vintage *Rear Window* poster and ordered coffee. Mackenzie also ordered a basket of fries, which I totally planned to pilfer.

"So," I said to Mackenzie, "how good did it feel? Honestly."

She cracked a wicked smile. "Damn good. That asshole deserved worse."

"What was that anyway? Kung fu? Karate?"

"Krav Maga."

"I figured it began with a *k*."

Mackenzie laughed. I liked the way she laughed. To be honest, I liked the way she moved her tight little body too. Suddenly I realized I was staring. She noticed it too.

"You okay?" she asked.

"Yeah. I just never met a woman who could probably kick my ass."

She arched a single brow. "Probably?"

This time I laughed, but immediately regretted giving her so much power. I didn't want to come off looking weak. Women don't respect weak. Weak men get banished to the friend zone. Maybe friendship was good enough for Mackenzie, but I wasn't quite sure yet. I'd have to be more careful.

When the coffee and fries arrived, Mackenzie sipped hers black. I usually took mine with a healthy dose of cream and sugar, but decided to follow Mac's lead. I needed to repair my earlier misstep by dialing up the masculinity a bit.

After a minute or so of quietly sipping coffee and munching on ketchup-dipped fries, Mackenzie sighed and said, "I thought we had that bonus in the bag."

"Me too. I had major plans for that cash."

"I was really looking forward to paying off all my credit cards," she complained.

"Really?" I said.

A smug smile eased across her lips. "Let me guess. Your first purchase would be a new suit, right?"

I sat more erect in the booth. "Most def. Along with some new rims and bigger surround-sound speakers for my home theater."

Mackenzie rolled her eyes and popped another fry into her mouth. "To each his own."

I was irritated that she was judging me, but let it go. "Well, Ashley's still out there," I said. "And so is that bonus."

"Right," she agreed. "I just hope one of us gets it and not that jerk Lance."

"Word."

We clinked mugs.

"Just to be clear," I said, "our fifty-fifty deal is off."

Mackenzie shot a hard stare across the table. "I know that."

"Cool." I reached for another fry, but Mackenzie yanked the basket away.

"You think I need your help finding Ashley?"

I gestured at the now-hostaged fries. "Really?"

Mackenzie's gaze didn't waver. "Answer my question."

"Let's look at the facts. I was able to get my hands on the actual video of Ashley and Lucius. You were not. Clearly my resources are superior to yours. I just don't want any hard feelings when I score that bonus."

She smiled. "You wish. Anyway, if you do win it, I can just beat you up and take it."

I laughed the comment off. "That's real funny," I finally said. "I do carry a gun, you know."

A tense moment hung in the air, thankfully interrupted by a chirp from Mackenzie's cell phone.

She glanced curiously at her screen. I could see that she had opened a text message, but I couldn't make out what it said from across the table.

Mackenzie noticed my prying eyes and placed the phone face-down.

"Guess who just got a huge lead?" Her face was lit up with excitement.

Before I could ask if she planned to share, Mackenzie shoved the basket to my side of the table. "You can pay the bill since you ate most of the fries."

With that, she slid from the booth and race-walked out of the diner.

I sat there alone with a half a basket of cold fries, jealous that Mackenzie had a new lead and I didn't.

Chapter 20

MACKENZIE

I jumped into the front seat of my Jeep with a massive smile on my face. Right about now, Jackson was probably stressing out about my big lead. Too bad I didn't actually have one.

All Jackson's bluster about winning that bonus was getting to me. But I couldn't let him undermine my confidence. So I'd lied and said I had a lead.

Let the head games begin.

The text I'd received was actually from Lance Brooks asking me to give him a call. He was probably trying to mess with my head too. Just as I was weighing whether I should bother calling him back, my phone rang.

"Hey, beautiful, how you doing?" Lance said in his gravelly voice.

"Why are you calling me?"

"Wow. So it's like that?"

"Just tell me what you want."

"Why the hostile attitude?"

Lance was trying to take me off my game just like Jackson had tried to do and I wasn't in the mood. "I'm busy."

"Okay, forget the small talk. I'd like to talk to you."

"So talk."

"I have a lead."

Sure you do.

Did this nutcase actually believe I trusted him? If he even had a lead, there was no way he was going to share it with me. He probably wanted to tie up my time by sending me on a wild goose chase. Maybe I would flip the script and play him.

"Great. So tell me about this lead you have."

"I think it's a damn good one. But it needs a female touch."

I chuckled. "Oh, so you need me to throw in a little skirt action. Is that it?"

"Aw, stop being so sensitive. That was just a joke."

"So you're going to just hand over your lead out of the goodness of your heart and let me walk away with the jackpot?"

"I didn't say that. But there's definitely something in it for you. Can you meet me at my office?"

I spent the bumper-to-bumper drive to Lance's office in the Valley plotting how I intended to turn the tables on him. If he did have some information about Ashley, I was prepared to double-cross him before he could do the same to me.

The San Fernando Valley used to be the undisputed porn capital of the world. But once California politicians started pushing laws requiring porn stars to wear condoms, the porn producers had packed up their cameras and migrated to Florida.

Not all of the Valley's old-time charms relocated. The Lucky Lancelot was a strip club off Ventura Boulevard surrounded by motels and liquor stores. The pickup trucks and motorcycles in the club's parking lot were an indication that the place wasn't frequented by high-rollers.

"Well, well, well. Welcome, little lady." A beefy guy with biceps the size of ham hocks greeted me at the well-lit entrance.

He grinned as he took his time looking me up and down. I was no doubt overdressed for this venue in my jeans and sleeveless black turtleneck. But Mr. Beefeater didn't seem to mind.

I returned the favor, leaning back so I could ogle him right back.

"If you like what you see," he said, grinning, "I can definitely make it happen."

I smiled sweetly. "How about a rain check?"

He waved a two-foot wand over my body, then gave me the go-ahead to walk through the metal detectors and pass four more bouncers who could've doubled as extras in a caveman flick.

The interior of the Lucky Lancelot induced a mind-numbing myriad of sensations: deafening music, flashing neon lights, rowdy catcalls, and boisterous laughter. Smoking was prohibited, but the strong smell of weed, tinged with the aroma of alcohol and buffalo wings, was overpowering.

I stood just inside the door, waiting for my eyes to adjust to the darkness. A near-naked contortionist was onstage twisting her body around a sparkly gold pole as a gaggle of men hurled dollar bills her way.

As I scanned the room looking for Lance, a tall, busty redhead wearing pasties and a Post-it note for panties appeared from nowhere. She practically grazed my nose with one of her big boobs.

"Hi, I'm Prissy. Can I get you a drink, sweetness?" She winked. "Or anything else?"

It hit me that she must've assumed I was here for a different kind of business.

"I'm straight," I said.

"Doesn't mean you can't appreciate a nice lap dance." Her thick eyelashes fluttered like two black butterflies.

I shook my head and tried to look regretful. "Where can I find Lance Brooks?"

She pointed over her shoulder. "Tell the bartender. She'll call him for you."

As I squeezed through the maze of tiny tables and chairs, I didn't garner even a glance from the all-male crowd. I was almost offended, but then again, I *was* a bit overdressed.

Taking an empty stool, I waited until the bartender—the only fully dressed woman in the place besides me—made it to my end of the bar.

"What can I get you?"

"I have an appointment with Lance Brooks," I said. "Can you tell him Mackenzie Cunningham is here?"

She nodded, picked up her cell, and turned her back to me. I assumed she was texting someone because she never placed the phone to her ear.

"Wait over there by the red curtain." She pointed to the far right corner of the club. "Someone will take you to Lance's office."

I stood in front of the curtain, watching a different stripper captivate the crowd. This one was Asian and not nearly as busty as the first. Still, the mob around the stage had doubled in size. When she squatted, opened her legs, and did a backflip, the crescendo of drunken cheers would've rattled the windows if there'd been any.

The red curtain behind me suddenly opened, revealing a door.

"Follow me, please."

I heard the female voice before I saw who it was attached to.

She was white, a foot taller than me, and also fully dressed—though I use the word *dressed* loosely. A leopard-print dress snaked around her body and her red, studded pumps could've doubled as stilts. Her face had a few miles on it, but not enough to distract from her prettiness.

"I'm Crystal Douglass, chief of operations. Mr. Brooks is expecting you."

Her professionalism didn't match her outfit or the Lucky Lancelot.

I followed her down a well-lit hallway, a stark contrast to the darkness on the other side of the red curtain.

Something told me she might appreciate a little ego stroking. "I'm sure a woman in this business has to be quite a badass to get men to respect her."

Crystal looked back at me over her shoulder. "Girlfriend, you don't even know the half of it."

Before I realized it, the atmosphere had gone from strip-club sleazy to workplace chic. It even smelled better back here. We stopped in an open area with a desk and a small couch. An eight-by-ten photograph on the corner of the desk showed Crystal wrapped around a candy-striped pole. She was gorgeous and I couldn't stop staring.

"Yep, that's me," she said wistfully. "I was really something back in the day. But since I got promoted to administration, I haven't looked back."

To the left of her desk were huge double doors that could easily have led into the Oval Office. She pressed a button underneath her desktop and the doors opened inward.

Crystal escorted me the few feet to the doorway and—seemingly for the benefit of Lance—announced, "Mr. Brooks can see you now."

Lance sat behind a huge oak desk, beaming like a baby walrus. His office was exquisite. Tasteful artwork, floor-to-ceiling curtains, modern Italian furniture. There was a sitting area with two velvet chairs, a couch, and a small coffee table. The *Playboy*, *Penthouse*, and *Hustler* magazines on the table were the only things that distinguished this place from the office of a Wall Street executive.

"So tell me about this lead you supposedly have?" I said, marching up to his desk.

"What do you think of my digs?" Lance rocked back in his leather chair, clearly hungry for approval.

I didn't bother to look around. "Nice. So what's up with this lead?" I was here for business and nothing else.

"I think I've found someone who may know where Ashley is."

"*May know*? Why are they holding back?"

"Well, it's this chick who doesn't really like me."

Surprise, surprise.

"But if you approach her, she may give up the goods."

"And why is that?"

"She's a soul sister. Like you."

Did he really just say that?

"What's her name?"

"I can't tell you just yet. We have to agree on your role."

I huffed. This was such bull. "I'm listening."

"If she gives you the four-one-one and I find Ashley, I'll pay you five grand."

All I could do was chuckle. "Oh, so you want me to be your gofer for chump change. Or maybe you're just sending me on a wild goose chase to distract me from finding Ashley myself. No, thanks."

I made a move toward the door.

"No, wait. That was just my opening offer." He stood up. "Let's get more comfortable."

He waddled over to the couch and plopped down. "C'mon, have a seat." He patted the cushion next to where he was sitting.

Really, dude?

I acted as if I was going to comply, but sat down in one of the chairs across from him instead.

Lance frowned. I smiled.

For the next five minutes, Lance kept upping my supposed cut of the bonus and I kept rejecting it.

"Okay, okay, final offer. Twelve grand."

"No, thanks. I only came here to find out what you had," I lied. "I have a few solid leads of my own."

Lance pursed his flabby lips. "Sure you do."

"This meeting is over." I got to my feet and rounded the chair just as Lance sprang off the couch.

"Wait. Okay. Fifteen grand. Final offer."

"I'll pass."

I took a step forward, but Lance blocked my path.

"You ever thought of stripping?" His bulging eyes glistened with lust. "My clientele loves black chicks with tight little bods like yours."

"I don't have time for this."

I moved sideways and so did he. His stale bourbon breath warmed my cheek.

A spark of anger raged through me, transforming Lance's head into a punching bag. *Jab, cross. Jab, cross. Jab, cross.*

"The minute you stepped into Patterson's office, I could see you on the pole." He licked his lips. "I bet you're a firecracker in bed."

Before I could strike, Lance pulled me into his doughy body and smashed his wet lips against mine.

"Excuse me," Jackson said, standing frozen in the doorway. "Am I interrupting something?"

Chapter 21

JACKSON

As I strode into Lance's office, the last thing I expected to see was that asshole locking lips with a beautiful black woman. When I realized that it was Mackenzie in Lance's embrace, I nearly fell over.

They both looked surprised to see me. Mac also looked infuriated. In two lightning-quick moves she broke free of Lance's bear hug and drove stiff fingers into his Adam's apple. I cringed as Lance crashed to his knees clutching his throat as if he were having a heart attack in his neck. His mouth moved like he wanted to scream, but only a thin rasp came out.

Damn. She really could beat me up.

Mackenzie pointed down at Lance's face like Zeus firing a lightning bolt. "If you ever touch me again, I'll rip out your fucking trachea."

Then Mackenzie whirled around to face me. "What the hell are you doing here?"

"He called me about some kind of lead," I said, gesturing toward a still-gasping Lance. "I'm guessing you got the same call."

"You guessed right."

As Lance struggled to his feet, Mackenzie turned back to him.

"What's the story? You taking lessons from Raymond Patterson? You planning to offer both of us the same *so-called* deal?"

Lance coughed, then replied in a hoarse voice. "What deal?"

"C'mon, I didn't hit you that hard. Did that jab wipe out your memory or something? The *soul sister* who supposedly knows where Ashley is. The one you wanted me to talk to in exchange for a cut of the fifty K. *That* deal."

Lance winced and held his throat as he laughed. "Yeah, you can forget that. There is no deal." Then he turned to me and said, "You can forget it too. I don't need either of you."

"Hold on," I said. "If this is for real, I might be willing to work with you. What's the split?"

Mackenzie shot me a look, obviously vexed that I was so willing to push her aside.

"Just get out," Lance snapped. "Both of you. No use trying to do business with you people."

Mackenzie and I traded *oh no he didn't* looks, then both glared at Lance and said, "*You people?*"

Lance defiantly returned our stares. "Yeah, *you* people! Now get the fuck out before I call my bouncers."

I'd gotten a good look at Lance's bouncers when I'd entered the club. Big white dudes with way too much Neanderthal DNA. Mackenzie must've noticed them too because, like me, she seemed to deflate a bit. I wasn't one to back down from a fight, but there was the right time and place for everything. Apparently Mac and I saw eye to eye on this snippet of Survival 101. A few moments later we were in the parking lot, walking back to our cars.

"Can you believe that asshole?" Mackenzie said.

"What I can't believe is that Lance is your type. Wow, that was some kiss."

Mac stopped walking. "What the hell are you talking about? Didn't you see the way I kissed him back with that throat strike?"

"I saw it, but what I don't understand is, with all your skills, how'd he get that close to you in the first place?"

Mackenzie crossed her arms. "Meaning what exactly?"

"Meaning maybe you wanted it to happen. Some women like the brutish oaf type."

Mackenzie balled her hands into fists and glared at me. Truth be told, in light of how she'd massacred Lucius and just brought Lance to his knees, her glare was pretty unnerving.

"I'm waiting for you to tell me you're kidding so I won't murder you where you stand."

"I'm not kidding."

She gritted her teeth. "I'm going to count to three. One. Two. Th—"

I burst out laughing. "Okay, okay. I'm kidding."

"Damn right you are." I caught the faintest smile on her face as she resumed walking. I went after her.

"Not very nice threatening a friend," I said.

"Oh, so we're friends now? Do you try to steal all of your friends' deals?"

"I would never team up with Lance," I told her. "I was just feeling him out. It's clear to me now what he was really up to."

Mackenzie stopped again. "And what's that?"

"There's no deal. No *soul sister* who knows Ashley's location. He made it all up to get us down here at the same time. Lance actually wanted me to catch you two doing the tongue tango."

"Yuck!"

"I bet he wanted me to think you two were in cahoots. If you and I got into it, that would throw both of us off our games. Only he made one big mistake. He didn't realize you and Bruce Lee were first cousins."

Mac screwed up her face. "You're giving Lance way too much credit. I doubt his game is that deep."

"Running a strip club in this town is no joke. Takes maneuvering around some very heavy hitters. After getting a load of this place, I wouldn't underestimate him."

Mac thought about that for a second. "Okay, maybe. But one thing doesn't add up. Why would fatso think you catching me with him would put us at odds?"

I shrugged. "Black man sees a black woman in a white man's arms. Lance is a racist fuckhead, so he assumed my reaction would be to go nuclear."

Mackenzie shook her head. "I just don't see Lance as the chess grand master you're making him out to be."

"I guess it could be something simpler. Perhaps he could tell that you clearly have a thing for me."

Mackenzie's head reared back and her hands flew to her hips. "Excuse me?"

I couldn't resist getting a rise out of her. She was such an easy mark. "Don't be embarrassed. I *am* pretty irresistible."

"You're quite full of yourself, mister."

I laughed. "I'm just messing with you. But my detective's instinct couldn't help noticing that you didn't deny it."

"Well, my detective's instinct tells me you're fishing." Her eyes narrowed. "Maybe *you've* got a thing for me."

Damn. Not only was she sexy, she was also quick with the comeback. I loved sassy, intelligent women. And I was also loving this little game.

"I like how you spun that," I said with a chuckle. "Nice try. But I still didn't hear a denial in there."

Mackenzie almost smiled. "Still fishing. And I really don't have time for your nonsense. I've got fifty thousand better things to do with my time. See ya."

I enjoyed the view as she strode away, then called after her: "That's still not a denial."

Never breaking stride, Mackenzie flipped me the middle finger and called out in a singsong voice, "Still fishing."

Chapter 22

MACKENZIE

I never slept in. So why was I still in bed at 9:07 a.m. on a weekday?

Yawning and extending my arms into a good stretch, I reveled in the luxurious feel of the bedsheets against my skin. For years I had rebelled against the extravagances of wealth my parents had force-fed my brother and me. But the one indulgence I still clung to was my eight-hundred-thread-count sheets. Except now I bought them at TJ Maxx instead of Saks.

Turning over, I buried my head under my pillow. I still wanted to puke at the thought of that pig putting his lips on mine. The entire trip to Lance's place yesterday had been one big bust. Well, not exactly. I had enjoyed the reaction on Jackson's face when he walked in on us. He'd tried to joke about it, but I'd seen more than a flash of jealousy in his eyes.

I rolled over and stared up at the ceiling. A rush of warmth eased through my body at the thought of Jackson. I wondered what kissing him would feel like. Maybe . . .

What the hell?

Why was my mind even going there?

It was definitely time to get up and rejoin the Find Ashley Cross search party. I checked my email, hoping to see a message from a friend at the Inglewood Police Department whom I'd asked to do a criminal records check on Ashley, as well as her parents and her most recent boyfriend. But there was no email from him.

I stretched again, just as my phone started ringing. I grabbed it from the nightstand without glancing at the caller ID.

All I could hear was gibberish. Hysterical gibberish. But I immediately recognized the voice of our receptionist, Joy.

I swung my legs to the floor and sat up. "Slow down, Joy. I can't understand a word you're saying."

More gibberish.

"Okay, stop," I ordered. "Just stop and take a breath."

Joy did as instructed, her frantic voice replaced by labored breathing.

"Are you okay? Now, tell me what's wrong. Slowly."

I was already on my feet, moving toward my jeans draped across a chair next to the bed. If Joy was calling me upset, it probably had something to do with the office.

"Somebody broke in," she sniveled. "You should see this place. Somebody tore it up. It's a mess!"

Placing the phone on the dresser, I hit the speakerphone button as I slipped into my jeans, then grabbed a bra and T-shirt.

I was already seeing red. What kind of scam were the two clowns I shared office space with involved in now? I knew they were criminals, but I liked the digs and the rent fit my budget, so I looked the other way. But now that I was part of the collateral damage, it was another story. When you lie down with dogs, you almost certainly get up with fleas. And in my case, bedbugs and ticks too.

"Have you called the police?"

"Yeah, but they said a break-in's not a high priority."

"Are Rod and Clint there?"

"Not yet."

Of course they weren't. My office mates strolled in on CP—criminal people's—time. No matter how many clients or patients were waiting in their offices.

"Well, call them and tell them to get their asses to the office now."

I was way too upset to trust myself behind the wheel of a car, so I jogged the four blocks to my office. I took the stairs to the second level of the strip mall three at a time. Charging past Joy's desk, I rushed to the doorway of my office—then froze, horrified.

The place looked like the aftermath of an FBI raid. It was as if someone had turned the room upside down and violently shaken it. My chair was lying on its side. Every piece of paper on my desk had been swept away. The drawers of my filing cabinet hung open, folders haphazardly sticking out. The cheap art pieces I had on the walls were now shards of broken wood and cracked glass.

My laptop!

I darted over to my desk. I kept my laptop locked up in a bottom drawer. It was halfway open, the lock broken. I held my breath as I pulled the drawer all the way out. My laptop wasn't there. I collapsed to my knees and searched underneath my desk, then crawled around the rest of my office grabbing papers, hoping and praying it might be hidden under the debris. I must have looked like a blind person reading a floor imprinted with Braille.

Just as I was about to implode, I remembered lying in bed last night, browsing the web. My laptop was safely buried underneath my comforter at home.

Taking a breath, I stared up at a wide-eyed Joy.

"How bad did they tear up Rod's and Clint's offices?" I asked.

Joy shook her head. "Not bad at all. Theirs weren't touched."

"What?" I would have been less stunned if she had slapped me. I slowly got to my feet, holding on to my fallen chair to boost myself up.

"Everything else around here is fine," she said. "I checked."

I pushed past her, determined to see for myself. I stepped through the work comp attorney's open door. Nothing had been touched. I dashed across the hall to the chiropractor's office. Again, everything was in its proper place.

WTF?

Joy followed me as I trudged back to my office.

"What time did you get in this morning? When did this happen?" My tone was angry and demanding.

Joy put a hand on her hip. "Don't start taking this out on me. I didn't do nothing."

I cupped my forehead. "I know, I know. Sorry. Did anybody around here see anything?"

"The guy from the Chinese place came up here right after I called you. He saw two guys looking through the window when he was closing up last night."

"What time?"

"About eleven fifteen."

I froze. That was around the time I had arrived at Lance's strip club. Jackson had surmised that Lance was trying to throw us off our game. Perhaps. But now I had no doubt the slob also wanted me away from my office so he could ransack it. I'd bet anything that he'd sent a couple of his goons to steal information I'd gathered on Ashley Cross. A folder I'd had on my desk with Ashley's name on it was missing. But that was no big deal. My most important research was on my laptop.

That worthless pig. His rep for dirty tricks was one thing, but this was nuts.

Picking up my chair, I flopped into it and promptly fell backward, crashing into the wall. One of the rollers was missing.

"It's gonna be okay," Joy said reassuringly. The despair on my face brought sympathy to hers. "We have a spare chair in the store-room. Want me to get it for you?"

"No, I'm fine." I positioned the chair against the wall and sat back down. "Just give me a minute."

Lance was not getting away with this. No friggin' way.

My next thought was to call Jackson. He'd be just as outraged as I was that Lance had pulled a stunt like this. I eased my phone from my back pocket, but I didn't dial.

If I called Jackson, he might see me as some helpless damsel in distress looking for a man to rescue her. I set the phone on my desk. A desk that hadn't been this decluttered since the day I bought it.

I leaned back in my unsteady chair and buried my face in my palms. I really needed to talk to Jackson. Hell, Lance might target him next.

That was it. That was my excuse. I would tell Jackson I was calling to warn him. I picked up the phone and dialed.

But before it even rang, I heard Jackson's sexy baritone.

Chapter 23

JACKSON

I pulled out my cell phone to call Mackenzie and was baffled to see her name already on my screen.

"Hello? Mackenzie?"

"Jackson?"

She sounded equally surprised. The realization that she was trying to call me at the exact same moment I was calling her came with a twinge of dread.

They'd got her too.

Ten minutes earlier, I had walked into my Century City office and found the place turned upside down. As I scanned the mess, I half expected to spot banana peels because it looked like I'd been robbed by a gang of monkeys. My beautiful Italian desk appeared to have been attacked with a sledgehammer. My file cabinet rested on its side, its contents strewn around the room. My bookshelves were toppled and splintered.

In an office tower filled with far juicier prospects, it struck me as odd that my humble little firm would be targeted. But a few minutes of rummaging through the debris confirmed my suspicions.

The only thing missing from my office was Ashley Cross's case file.

When I left yesterday, that folder had been on my desk along with a few others. After a search of the paperwork carpeting the floor, not one document connected to Ashley's case could be found. Because of the case's urgency, I held out a sliver of hope that Nadine might've taken Ashley's folder home with her. My cousin did that occasionally to continue her research from the comfort of her living room, as opposed to working overtime in the office. But my hopes were obliterated when Nadine walked into the office, late as usual, her mouth agape and her hands empty.

She did not have Ashley's file.

Nadine asked the obvious question: "Who would do this?"

I already knew the answer. The bit of cheap theater that had unfolded in Lance's office the previous night was even more calculated than I had first theorized. Reaching this conclusion, it struck me that in all likelihood Mackenzie's office might have been targeted too.

That's when I'd reached for my phone.

"How bad?" I asked Mackenzie.

"Bad. They didn't just take Ashley's files. They wrecked the place. I'm seriously fighting the urge to go kick Lance's ass."

It was no surprise Mackenzie had reached the same conclusion regarding Lance's complicity. And while I understood her desire for a little street justice, that wasn't a good idea.

"If we play this wrong, we'd pretty much be handing that bonus to Lance."

"I see that. But we can't just let that asshole get away with this."

"No. We can't. But the way I see it, we only have one choice. And it's not a great one."

Chapter 24

MACKENZIE

Just over an hour later, I parked my Jeep outside the Inglewood substation on Prairie Avenue.

Jackson was right. Our one choice—filing a police report—wasn't a good one. But I agreed to go through the motions anyway. When I told him I knew a detective in the Inglewood Police Department who might make a serious effort to investigate the break-in, Jackson volunteered to tag along.

Initially I tried to blow him off, reminding him that he needed to file his own report since the Inglewood PD didn't have jurisdiction over a break-in in Century City. But seconds after saying that, I heard his assistant announce that two burglary investigators had just arrived. Of course they had. That's how it worked on the other side of the tracks.

As I climbed out of my Jeep, Jackson cruised up in his flashy Benz. I could only shake my head. I hoped he owned a less conspicuous ride for stakeouts.

Jackson sprang out of his car with extra pep in his step. I couldn't help but smile.

"You like it, huh?"

I quickly wiped the smile off my face. "What are you talking about?"

"I saw you admiring my ride."

"Actually," I said, laughing, "I was fantasizing about landing another knifehand strike to Lance's throat. I couldn't care less about cars."

I noticed a spark of disappointment on his face as I brushed past him and into the station. Giving Jackson access to one of my best contacts wasn't a decision I'd made lightly. But Lance's antics made teaming up against him a sensible thing to do.

I'd called ahead, so we were escorted into the office of Detective Frank Mason right away. He was a good-looking, solidly built man with a close-cropped beard. We took seats in front of Mason's desk in his crappy office and shared the long and short of our story.

When we were done, Frank spread his hands, palms up. "Without more, I don't see how we can go after this guy. He was with you at the time of the break-ins. You two are his best alibi." He directed his gaze toward Jackson. "You're an ex-cop. One would think you'd know that."

Whoa.

As soon as I'd introduced the two of them, a funky vibe had infiltrated the room. Frank and I did have a past—a short one—but that was more than five years ago. He'd been on the jealous side, which was one of the reasons we didn't make it. Frank had apparently jumped to the conclusion that Jackson and I had more in common than Ashley Cross and Lance Brooks.

Jackson massaged his jaw and turned away for a fraction of a second. "I'm well aware of that, *Detective*." He practically spat that last word across Frank's desk. "But it's clear to us that Lance sent his guys to do it."

Frank rocked back in his chair and hunched a shoulder. "Well, show me some evidence that makes that clear to *me* and I'll hop right on it. In the meantime, I wouldn't go around making baseless allegations against the guy. You, of all people, should know how that could turn out, *partner*."

The amplified testosterone level in the room wasn't all about me. Even though the Inglewood Police Department and the LAPD were separate entities, the black cop community in the Los Angeles area was small and close-knit. Frank obviously knew about Jackson's breaching of the blue wall. Reporting his partner's criminal activities had taken courage and I respected Jackson for it. Frank obviously didn't.

I needed to jump in and steer this ship in another direction before they whipped out their dicks and forced me to pick the biggest one.

Jackson opened his mouth to fire off the next shot, but I intercepted it.

"Look, we hear you. We'll work on getting some evidence that ties Lance to the break-ins. In the meantime, could you check to see if you have any info on Ashley Cross?"

"Sure, babe," Frank said, turning back to his computer screen. "Anything for you."

Babe? Really? He hadn't called me that even when we were dating.

"What kind of info you looking for? And why?"

I didn't want Frank to know Jackson and I were working the case together. He might withhold information just to get under Jackson's skin. So I responded to his first question and ignored the second one.

"Just wondering if she's had any run-ins with the law."

As Frank pecked his keyboard, I stole a glance at Jackson. His jawline was taut, his lips pursed and twisted to the side. I appreciated his restraint.

"Hmm," Frank mused. "Arrested for credit card fraud two years ago. Looks like she had an accomplice. A woman a bit older than her. Marva Vargas."

My heart began to pound with hopeful excitement. Maybe this could get us someplace.

I kept a straight face, not wanting to reveal my emotions. "What can you tell us about that case?"

"Not much here. It was dismissed pretty early on, doesn't say why. Vargas has a long record, but nothing serious. Mostly credit card fraud and petty theft. Looks like this was Ashley's first tango with the law."

Jackson and I exchanged stone-cold gazes; then I turned back to Frank.

"Do you have an address for Vargas?"

"And maybe a photo?" Jackson added.

Chapter 25

JACKSON

Hold up. Why don't you ride with me?" I said, as Mackenzie headed for her Jeep.

She pulled the door open. "No, thanks."

Marva Vargas lived in downtown Los Angeles, only twenty minutes from Inglewood, but I didn't see the sense of driving separately into the only area in LA notoriously unfriendly to automobiles.

"C'mon, hop in. Parking's a nightmare downtown, plus we could use the time to strategize."

I swung open the passenger door and gestured toward the front seat with a regal flourish.

Mackenzie hesitated, then gave in. "Okay, fine."

En route to the Harbor Freeway, we rode along Manchester Avenue in silence for the first ten minutes.

"You mind putting the top up?" she asked.

"Why? You look good in a convertible."

In fact, at that moment she looked fantastic. The midday sun kissing her bourbon-brown skin, her eyes glittering with anticipation.

Mackenzie made a face. "It's just too much air."

"No such thing in LA."

I merged onto the freeway. As usual, traffic was just above a crawl. The quick twenty-minute ride downtown now seemed like a dream. I occasionally stole a glance at my gorgeous passenger. I found myself wishing our destination was someplace romantic. Like a hotel suite overlooking the ocean. A little voice in my head warned me to check myself.

Don't get distracted, Jackson.

Seeing she was truly uncomfortable, I decided to comply with her request. Her dislike of convertibles registered as a negative in my mental Mackenzie checklist. She'd been batting a thousand up until she mentioned that she didn't care for cars, so no real damage done. Nobody's perfect, after all. For example, Mackenzie's choice of romantic partners definitely needed some work.

As the retractable hardtop closed, I said to her, "Your boyfriend's kind of an asshole."

"My boyfriend?"

"You know, Deputy Ass Clown. And don't deny it. When he called you *babe* you didn't even blink."

Mackenzie frowned. "Frank's ancient history. Nothing else."

"Whatever. I gotta be honest. It's hard to picture you with a low-brow like that."

Mackenzie shot me a look. "Didn't you say we needed to strat-egize? Shouldn't we be discussing Vargas?" She waved the photo-copied black-and-white image of Marva Vargas provided by Lover Boy. Marva looked pretty enough to star in one of those Mexican soap operas, but there was a hardness in her eyes, so she'd have to play a villain.

"Seriously," I said, "how long did it take you to dump that mouth-breather?"

"We are not discussing this," she hissed.

"Wait. Don't tell me he dumped you."

"I'm not going to discuss my private life with you. I don't know you. Hell, we're practically strangers."

"Yeah? Then what the hell are you doing in my car, lady?"

Mackenzie tried her damnedest not to laugh, but I spotted the faintest hint of a smile.

I plucked Marva's photo from Mackenzie's hand. "Okay, let's strategize."

"Yes. Let's."

"If it turns out that Ashley is actually holed up with this woman, we'll blackjack her, toss her in the trunk, drive her to Patterson's office, and collect the prize."

"Blackjack her? You mean 'jack' her, right?"

I sighed. "I don't know what irks me more, that you don't get that reference or that you ruined my joke."

"Hate to bust your bubble, but you're not as funny as you think."

"I think I'm hilarious, so if I fall a little short, I'm still pretty damn funny."

Mackenzie chuckled. I liked the sound. There was something sexy about it. I couldn't help wondering what other sensual sounds I could coax out of her.

Jackson, cut it out.

"Look," Mackenzie said, "is our fifty-fifty deal still in effect or what? We need to be clear on that."

"Going forward, if we find Ashley while we're together, the deal's still in place. You cool with that?"

"Works for me. And for the record, I know what a blackjack is."

"You're not talking about the card game, right?"

"Shush. Put on some music or something . . . and get better jokes."

After a few minutes a bona fide miracle occurred. The freeway cleared up a bit and we cruised the rest of the way at damn near the speed limit. Before I knew it, LA's anemic skyline loomed ahead.

Taking the Fourth Street exit, we drove past luxury hotels, towering office buildings, and block after block of homeless encampments. Makeshift shelters crowding trash-ridden sidewalks. Signs appealing for donations wielded by smudged-faced men and women who somehow were still able to smile. Abject poverty festering in the shadow of obscene wealth.

Mackenzie and I exchanged frowns. It's a fucked-up feeling to cruise by legions of needy souls in an $80,000 sports car. I wouldn't call it guilt. It just felt off. At a red light a Latino man, about sixty, approached wearing a soiled Raiders jersey. His sign consisted of just a single word, but it was the magic word. PLEASE.

I handed the Raiders fan a ten-dollar bill. He smiled and raised a fist in thanks as I drove on.

Marva's address brought us to an unsightly neighborhood bordering the fashion district: an urban planning goulash of shoddy storefront shops, strip malls, gas stations, graffiti-covered industrial structures, and small apartment buildings. The only plus to living in a low-rent 'hood like this was, well, the low rent.

Marva's building, three stories of lopsided red bricks, appeared ancient. The ground floor was occupied by a bodega, a cellular store, and some kind of electronics repair shop. All three establishments featured poorly hand-painted signs.

I got lucky and found a parking space directly across the street. Normally, in a neighborhood where my car was the most expensive object within a one-mile radius, I'd never park on the street. I'd seek out a local garage and tip well. But I didn't want to hear the snippy comments that were sure to come from Ms. Cunningham. So I decided I'd rather roll the dice than give her the satisfaction.

As Mackenzie and I climbed out of the Benz, she said, "Nice neighborhood."

I chuckled. "Yeah. Good place to hide for sure."

"Very true." She smiled. "Suddenly I have a good feeling about this."

"Me too. What are you going to do with your thirty percent?"

"Not funny."

We crossed the street and found the building's entrance, an unmarked red door tucked between the cellular store and the bodega. We had Marva's apartment number, 3A, but there was no tenant directory or intercom to speak of.

Mac said, "Maybe it's unlocked."

"In this neighborhood? Doubtful."

Mackenzie grabbed the knob and pushed the door open. "You were saying?"

"That right there is a lawsuit waiting to happen."

Mackenzie chuckled. "Okay, that was kind of funny."

We entered a dimly lit lobby the size of a large closet that smelled like rotting wood and plantains. There were eight battered mailboxes on one wall and a narrow stairway leading up. A handwritten sign posted over the mailboxes read PLEASE KEEP THE FRONT DOOR LOCKED.

As we started up, the steps creaked and groaned like something out of a haunted house flick. The handrail was clammy but the rickety nature of the stairs practically dared you to let go.

As we turned onto the second landing, we were greeted by the sound of muffled opera music from one of the apartments. I couldn't help commenting, "Opera? Here? Really?"

"That's racist," Mackenzie said.

I scratched my head. "That song sounds very familiar."

"That's 'Habanera' from *Carmen*."

"Right. I knew that."

Mackenzie chuckled. "Sure you did."

We continued up to the third floor. There were two stickers decorating apartment 3A's front door. One was a Mexican flag. The other featured a raised black fist over the caption *Black Lives Matter*.

No doorbell, so I knocked.

As footsteps approached, Mac and I traded hopeful glances, our concern that Ms. Vargas might not be home instantly quelled.

There was a fidgeting sound from the peephole accompanied by a Spanish-accented female voice bent with suspicion. "Who is it?"

I shot Mackenzie a glance and she immediately got the message. *Better if a female answers.*

"Hi, my name is Mackenzie Cunningham. I'm looking for Marva Vargas."

"Why?"

"I just want to ask a few questions."

"About?"

"Are you Miss Vargas?"

"Are you the police?"

"No. Actually, I'm a private investigator." Mackenzie pulled a business card from her pocket and raised it to the peephole. "See?"

"Okay. What about him?"

I held up my business card. "Also a private investigator. My name's Jackson Jones."

"Please, Ms. Vargas," Mackenzie went on. "You're not in any trouble. We're here about an old acquaintance of yours. Ashley Cross?"

"What about her?"

"She's missing. We were hired to locate her. We thought maybe—"

"That bitch ain't here. And Marva's not here either."

Mackenzie shot me a puzzled look.

"Wait," I jumped in. "Then who are you?"

Locks clicked, then the apartment door swung open. A thick, twentysomething Mexican woman filled the doorway. A huge rose tattoo on her neck peeked from beneath the collar of the McDonald's uniform she wore. Instead of giving her name, she tapped a glossy red fingernail on her nametag: ROSA.

"This is my place," Rosa said. "Marva used to live with me, but that was a while ago. We dated, you know. Ashley, I never met, but Marva used to talk about her all the time. Called her a bitch. A user. Sounds like someone who might go missing, right?"

There was an awkward pause as Mac and I recovered from surprise and disappointment.

"As you can see," Rosa said, "I'm about to leave for work, so . . ."

"Are you still in touch with Marva?" I asked.

"Do you know where we can find her?" Mackenzie added, completing my thought.

An opportunistic smile creased Rosa's red-painted lips, and instantly I knew where this was headed. Stupid detective shows had everyone believing PIs were human ATMs. Feed us info and we spit out cash. Getting the pinch from bartenders and bouncers I can understand, but from a goddamned McDonald's worker? Come on.

Mackenzie just smiled at me and shook her head, the message clear. *Here it comes.*

"Actually," Rosa said. "I know exactly how to contact Marva. What's it worth to you? And I know that's your sweet-ass Mercedes parked downstairs, so don't try to lowball me."

Chapter 26

MACKENZIE

As Jackson drove north on the 405 toward Marva Vargas's Porter Ranch address, I gazed out blankly at the sliding landscape. Silent. My mind consumed by a nagging question. I wanted to let it go, just forget about it and keep pushing forward with the case, but it was no use. I couldn't get the damn question out of my head.

Should I or should I not ask Jackson to reimburse me for half of the lip-loosening money I'd just paid Rosa?

After a brief negotiation with the tattooed Hamburglar, we'd settled upon the price of $250. A bit high for the average pinch, but considering Rosa's street savvy and our eagerness to score that fat bonus, I considered it a bargain. Unfortunately, neither Jackson nor I was carrying anywhere near that amount of cash. Without skipping a beat, Rosa had informed us that she didn't trust Cash App or Zelle due to some conspiracy nonsense she learned on TikTok, but that she'd gladly accept Venmo. Since Jackson didn't have the Venmo app on his phone and I did, it fell to me to send Rosa the payment.

The McDonald's employee had served up more than just an address. Making no effort to hide her bitterness, Rosa had detailed how Marva pregnancy-trapped a rich nerd and was now playing housewife and mom in the suburbs.

As Jackson and I made our way back to his car, he actually made a comment about how we'd gotten our money's worth.

Our money's worth? Really?

I considered reminding my partner that I alone had fronted the cash, but not wanting to sound petty, and deciding I could casually bring it up later, I'd bit my lip and kept my mouth shut. Also, I was hoping Jackson would bring it up. In fact, that's what should've happened. That would've been classy. But he never went there. Instead, he made a crack about Rosa, griped about how long it would take to drive to Porter Ranch, and fiddled with his damn phone. By the time we were back on the highway my internal tussling had left me good and pissed.

Just let it go, girl.

Maybe, distracted by the scent of that fifty K bonus, Jackson had genuinely forgotten. Then again, maybe I'd fallen victim to the *I left my wallet at home* routine. Come on, who the hell doesn't have Venmo? As I weighed the possibility of getting my hands on his phone to check the apps, his voice interrupted my scheming.

"Is something bugging you?" Jackson asked.

I couldn't hold it in. "Yeah. You."

Confusion leapt onto his face. "Me? What did I do?"

"It's not what you did. It's what you didn't do."

"I have absolutely no idea what you're talking about."

"I just paid Rosa two-fifty. We're partners, you should've volunteered to pay half."

Jackson actually chuckled and shook his head. "I disagree completely."

The back of my neck went hot. "Excuse me?"

"I figure Rosa would've cost us fifty bucks, tops, if not for my Mercedes. So just keep it. No worries."

I flinched. "Just keep it? What the hell are you talking about?"

Jackson raised what he intended to be a calming hand. I wanted to bite it.

"I refuse to argue about it," he said. "And if you try to send me back half, I won't accept it. End of discussion."

With that he returned his full attention to driving.

Jackson and I clearly weren't having the same conversation. Before I could ask for clarification, my phone dinged with a text. Right there on the home screen was a notification banner from Zelle.

Jackson Jones sent you $250 using Zelle.

I nearly dropped my phone. My embarrassment was so intense I winced. Here I was accusing Jackson of being a deadbeat, while he was being . . . amazing. I looked over at Jackson as he drove, taking him in with new eyes.

Sensing my gaze, he glanced at me. "We good?"

I considered confessing my blunder, but shoved back the notion. At that moment Jackson was looking particularly sexy. No point making myself appear foolish when there was no telling what kind of partnership this would ultimately turn out to be.

"You win," I said, settling back into my seat. "Thanks for being so considerate."

In response, Jackson actually winked at me. A big, bold, cheesy wink, like something you'd see in a movie. Who does that? But the truth was, throughout my life I've been winked at a lot, and that was the first time the gesture genuinely made me quiver inside.

Porter Ranch was an affluent suburb approximately thirty miles north of Rosa's janky 'hood. Tree-lined winding streets. Custom-built mini-mansions. Mountains in the near distance framed by endless blue sky. Postcard material for sure.

From the looks of the two-story residence Jackson parked in front of, Marva Vargas had indeed done well. Meticulous geometric landscaping kicked curb appeal's butt. The place looked pristine and untouched, like a model home. Even the tipped-over tricycle on the perfect lawn appeared staged.

As we followed a polished-stone walkway to the front door, Jackson once again suggested that I do the talking. I understood his Neanderthal-rooted reasoning, but the truth was not all women responded better to other women. In fact, sometimes it was just the opposite. I made a mental note to chop this subject up with Mr. Jones at a more appropriate time.

I pressed the button on the Ring doorbell and chimes filled the multimillion-dollar house. Expecting to be greeted by a disembodied voice over the Ring intercom, Jackson and I were a bit startled when the front door suddenly swung wide open. Disregard for home security like that only happened in movies and in cozy little suburbs like Porter Ranch.

The woman in the doorway was almost a perfect match for the photo Frank had given us. Marva Vargas's striking eyes retained their edge, but now they were etched with fine lines of stress and fatigue. I'd wager my PI license that the tow-haired three-year-old boy clinging to her leg was at least partly responsible.

Marva took in Jackson and me with a look of blatant surprise. When she'd opened her door, she'd apparently expected to see a neighbor standing on her doorstep, not two black strangers.

"May I help you?" she asked guardedly.

I flashed my best put-'em-at-ease smile. "Hi, Mrs. Vargas. My name's Mackenzie Cunningham and this is Jackson Jones. We're—"

"Vargas?" she interrupted, shaking her head. "No."

"I'm sorry. You are Marva Vargas, correct?"

Her kid tugged at her yoga pants with jelly-stained hands, trying to pull her back inside. She explained to him that Mommy was talking, then rejoined the conversation. "I haven't been Vargas for a while. It's Dawson now. Like it says on the mailbox."

"Of course. I apologize, Mrs. Dawson."

For some reason Jackson pointed to the sleek pedestal-mounted mailbox at the curb and said, "That's a really snazzy mailbox, by the way."

It took real effort for me not to kick him in the shin.

"Thank you," Marva said, then narrowed her eyes. "Now, who are you two again?"

Before I could respond, a man's voice boomed from the house: "Who is it, babe?"

"Hold on," Marva called back.

"I'm Mackenzie Cunningham," I went on, "and he's Jackson Jones. We're private investigators. We're working on a case involving Ashley Cross."

Marva shook her head. "Sorry. I don't know anyone by that name."

"Ma'am, I assure you we're not here to cause you any inconvenience or accuse you of anything, but we do know that you were arrested with Ashley back in—"

She raised a hand. "Shhhhhh. Okay. Please keep your voice down."

"Babe?" her husband's voice surfaced again from the distance, as if on cue. "Everything okay?"

"Just a salesman, honey," she replied.

"Send him away."

"It's okay. I'm handling it."

Marva gently peeled Junior off her leg and steered him into the house. "Go to Daddy, sweetie. Go on." The kid did as he was told.

Marva stepped out of the house and quietly shut the front door behind her. Lowering her voice, she said, "Ashley was part of another life. As you can see, I'm not that person anymore. Not even close. That's all behind me now. Especially *that* woman."

"Ashley's missing," I said. "We thought maybe she might've contacted you."

Marva snorted. "No way. If she did, that would've been the shortest phone call ever."

Jackson jumped in. "We were under the impression you two were friends."

"Oh, Ash and I were more than friends. We met at a club, and she fell hard for me. Not just a sex thing, she adored my lifestyle. I was heavy into hacking fullz and cloning. Living the swipe life. I taught her everything I knew, and we were running good for a while. Then the bitch ratted me out. Ash looks like an angel but schemes like the devil. Anything else?"

I shook my head, but was surprised to see Jackson raise a finger. "Just one more thing. You knew Ashley well. If she wanted to hide, where do you think she'd go?"

As Marva pondered the question, my phone rang. I was surprised to see that it was Frank. Signaling Jackson to continue without me, I walked a few feet away and answered the call.

"Guess whose name just popped up in the system," Frank said.

The irony in his voice made the answer obvious. "Ashley Cross."

"Correct."

My heart began to beat faster. Had Jackson and I just hit the lottery? "Please tell me you have a location."

"I do," Frank said. "A unit responded to a domestic dispute call at a motel in Santa Monica. Turned out it was your girl. And take one guess who the guy was?"

Damn it. There was that tone again and I knew exactly what it meant. Jackson and I hadn't won the lottery, we'd just got our asses kicked. With a sigh I replied, "Lance Brooks."

"Correct again."

I clenched my eyes shut against a tsunami of disappointment. Finally I said to Frank, "That wasn't a domestic dispute. Trust me."

"Well, that's what they told the responding officers. Report says the couple apparently settled everything on-site. No arrests were made."

"Wonderful."

I listened to a few more meaningless details, then hung up and resisted the urge to hurl my iPhone toward the distant mountains.

Chapter 27

JACKSON

Mackenzie rejoined me at Marva Dawson's front door just in time to thank the rehabilitated scammer for her help.

As Marva withdrew into the American dream and shut the door, I was eager to fill Mac in on what I'd just learned. That Ashley had a thing for vinyl records and the specialty shops that sold them. How we could visit those shops with Ashley's photo and maybe get lucky. A solid lead for sure that made our excursion all the way out to Porter Ranch actually worth it.

Before I could get a syllable out, I was struck by the decidedly less-than-cheerful look on my partner's face. Typically, I'd lob a classic crack like "Who pissed in your cereal?" But from the dejected way Mac stared at me, I had a bad feeling that my Cheerios had been polluted as well. That must've been some phone call.

"Okay," I said. "What's wrong?"

"Everything."

"That bad, huh?"

"Worse."

"Let me guess. Kanye and Kim are getting back together."

"Would you stop?" She meant it.

"Sorry." I meant it too.

"It's over," she said.

"What's over?"

"Lance found Ashley. He beat us."

I heard her perfectly, but shock took control of my mouth. "What, what, what?"

"That's all you have to say?" Mackenzie rolled her eyes and stomped toward the car. "Let's just get out of here."

"Wait." I trailed after her. "How do you know that?"

She quickly filled me in on everything she'd learned from Detective Dickhead. It didn't sound good, but it also didn't sound final. "We don't know for sure that Lance scored that bonus," I said to Mackenzie, pulling out my phone. "I'm calling Patterson."

"Good idea."

While I waited for the call to connect, Mackenzie crossed her arms and leaned on my car. While I recognized we were in crisis mode, that was no reason to overlook common car etiquette. "Do me a favor," I said. "Please don't lean on my ride. Scratches are pricey to fix."

She glared, huffed, then stepped away from the car.

Patterson's assistant put me on hold for several minutes. When the lawyer finally came on the line, I put the call on speaker. Patterson was short and gruff. Lance found Ashley. Lance got the bonus. Our services were no longer needed. Click.

Mackenzie looked at me. I looked at her. Neither of us uttered a word for a long while. The fact that we stood surrounded by mansions and the trappings of wealth made the sting of losing that bonus all the worse.

The silence was shattered by Mackenzie's fist hitting her palm. "Okay, now I'm ready to kick Lance's ass. At a minimum, he should pay both of us for the damage to our offices."

Before I could agree, Mackenzie snatched open the passenger

door of my Benz and climbed in. "Let's go get us some payback," she hissed.

As I slid behind the wheel and started the engine, images of a hospitalized Lance in traction filled my head. I was all for getting what Lance owed us and even hurting him a little, but I wasn't trying to catch a case or a lawsuit.

"Look," I said to Mac, "when Lance starts bragging about that bonus, I want you to count to ten before reacting. You're a bit of a hothead. We need to set some ground rules about what we're going to do and what we're *not* going to do when we get there. I've seen the Mac Attack in action."

She smiled. "Mac Attack. I like that."

"I'd just like to stay out of jail."

"Okay," she said, her head tilted. "Don't murder him. Check."

"Or cause any major injuries."

"Define *major*."

"Broken bones, severed limbs, gouged eyes, etc."

"He doesn't need two eyes."

"Mac!"

"Check, check, check. Can we go now?"

"And let me do the talking," I added. "You just hang back and crack your knuckles. Got it?"

"Yes. Fine. I really need a T-shirt that says *Mac Attack*."

"Oh boy."

Close to an hour later, Mac Attack and I were intercepted at the club's entrance by two hairless apes Lance called bouncers. They appeared to know us on sight and apparently had strict orders to keep us out. Undeterred, I demanded that they ask their boss to step outside. To my surprise, we were told to wait as one of the bouncers disappeared inside.

Instead of Lance, the bouncer returned with his apparent

second-in-command, Crystal Douglass. The skintight, green satin minidress she wore clashed with her job title.

Framed in the doorway, she declared dismissively, "Mr. Brooks isn't here at the moment. Is there something I could help you with?"

I opened my mouth to reply, but Mackenzie beat me to it. "Tell that snake to stop hiding in his office and come out and play."

Crystal smiled politely. "Like I said, he's not here. I have no reason to lie. If Mr. Brooks were here and simply didn't want to see you, that would be the end of it."

Her words held a ring of truth. I could tell Mackenzie felt it too because her balled fists began to relax.

During that uneasy pause, a FedEx driver approached Crystal carrying a clipboard. "I have a package that needs a signature. That guy over there told me to see you."

Crystal reached for the clipboard and signed it.

As the FedEx driver walked away, she tucked the package underneath her arm, then returned her attention to us. "If there's nothing else, I'll be sure to tell Mr. Brooks you two stopped by."

"Also tell him we know he trashed our offices," I said.

"Yeah," Mackenzie added. "And tell fat ass he's going to make it right or he and I are going to go another round."

Hearing the threat, the two bouncers took a step forward, flexing their muscular arms like gorillas.

Instinctively, my hand eased toward my holstered Glock.

Mackenzie just stared the two goons down like she didn't give a shit. She was practically licking her chops. What a woman.

Crystal defused the situation by waving the bouncers off. She leveled hard eyes at Mackenzie. "You should leave before I call nine-one-one and report you for making terrorist threats." She nodded toward a security camera mounted over the front door. "Smile for the camera."

Needless to say, Mackenzie did not smile.

Chapter 28

MACKENZIE

Jackson and I performed a slow-moving death march back to his car.

He opened the door for me and I let him. Normally I would've made some smartass remark about him thinking I was too fragile to open the door for myself. But rage had rendered me unable to speak.

Jackson must have felt equally dejected. He started the car and eased away from the curb without even glancing my way. The silence gave both of us time to lick the wounds we'd suffered in Lance's $50,000 daylight robbery.

As my own despair sank in, I wondered why Jackson was so down. He had a thriving investigations business with a ton of corporate clients. I, on the other hand, didn't know where my next dime was coming from.

I stole a glance in his direction. The way his knuckles gripped the steering wheel, he could easily break it in two.

What I'd usually do when I was down was go home and drown myself in a bottle of Trader Joe's wine. But for some reason, I didn't want to be alone.

"My mom might be sick," I blurted out, surprising myself. "She's acting like it's no big deal, but I'm worried that it is. I could really use a drink."

Jackson glanced over at me, concern blanketing his face. His voice softened. "Sure, I know the perfect spot."

The Benz picked up speed and in no time we'd hopped off the 405 freeway and were gliding up Hawthorne Boulevard.

"Do you mind if I ask what's wrong with her?"

I shrugged. "She found a lump in her breast. She hasn't had a biopsy yet. But it's scary because her mother and a first cousin died of breast cancer."

"Today's breast cancer technology is a lot better than when your grandmother had it. And if it makes you feel any better, I dated a woman more than ten years ago who had breast cancer and she's still alive and well."

I wasn't used to sincerity from my PI rival. I found myself smiling warmly. "Thanks for sharing that."

"Are you and your mother close?" he asked.

"Nope." I turned to look out of the window. "She doesn't exactly approve of my chosen profession. Or anything else I've done in life since graduating from college."

Jackson let it go. He seemed to sense that I didn't want to answer any more questions, which I appreciated.

As we began a leisurely, winding ascent up Hawthorne Boulevard, our surroundings slowly changed. The visible shift from congested city life to sprawling suburbia could not be missed. Somewhere along our drive, we had crossed a dividing line from middle class to moneyed.

"Where are we going?" This was a long way from the Inglewood Police Department, where I'd left my Jeep.

"A really nice spot. Trust me."

Minutes later, we came to a stop in a circular driveway in front of a huge Mediterranean-style building that resembled a billionaire's mansion. The Terranea Resort rested on a bluff above the coast of the Palos Verdes Peninsula. I knew about the luxury resort because it was one of my parents' favorite weekend getaway spots. Five or six times a year, they'd lapped up its lavishness, while my brother and I terrorized some ill-equipped nanny back at home.

Jackson looked at me, excited. "Wait until you see the view."

The valet handed him a ticket and we walked inside. The atmosphere exuded wealth, but in a refined way. Large expensive furniture, eye-catching artwork, a decorative ceiling as high as the sky. Jackson was obviously familiar with the place. My parents would like that. He led me past the reception desk to a bank of elevators, and then to a restaurant called mar'sel.

My first thought was why they didn't capitalize the *m* in mar'sel. I tended to be anal about things like that.

A scrawny blonde standing inside the doorway lit up at the sight of Jackson. "Nice to see you again, Mr. Jones. Your usual table?"

He smiled and winked at her. "That'll work."

If he was trying to impress me, it was working.

The hostess led us to a table on the rim of the circular patio. He was right about the view. The boundless blue waves of the Pacific Ocean seemed to immerse me in serenity. There were only three other couples seated on the patio.

"Nice spot," I said as he pulled out my chair.

"I thought you'd like it."

The waitress, who also knew Jackson by name, asked for my order, but not his. She quickly returned with my apple martini and a scotch for him.

"You hungry?" he asked, picking up the menu.

"Yeah. Hungry to kick Lance's ass. Beating us out of that bonus is one thing, but we can't let him get away with trashing our offices."

Jackson nodded. "Agreed. But before we plot his demise, how about sixty uninterrupted minutes with no thoughts of Lance Brooks, Ashley Cross, or Raymond Patterson."

"I'll give it a try."

After ordering appetizers, Jackson leaned back and folded his arms across his chest. "I'm dying to know what made you get into the PI business."

"My rebellious streak."

Thin lines creased his forehead. "I'm not following."

"I tried to pick the one career path that would piss off my parents the most."

He laughed.

"What about you?"

He shrugged. "An honest cop who snitched on his dishonest partner couldn't get hired to clean the toilets at a rent-a-cop office. PI work was a logical choice."

The warmth of the martini easing down my throat was already working its magic. I shifted in my seat, no longer fueled by fury.

"Business must be good," I said.

He squinted. "What makes you say that?"

"Benz. Office in Century City." I glanced around the patio. "This isn't exactly Denny's."

Jackson's lips pursed into an almost smile. "When it's good, it's really good. But the occasional dip can be rough. Also, dealing with entitled assholes takes its toll. Do you know how many times I've been sued?" He grimaced, then asked, "How's business for you?"

"Could be better." I took another sip. "A whole lot better. I never should've started accepting payment plans. I spend as much time chasing down clients who owe me money as I do on actual investigative work."

Our conversation was interrupted by Jackson's ringing phone. After glancing at the screen, he apologized and answered the call.

"Hey, sweetie."

A flash of heat stung the back of my neck. Was he actually going to sit here in front of me and talk to some woman?

"Of course. I didn't forget," Jackson said into the phone. "And you have nothing to worry about. You've got all the moves down pat. You're going to walk out of there tomorrow with that orange belt and make Daddy proud."

In a flash, I cooled off. He was talking to his daughter, not some love interest.

He spent the next couple of minutes pumping up his daughter.

"Sorry about that," Jackson said, returning his full attention to me.

"Is your daughter taking karate?"

"Naw, jujitsu, and she's a natural." He smiled like a proud papa. This was a side of him I'd never seen. Soft-spoken. Loving. A caring father stopping the world to build up his little girl. The sight ignited another wave of warmth inside me. It was almost as if someone had turned up Jackson's attractiveness meter a few notches.

From there we talked easily about everything from PI work to politics. By the time we were on our third round of drinks, we were giggling like two buzzed high school seniors.

I glanced at my watch. "Okay, your hour is up. Time to get back to Lance. I say we hire a couple of ex-cons from San Quentin to break his kneecaps."

Jackson shook his head. "That would be going too easy on him. I say run him over. Not with my Benz, of course. Your Jeep would do a much more effective job."

"Oh, so you want his fat ass to dent *my* bumper but not yours?"

We laughed together. A moment that felt surprisingly natural.

Jackson reached for a huge, spicy shrimp and stuffed the whole thing into his mouth. "You ever been married?" he asked, chewing.

The abrupt topic switch caught me off guard. "Nope."

"Why not? You're beautiful." His face was relaxed, his eyes narrowed into slits.

I pretended not to blush. "Beauty has nothing to do with marital eligibility," I replied. "And you, sir, are definitely buzzed."

Jackson lifted his glass and pretended to examine it. "Not yet. But I'm getting there."

Another giggle-fest erupted.

"Shhh," he whispered, placing a finger to his lips. "You're going to get us thrown out."

My head was starting to spin, so I tried to steer our conversation back into the serious zone. "So how many times have you been divorced?"

"Aw, that's cold. Why would you assume I've been divorced at all?"

I smiled sheepishly. "Just a hunch."

"For the record, one marriage, one divorce."

"Any other kids besides your daughter?"

"Nope."

"How old is she?"

"Thirteen. And she's amazing. I want her to be just like you when she grows up."

"Yeah, right."

"I'm serious. I want her to be able to hold her own. She's one of the few things in my life that I did right."

"What happened with the marriage?"

His shoulders sank a bit. "I wasn't ready. She wasn't ready."

"So what does it take to be ready?"

He paused for a long time, his eyes focused skyward. "You have to be willing to share your innermost thoughts with your partner. And not be afraid to admit your vulnerabilities."

Jackson gazed across the table, his stare so intense it made me shudder. Then he cracked a lopsided smile. "Please tell me you didn't believe that bullshit."

This time we laughed for a good long time.

"Okay," Jackson declared, "I am now officially buzzed."

I propped an elbow on the table and cupped my chin in my hand. My body felt light enough to float away. "I will have to admit that I, too, am on the buzz train with you."

More laughter.

The waitress approached and retrieved our empty glasses. "Another round?" she asked.

Jackson stared across the table, signaling that the decision was up to me.

I checked the time, though I didn't know why. It wasn't like I had anyplace else to be. I couldn't remember the last time I'd laughed this much. Enjoying Jackson's company helped me forget Ashley Cross and Lance Brooks. More importantly, it helped me keep my mind off my mother.

"Sure," I said against my better judgment. "Another round for sure."

Chapter 29

JACKSON

The next round of drinks was more of the same: an apple martini for Mackenzie and two fingers of Macallan 18 for me. I decided to slow down my drinking to occasional tiny sips. I wasn't on the buzz train, as Mackenzie put it, but I was certainly close to boarding.

I hadn't imbibed this much scotch since my ex hit me with divorce papers, and I also couldn't remember the last time I'd had so much fun with anyone. I could tell Mackenzie was worried about her mother even though she didn't say so. I got the sense that she needed to blow off some steam.

Beneath her armor of tough talk, Mackenzie was vulnerable, something she didn't want me or anyone else to see. Even in my fuzzy-headed state, I knew that if I said any of that out loud she'd probably toss her drink in my face. Still, there was no denying that Mackenzie was funny, smart, charming. On top of that, rimmed by the restaurant's subdued lighting she looked absolutely gorgeous. I couldn't help wondering what she was hiding underneath all those clothes.

Mackenzie's amused voice interrupted my reverie. "Why are you looking at me like that?"

I blinked. "I wasn't looking at you."

Mackenzie giggled. "You're right. It was more like staring." She leaned closer and whispered, "Penny for your thoughts."

I reclined and took an easy sip of my drink, trying to regain some of my cool. "You know, people always say that, but they never cough up the cash."

Mackenzie fished around in her small shoulder bag, then slapped a dollar on the table and slid it across to me. "I don't have a penny so I'll take a dollar's worth."

"You sure you can handle a dollar's worth?"

She relaxed in her chair, sipped her drink, then gestured for me to bring it on.

There was no way in hell I was going to confess what I was really thinking. I scrambled to come up with something intriguing and fun to placate her curiosity. Unfortunately Mackenzie was also amazingly observant.

She waggled a finger at me. "Oh, no. You're taking way too long. I want the truth. What were you thinking when you were lost in my eyes."

I chuckled. "I wasn't lost in your eyes."

"Yes, you were. Come on, just tell me."

"Fine. I was thinking that you're not so bad. Happy?" With that, I snatched up the dollar and pocketed it.

She made a face. "That's it?"

"That's what a dollar gets you. If you want more, it's really going to cost you."

She laughed, then smiled and said softly, "You know . . . you're not so bad yourself."

Then, like some cheesy romance flick, Mackenzie and I just gazed at each other. Deep, earnest, soulful.

When the waiter appeared and informed us that the restaurant would be closing in fifteen minutes, I was grateful for the interruption and I got the feeling Mackenzie was too.

She smiled and said, "We should go."

"I absolutely agree. Your place or mine?"

Mackenzie raised a single eyebrow. "Oh, really?"

"Yes, really. Neither of us is in any condition to drive so we should share an Uber. We'll have to tell the driver where to stop first. So like I said . . . your place or mine?"

"Hmmm," Mackenzie uttered, narrowing her eyes and tilting her head ever so slightly. "Looks like my dollar might just pay off after all."

I chuckled. "I have no idea what you're talking about."

That, of course, was a lie. The fact that Mackenzie was playing along with my flirting left me pleasantly confused. A moment ago, I'd thought I knew how our interlude would end. A friendly hug. Maybe a peck on the cheek. Promises to get together for coffee in the future.

But as Mackenzie and I floated toward the exit, her arm looped through mine, I was only sure of one thing. I didn't want this evening to end.

Chapter 30

MACKENZIE

By the time we teetered our way to the Terranea lobby, our Uber driver was already waiting. I couldn't help but smirk. Of course Jackson had sprung for the more expensive Uber Black. If I had ordered the car, we'd be climbing into the back seat of a Prius, not a Lincoln Navigator.

The driver greeted us like royalty as he opened the back door. As soon as my body melted into the soft leather seats, an overwhelming yearning for sleep consumed me.

"You okay?" Jackson asked as the driver eased the car onto Palos Verdes Drive.

The little voice in my head that usually kept me from going with the flow had been temporarily muted by alcohol.

"Yup. I'm great," I said as I closed my eyes and sank into my seat.

It had been months since I'd had the pleasure of cuddling up with a guy handsome and sexy enough to make me drop my guard like this. Okay, who was I kidding? It was actually more like two years since I'd even been close enough to a man to smell his cologne.

My evening of excess would no doubt extract some serious payback, initially in the form of a raging hangover. At that moment, I didn't care. I closed my eyes and reveled in my beautiful buzz and the equally beautiful Jackson Jones.

In what seemed like mere minutes, Jackson was gently tugging at my arm.

"Hey, wake up. We're here."

I didn't move. "And where is here?"

He laughed. "Your place."

Struggling to sit up, I reached out for the car door at the same time our Uber driver opened it for me.

I tried to swing my legs around so I could step out of the car, but my feet had turned into cinder blocks.

Like magic, Jackson was no longer sitting next to me, but was peering down at me from the open car door.

"I got you," he said, taking my hand and helping me out.

A rush of cool air tickled my face as I savored the touch of his huge hand encasing mine.

I took a wobbly step forward and tumbled into him, our foreheads almost touching. For an instant, our lips brushed.

"Whoa, there," he said, his left arm securely around my waist.

Had Jackson not been there to catch me, I would've hit the ground headfirst. And if I weren't such a coward, I wouldn't have let our lips just brush, I would've . . .

"You okay?" Jackson placed a finger underneath my chin, tilting my head up.

"Of course. I'm fine." I tried to stand more erect and pretend my neck wasn't balancing a bowling ball.

Get it together, girl. I will never drink this much again.

Despite my objections, Jackson insisted on escorting me to the entrance of my town house complex.

"Where's my purse?" I said, still relying on Jackson to stay afoot.

"Right here."

He handed it to me and waited as I took forever to dig out my keys.

"Thanks for a fun evening," I said, finally getting my key into the lobby door on the third attempt. "Maybe our paths will cross on another case."

"I think I better see you to your door."

"No need. I'm good." I pulled away from him and swayed through the double glass doors and into the lobby. Jackson followed.

"I'm sure you are, but can't be too careful," he said, standing close enough to catch me if I took another tumble. "I wouldn't feel comfortable unless I walked you to your door."

"I guess I might have had one too many," I said, wishing I had my sunglasses to shield my eyes from the lobby's bright lights.

Ignoring my protests, Jackson slid his arm back around my waist and we trudged over to the elevator. I jabbed at the button, but hit the wall instead. "You don't need to do this. I told you, I'm fine."

Jackson's perfect lips angled into a grin as he reached out to press the button. "We can stay here and debate this for as long as you want." His voice was firmer now. "But I'm definitely walking you to your door. So you might as well just let it go."

"Fine," I said with a phony pout.

Like Siamese twins, we stumbled into, then out of the elevator. As we approached my unit, with Jackson's arm snaked around my waist, I felt a sobering moment of coherence.

That always uptight voice in my head was firing off a warning call. But I refused to listen. Our case was over. After tonight, I would never have to see Jackson Jones again. I deserved this. So did he.

It's about to be your lucky night, Mr. Jackson Jones.

I repeatedly tried putting my key in the door without success. Jackson took it from my hand.

"Let me do it."

I started to giggle. *Yep. I'm definitely going to let you do it.*

He glanced over at me, puzzled. "What's so funny?"

"Nothing." I covered my mouth in a halfhearted attempt to stifle my giggles.

Jackson pushed open the door and we staggered across the threshold.

"Where's your bedroom?" he asked, still holding me up.

Okay, now you're talking. A rush of desire fluttered between my legs as my whole body quivered with anticipation. Thank goodness it was too dark for Jackson to see the eagerness on my face.

"Make a right and a quick left." *Damn, you smell good.*

We made it to the bedroom and Jackson flicked on the light switch. He led me over to the bed and threw back the comforter.

"Have a seat," he ordered.

"Yes, sir." I giggled again, raising my hand to my forehead in a drunken salute.

He knelt to take off my shoes, handling my feet so delicately that his touch fired warm embers of passion up my legs. A knowing smile eased across my face. A brother this gentle had to be a good lover.

That warning call blared again. *What are you doing?*

Shut up! For once, don't think. Just enjoy.

Still not saying a word, Jackson took me by the shoulders and eased me flat onto the bed. As he moved toward the door and turned off the light, my hunger for him was so intense, I forgot how to breathe.

In the darkened room, I lay there, as excited as I was nervous, waiting for Jackson to walk back over to the bed.

Chapter 31

JACKSON

She was clearly wasted. I did the right thing," I muttered under my breath.

The Uber driver glanced at me in the rearview mirror. "You say something, sir?"

Slumped in the back seat, I flashed a foolish smile. "Just talking to myself. Sorry."

As the driver continued to speed toward my apartment, the ever-horny wingman who resided inside my head protested again.

Come on. She wasn't that wasted. She wanted you, dude. Couldn't you see that?

I could. I mean, I thought she did. It sure felt that way. Mackenzie was gorgeous as hell, and at the restaurant I'd definitely felt a connection. During the Uber ride, as she nuzzled up against me, I don't think I'd ever wanted a woman more. In fact, I was nervous she'd notice just how rock-hard my attraction to her truly was. It took every ounce of my willpower not to pull her into my arms, tear off her . . .

I used to always roll my eyes when I saw a limo back seat sex scene in a movie. The couple, raging with lust, ripping off each other's clothes and getting it on. Not giving a fuck about the driver.

Now I got it.

When we'd arrived at Mackenzie's place, the pull of raw lust was ten times worse. Yes, escorting her inside was the gentlemanly thing to do. She was way too messed up to even consider letting her make the trip solo. But, damn, walking out of that bedroom was hard. I'd be lying if I didn't admit part of the reason I put her to bed was the hope that we'd end up beneath the sheets. Naked and sweaty. Me exploring every inch of her tight little body.

And it could've happened. I knew it. When I laid Mackenzie down on the bed there was a look in those beautiful eyes that seemed to whisper: *Take me.* No. *Fuck me!*

Then why didn't you fuck her fine ass? There's still time to turn this ride around.

"No. It wouldn't have been right, damn it!" I punched the seat.

This time the driver glanced back over his shoulder, his eyes uncertain, questioning whether he had a deranged passenger. "Are you okay?"

I winced with embarrassment. "A little too much to drink, I guess."

He nodded warily, then returned his eyes to the road. "Hang tight. You're almost home."

Deciding to leave the dude a generous tip, I peered out as the dark streets of Venice slowly rolled by.

Fueled by four rounds of scotch, that nagging voice in my head continued to cast doubt, but I ignored it. Pushing up on Mackenzie when her guard was completely down wouldn't have been right. And as the Navigator wheeled into my building's driveway, something occurred to me that finally silenced that pesky voice.

I really liked Mackenzie.

She was smart, funny, and tough, and we shared the same career. It was like we were born to be buds.

After my divorce, I'd found myself craving a real female friend. Someone of the opposite sex I could chop it up with, like I did with my buddies. Although I'd met a few women who could fill that role, hormones always got in the way. And once the sex started, the friendship's days were numbered. Sex with Mackenzie, no matter how amazing, would eventually ruin our relationship. No, it would be better if we just kept our hands to ourselves and remained solidly in the friend zone.

Yeah, right. Quit making excuses for being a pussy. That ain't your style. You know you're gonna hit that someday.

"Shut up!"

The driver, now holding the rear door open, stared at me in confusion.

"No. Not you. I was just—"

No doubt happy to see me go, he smiled and nodded. "You have a good night, sir."

. . .

Just before eight the next morning, despite a Tylenol-resistant headache, I wheeled into a parking space outside Gentle Fist Dojo ten whole minutes before the belt tests were scheduled to begin. The small jujitsu school was located in a strip mall between Loretta's Hair Salon and Dreamscape Comic Books. A beautifully hand-painted sign above the storefront depicted a taut fist clutching the stem of a perfect Japanese sunflower.

Leaving my shoes on a rack by the entrance, I entered the spacious padded gym area. It was buzzing with excitement. Parents, with their son or daughter, stood waiting around the periphery of a huge red mat. The dozen or so students stood barefoot and wore crisp white gis, cinched tight with rank belts of varying colors.

"Dad, over here."

I spotted Nicole across the room, her braids swaying as she waved. She sported a white gi like the other kids and her rank belt was yellow. After today, if she passed the test, she'd advance to an orange belt. Seeing her in her martial arts gear always stirred something inside me. Seemed like only yesterday my baby girl and I were tickle-fighting on the floor. Now Nicole was a blossoming woman warrior. I was getting a little misty-eyed until my ex, who stood beside Nicole, summoned me over with an impatient wave.

Careful not to step on the center mat, I made my way toward them. Robin possessed a figure like a Fashion Nova model and took every opportunity to flaunt it. Inspired by the event, she'd donned a stylish pink tracksuit that clung to her curves. In other words, Robin looked fine as hell, as always. I couldn't help wondering how much of my child support payments went to her Pilates instructor.

"Hi, Daddy." Nicole enveloped me in a warm hug.

"You ready to kick some butt?"

She rolled her eyes. "There's no sparring, Dad. Just forms and strikes."

"Whatever it is, you kick butt. That's an order."

Nicole giggled. "Okay. I will."

"You're on time," Robin said, glancing at her watch as though she were my boss. "Good job."

The tiny hairs on the back of my neck stood up. When it comes to Nicole, I'm never late. But this was Robin's modus operandi. She invents ways to belittle me. Constant microaggressions hidden behind a gorgeous smile. If I pushed back and defended myself, I'd look like I was being overly sensitive or instigating a fight. What really irked me was when she disparaged me in front of our daughter. For that reason, I preferred to spend time with Nicole alone, and avoided joint parent events like this belt test as much as possible.

But when Nicole personally invited me, I knew there was no way I could let her down, no matter how stressful the morning was likely to be.

So when Robin began her verbal sparring, I did what I always do. I smiled and slipped on my imaginary protective headgear to absorb the blows.

To my relief, before Robin could land another jab, the dojo went respectfully silent as Nicole's instructor, Sensei Linton, strode to the center of the red mat. Sensei Linton was black with a mane of shoulder-length dreadlocks. Like his students, he was barefoot and garbed in a white gi, but his uniform was adorned with colorful patches, including a large Gentle Fist Dojo logo on the back. During the three years Nicole had attended the school, I'd only spoken to the sensei once, but never forgot it. He was soft-spoken and exceedingly polite, but there was a confident power about him that you could sense in his rock-solid handshake.

Sensei Linton wasted no time. After greeting everyone warmly, he instructed all twelve students, including Nicole, to line up on the mat. With quiet authority he guided the kids through an extensive series of kicks, punches, rolls, and crawls. Next the sensei had the kids pair off to demonstrate holds, takedowns, and wrist breaks. When the drills were completed, the kids knelt, heads down, as Sensei Linton walked the line, bestowing new rank belts on those who had passed. The few kids who'd failed the belt test received only an encouraging pat on the shoulder and a respectful bow.

My heart ached to see tears streaming down Nicole's face as she bowed back to Sensei Linton, then trudged across the mat toward us. "I t-tried my best," she stammered. "I d-did."

"We know that, baby," Robin said, pulling Nicole into a hug. "And you looked great. You get to try again in a few weeks, right?"

"Yeah, but—"

"But nothing," I said, jumping in. "Practice a bit more and I know you'll nail it. Come here."

It was my turn to give Nicole a big comforting embrace. She sniffled and frowned up at me. "Guess I'm not so good at kicking butt, huh?"

"Believe it or not," I said, "there's a silver lining to you failing the test."

Robin's eyes narrowed at me. "Just because you're comfortable with failure doesn't mean she should be."

Maintaining a smile, I replied, "That's not what I mean."

"What silver lining, Daddy?"

"A lot of these martial arts schools hand out belts like birthday presents, just for participating. At least we know that Sensei Linton is legit. You're really learning how to become a lethal weapon."

Nicole giggled and brushed away tears. Even Robin couldn't help but chuckle at my optimistic perspective. Apparently sensing that this tiny crisis was a good time for a little family bonding, Robin suggested that we all go to a nearby Starbucks. Nicole's favorite drink in the whole wide world was a Starbucks concoction called a Dragon Drink, or something like that.

When Robin wasn't attacking me, she worked hard at being a damn good mom and a well-connected publicist. For Nicole's sake, Starbucks was a good idea. I was about to once again suspend my joint-parent-activity embargo and say yes when my phone chimed.

I glanced at the screen, and what I read nearly made me drop my iPhone.

"Are you coming, Jackson?" Robin asked.

"Please, Daddy," Nicole said. "Please come with us."

Ordinarily I would never prioritize my job over my little girl, but this situation was far from ordinary. This couldn't wait.

I said to Nicole, "I'm so sorry, baby, but an emergency has just come up. I have to go. We can all go to Starbucks another day, okay?"

Nicole frowned but nodded understandingly.

Robin drilled me with a skeptical gaze. "What emergency?"

"I'll explain later." I kissed Nicole's forehead. "I'll make it up to you, baby. I promise."

"Sure you will," Robin said over my shoulder.

I hurried toward the exit, and less than thirty minutes later I rushed through my front door, turned on the TV, and started flicking through the local news stations to see if they were covering the story. It didn't take me long to find it on KABC. Even as their photos flashed on the screen along with live footage from the crime scene, I couldn't believe it.

I also couldn't believe that Mackenzie hadn't answered her damn phone, despite me calling her at least a half dozen times as I sped home. Where the hell was she?

And as I continued to watch the grim news feed, I began to get very worried.

Chapter 32

MACKENZIE

I awoke to the sound of my phone blaring. With each sharp ring, it felt like somebody was whacking me upside the head with the large end of a pool cue. All I could do was whimper like a lost puppy. Whoever was calling would have to wait until the agony ended.

After six rings, the phone stopped torturing me. The silence brought instant relief.

"Alexa, what time is it?" I mumbled.

"The time is nine fifty-seven a.m.," Alexa dutifully replied.

I couldn't believe it was almost ten. I never slept in this late.

I will never drink that much again. Never ever.

This was so humiliating. A lady-killer like Jackson Jones had made it all the way into my bedroom, but I was so sloppy drunk he took a pass. How sad was that? But in retrospect, I should be thanking God nothing happened between us. If it had, my hangover would now be accompanied by nagging regret.

The phone came gunning for me again. *God, please make it stop.*

I reached for my purse on the nightstand and fumbled inside until I found my phone. It was Jackson. I was far too humiliated to face speaking to him right now. I promptly declined the call, threw the phone down next to me on the bed, and buried my face into my pillow. At least the investigation was over and I'd never have to see him again.

Seconds later, my phone dinged, signaling a text message. Jackson again. When I read his message, the fog in my head made room for a few seconds of clarity.

Answer the damn phone! Lance and Ashley are dead!

What the hell?

I sat up and dialed Jackson's number. He picked up before I even heard a ring.

"Turn on the TV," he yelled. "Channel nine. Hurry up."

"What happened?" I asked as I staggered into the living room and snatched the remote.

"Just hurry up," Jackson said again. "They teased the story before the commercial break and are about to go to it."

The television seemed to take forever to come on. The news anchor answered my question before Jackson did.

Early this morning, the bodies of Lance Brooks, a local private investigator, and a woman identified as Ashley Cross were found in an abandoned building near the Lucky Lancelot, a strip club in the San Fernando Valley owned by Brooks. A police spokesperson declined to disclose exactly how Brooks and Cross were killed. Police say they have no motive for the murders at this time and refused to divulge additional details pending completion of their investigation.

"Oh my God!" My drunken haze instantly dissipated, replaced by an icy chill that made me shiver. "What does this mean? Why would someone kill them?"

"Hell if I know," Jackson said. "But maybe it's a good thing that we didn't find Ashley."

I let that sink in. "You think Lance was murdered because he found Ashley?"

"We can't know that for sure. But it's awful strange that the missing woman we were trying to track down and the man who located her are both dead the day after she was found."

I wondered if Jackson was thinking what I was thinking. "Maybe Patterson wanted us to find her because he wanted her dead."

"Possible," Jackson replied. "If Ashley really was from a wealthy family, why wasn't that reported in the news story?"

"Maybe Patterson made up all that stuff about her dying mother?"

"Again, possible. Very possible," Jackson agreed.

"But I checked. Ashley's mother *was* in a hospice facility."

"It wouldn't be hard to set something like that up. We never actually saw Ashley's mother and we never spoke to her. That would definitely explain why Patterson was so insistent that we didn't contact her. Maybe she doesn't exist."

"Wait, hold on," I said. I needed a minute to process all of this. "Do you think—"

I heard a thunderous knock at my front door. Not a knock really. More like someone was pounding on it with a battering ram.

Annoyed, I headed down the short hallway. "Just a minute, Jackson," I said. "Somebody's banging on my door like the place is on fire."

I peered through the peephole. Standing on the other side was a tall, stern-looking white guy who bore all the markings of a police detective. Cheap sport jacket, broad shoulders, and an aura of sullen arrogance that I could almost smell through the door that separated us.

"I think it's a detective."

"What do you wanna bet the cops are at your door to ask about the murders?" Jackson said, his voice infused with alarm. "Somehow they know we were searching for Ashley. Another detective is probably on the way to my place as well."

"Who is it?" I asked through the closed door.

"I'm Detective Crawford. LAPD. I'd like to ask you a few questions about Lance Brooks. May I come in?"

I stuck my phone into the front pocket of my jeans, leaving the microphone exposed so Jackson could listen in.

"Now's not a good time," I said.

"It's important that I speak to you right away. Could you please open the door?"

I waited a beat, then cracked the door open, but didn't unlatch the chain.

When our eyes met, I hesitated. His clear blue eyes radiated a cold callousness. My instincts were a natural gift. Right now, they were flashing a yellow caution signal.

"Let me see your badge," I demanded.

He held it up and I took my time studying it. It appeared to be legit. I unlatched the chain, but didn't invite him in.

"So what do you want to know?"

"May I come in?"

"No, you may not. I was up late. Now isn't the best time."

His lips angled into a smile that really wasn't a smile. It was probably rare for this guy to be denied entry anywhere. It perturbed him that his law enforcement status didn't intimidate me.

"Are you aware that Mr. Brooks is dead?"

"Yep. Saw it on the news just a second ago." I wondered why he didn't mention Ashley.

"It's my understanding you were at his club last night."

"Yeah. So what?"

"And you were supposedly pretty angry with the guy."

I chuckled. "You can't possibly think I had anything to do with his death. So I really don't understand why you're even here."

He forced his lips into another faux smile. "I'd be glad to explain if you'd allow me to step inside." He flexed the fingers of his left hand.

"As I said, now's not a good time. I'll be at my office later today. You can call my assistant to make an appointment."

I was about to shut the door when the man stuck his foot forward, preventing me from closing it.

All of my senses were now on full alert.

"I only need a moment." His voice hardened along with his frosty blue eyes.

"I *said* now's not a good time."

As I pressed the door against his foot, expecting him to move it, he turned sideways and rammed his shoulder into the door. Before I could react, he reached forward and grabbed me by the neck with both hands.

I tried to scream, but the massive hands encircling my throat reduced my voice to a squeal.

As I stumbled backward, he charged inside.

I was in full Krav Maga mode now. I could hear my instructor over my shoulder. *Be quick. Be efficient. Be aggressive.*

I pressed my full weight forward, ducked my head down between his extended arms, twisted my body to the left, and freed myself from his grasp. Spinning around, I kicked him hard in the groin.

"Ugh!" He winced as his body folded forward in pain. "You bitch!"

Before I could take a breath, he was upright again, slamming me against the wall.

I darted to the right, but he cornered me and tried to press his thick forearm against my neck. I head-butted him in the nose, spewing the wall with splotches of blood.

"Owww," he yelped.

I could hear Jackson shouting something from the phone, but I couldn't respond. Right now, I was concentrating on fighting with everything I had. This man had come here to ensure I met the same fate as Ashley and Lance. And I wasn't about to let that happen.

He pressed his nose into the crook of his arm, blood soaking his jacket. I leaned back, preparing to land another kick to his nuts when my leg froze in midair.

With wild, fuming eyes, the man aimed a snub-nosed revolver inches from my chest, squarely at my heart. I froze with fear. The same way I had when Lucius stopped us with his .38.

I couldn't believe it. For the second time this week, I was staring down the barrel of a gun.

Chapter 33

JACKSON

The sounds of a struggle spilled from my phone's speaker. Grunts, groans, crashes, body slams.

Images of Mackenzie being violently assaulted flooded my mind, accompanied by a feeling of utter helplessness.

"Mackenzie!" I shouted at my phone. "What's happening?"

Crack!

A muffled sound caused me to recoil as if I'd been punched. I knew that sound. It was a gunshot. A shot fired from a gun with a silencer.

"Mackenzie!"

Then the phone went dead.

No! No!

Hands trembling, I dialed 911 as I grabbed my keys and hurried across the living room toward my front door.

"Nine-one-one, what's your emergency?"

"I want to report a shooting. You have to hurry!"

"What's your address?"

"No. Not here. I was on the phone. I heard a gunshot. At my friend's place."

"What is your friend's address?"

I stopped in my tracks as I rifled my mind for Mackenzie's address. "Shit! I don't know. She lives in Inglewood. On Hillcrest. I know how to get there but I can't remember the—"

"What is your friend's full name?"

"Mackenzie Cunningham."

"Sorry. Was that Cunningham or Dunningham?"

Exiting my apartment, I was about to reply when I spotted a man marching down the hall toward me. He was dressed in an expensive suit but I instantly sensed trouble. Maybe it was because this dude was linebacker big and eyeballing me like I was a football.

"Mr. Jones, hold it right there," he said.

His robotic gait screamed law enforcement, so I wasn't surprised when he flashed a gold shield. He was still about six feet away.

"I'm a detective. I'd like a few words with you about Lance Brooks."

Remembering that Mackenzie's attacker had also claimed to be a detective, I couldn't be sure if this guy was legit or not. I instantly came up with a way to draw him out. Waving my iPhone, I said, "Listen, I'm on with nine-one-one right now! My friend was attacked and—"

Big Man reached into his jacket and pulled out a Glock. "Hang it up."

Wonderful. Now that I had my answer, I had to figure out how to make him eat that gun.

"Hey. Easy. I'm trying to tell you my friend is in trouble—"

He leveled the weapon at me. "I said, hang it up. Now!"

I held out my phone to Big Man. "Here, you talk to them!"

"Hang up the fucking—"

I hurled my iPhone at his face.

Just as it crashed into the bridge of his nose, he fired.

But I was already moving toward him. I closed the distance between us in two steps. Snared the wrist of his hand that held the gun and used a close-combat technique I'd picked up in the police academy. With everything I had, I bent his hand forward, hyperextending the limb. Forcing his fingers to spring open.

He cried out as the gun clattered to the hallway floor.

Almost simultaneously, his fist slammed into the side of my head. The world tilted and my ears filled with a piercing ring. He unleashed another blow, this one to my left eye. When he reared back for a third punch, I blocked it and pile-drived my right fist into his gut.

The groan that escaped as he doubled over jolted me with hope.

I fired an uppercut.

He dodged and barreled headfirst into my midsection.

We crumpled to the floor. Suddenly I was pinned beneath 250 pounds of snorting rage.

He clawed forward, over me, groping for his dropped weapon.

No way I was going to let that happen.

I hammered my fist into his kidney. *Wham!*

Again. *Wham!*

Wincing and clutching his side, he curled into a ball.

I rolled clear and sprang to my feet.

He tried to grab me and stagger up, but I introduced my shoe to his face. *Bam!*

He crumpled back to the floor, blood gushing from his snout. It bugged me that he still had his front teeth, so I kicked him again.

Finally, Big Man withered completely. Out cold.

Panting, staggering, I snatched up my phone. The screen was shattered, but the call was still connected. The 911 operator's frantic voice squeaked from the speaker. "Sir, are you okay? Hello? Hello?"

Bringing the phone to my ear, I picked up exactly where I left off. "I told you, her name is Cunningham. Mackenzie Cunningham!"

"Yes. We got it. Units are on their way to her address. But what's going on there? Are you under attack as well?"

I hung up the phone and raced downstairs to my building's garage. My parking stall was empty.

Damn!

My Benz was still at the resort. I hopped into my ancient Toyota 4Runner and prayed it would start. I only used it on stakeouts and hadn't driven it in a while. After a couple of tries, it roared to life.

As I sped toward Inglewood, I called Mackenzie's phone over and over, but there was no answer.

I slammed my fist against the dashboard. "Pick up the damn phone!"

The sound of that gunshot kept reverberating in my head. My breaths started to escape in short, panicked bursts. My vision seesawed between haziness and clarity.

When I finally arrived at her building, what I saw made my heart lurch into my throat.

Several police cars and an ambulance, lights blazing, were parked out front.

Rushing through a small crowd of gawkers, I approached a uniformed officer standing in front of the lobby doors.

"I'm the one who called the police. Is Mackenzie okay?"

The officer reared back. "What happened to your face?"

"Nothing. Is Mackenzie okay?"

"How do you know Ms. Cunningham?"

"We're friends. We work together. Is she okay or not?"

The cop shook his head. "I don't know. There's no sign of her in her apartment. It's a mess up there."

I could feel my pulse throbbing in my neck. "You gotta let me in. She might've been kidnapped."

I tried to push forward but he blocked my path.

"You're not going up there," he said, placing a hand on his weapon. "I need you to stay right here while I get one of the detectives. I'm sure they'll want to speak to you."

As he turned away and raised his walkie-talkie to his lips, my iPhone pinged.

When I looked down at my spiderwebbed screen, I reflexively clenched my phone almost hard enough to crush it. I had a text message.

From Mackenzie.

Chapter 34

MACKENZIE

It wasn't until I heard Jackson hop into the driver's seat of his 4Runner that I finally let myself breathe again.

I was crouched in the back seat, my face kissing the floorboards.

"Are you okay?" Jackson's words were low and rushed.

"Please," I said, fighting off a panic attack, "just drive. Get us the hell out of here."

He couldn't possibly know how glad I was to see him. My horrifying clash with death was still running through the spin cycle in my head.

As Jackson's SUV sped away from the curb, there were no more words between us. Jackson apparently needed this bout of silence as much as I did.

"Okay," he said a few minutes later. "You can get up now."

I groaned as I lifted my battered body. I'd never been so stiff and achy. Then again, I'd never stuffed myself into a space meant for feet, not bodies, immediately after engaging in mortal combat. As I settled into the back seat, my eyes met Jackson's in the rearview mirror.

"What the fuck!" we both exclaimed at the same time.

I'd taken a punch or two from my assailant, but my bruises

couldn't be half as bad as Jackson's. He looked as if he'd volunteered his face for punching-bag practice. His left eye was twice the size of the other, his right jaw protruded like it was holding a golf ball, and bruises spotted his face.

Jackson swerved off the road, then leaned over and threw open the passenger door. "Come sit up front."

I gingerly stepped out of the back door and eased myself into the passenger seat.

"You sure you're okay?" he asked.

"Yeah, just sore as hell. I can't believe they came after you too."

Jackson quickly recounted his run-in with a goon as bent on murder as my assailant had been.

"Honestly, there was a point when I didn't think I was gonna make it," he said. "And after hearing that gunshot on the phone, I was scared to death that you didn't either. What happened?"

I sucked in a long breath before recounting my early morning nightmare. . . .

When the bloody-faced detective pulled out his 9mm, I instantly suppressed my fear and took control of the situation.

"I don't think you want to do that," I said quietly, trepidation ballooning in my chest. "The walls in this complex are pretty thin. As soon as you pull that trigger, fifty people will spot you running out of here."

His lips slanted like a seesaw and he chuckled indignantly. "You let me worry about how I get out of here. I'm a cop, remember?"

In a flash, I jerked to the left, then swung my leg upward, knocking his extended arm to the right. A gunshot plunged into the wall, inches from my head, as the weapon tumbled to the floor and skittered several feet down the hallway. As he started to go after it, I immobilized him with a hard jab to his Adam's apple, then maneuvered him into a chokehold designed to cut off his air supply.

He charged backward, slamming me so hard against the opposite wall it sent spasms of pain up and down my spine. But I continued to squeeze his thick neck in the crook of my arm with every
ounce of strength I could muster. Just as I thought he might be able
to wrestle himself free, his massive frame crumpled to the floor.

I ran into my bedroom and grabbed my purse and shoes. Jumping over his unconscious body, I charged out of the place. I raced to
the stairwell, taking the three flights down five or six steps at a time.
I must've looked like an Olympic long jumper. . . .

"Wow, that's impressive," Jackson said. "I'm glad you're okay.
But it took me close to thirty minutes to get to your place. Where
were you all that time?"

"I hid out at a barbecue joint on Prairie to gather myself, then
I headed back home to get my Jeep. I was almost there when I re-
membered that we left it at the police station before driving out to
Lance's place."

Our fun night of excessive drinking and incessant laughter now
seemed like ages ago.

"Jackson, you have no idea how relieved I was when you texted
me back and told me where your car was parked," I said. "But I have
to say, I never expected a flashy guy like you to drive a Toyota. I
figured your second car would be a Bentley or a Jag."

"I'm not flashy," Jackson said, a hint of hurt in his voice.

I immediately regretted the playful jab. Not cool, when someone
just tried to save your life. A change of tone was in order. "I appreciate what you did today." I glanced over at him, hoping he could see
the earnestness in my bruised face. "Actually, it was pretty amazing."

Jackson kept his eyes on the road. "What are you talking about?"

"I wasn't there to see it, but I can just imagine you speeding
across town to my place and leaping out of your ride like Black
Panther coming to my rescue."

Jackson grinned. "Black Panther doesn't have a car. More like Batman, maybe."

I laughed. "Let's head over to the police station to get my car."

"No way," Jackson said, his tone full of finality. "I'm not letting you out of my sight."

I wanted to say something snarky, like pointing out that I wasn't a child. Or that I could take care of myself. But what he'd just said and the way he said it gave me goose bumps. Literally.

Once again, we didn't speak for a while.

"I think someone wants us to join Ashley and Lance in the after-life," I said, cutting into the silence.

He nodded. "Yep. We're mixed up in something really big here."

"The guy who came after me bore all the markings of your standard-issue cop," I told him. "And the badge he flashed looked real."

"Same here," Jackson replied. "If the cops are involved, no telling who else could be."

Glancing out the window, I realized I had no idea where we were. "Where are we headed?"

Not that I really cared. In light of what had just happened, I couldn't think of anyplace I'd rather be than with an honest ex-cop who cared enough to dash across town to rescue me. The signifi-cance of what he'd done was too much for my flustered brain to fully take in right now.

"Someplace safe," he said quietly. "Where we can clear our heads and figure this shit out."

"And exactly where is that?"

"A cabin deep in the mountains where no one can find us."

Chapter 35

JACKSON

With Mackenzie by my side, I sped east on the 10 freeway through surprisingly light traffic. An overcast morning had blossomed into clear skies and lots of sun. As the Los Angeles skyline shrank in my rearview mirror, beautiful snowcapped mountains loomed ahead in the distance. It almost felt as if Mackenzie and I were headed for a weekend getaway, but nothing was further from the truth.

We were fleeing for our lives.

I glanced over at Mac, still a little unnerved by her battered face. She was on her phone trying to reach Raymond Patterson. Since he'd hired us, we were hoping the lawyer could answer two questions: Why were we on a hit list along with Lance and Ashley, and who might've written that damn list?

From the look on Mackenzie's face as she lowered her phone, it appeared that we weren't about to get any explanations.

"No answer?" I asked.

She shook her head. "Nothing. The line's disconnected. Hell, maybe they got him too."

"Nah. A big-time lawyer gets murdered, it makes the news.

Also, his death wouldn't account for his phone being disconnected. The police would leave it active to monitor who does and doesn't call. That's standard investigative procedure."

"You're right." Mackenzie bit her lower lip. "You know, there was something janky about Patterson from the start."

"Agreed. He did make my spidey senses tingle."

Mackenzie sat straighter. "I'm sorry. Your what?"

"You know, Spider-Man's powers to detect trouble. Spidey sense."

Despite her earlier Black Panther reference, Mackenzie's look of absolute incomprehension made it clear that she was not a superhero fan. Although I hadn't cracked open a comic in decades, as a kid my face was always buried in those colorful pages. In fact, it was my love of superheroes that inspired me to become a crimefighter in real life. Although I no longer carried a badge, my private investigation business still kept me on the side of justice. Usually.

"Anyway," Mackenzie pushed on, "I'm thinking Mr. Patterson may've set us up. That fancy office was all for our benefit. I bet his name isn't even Raymond Patterson."

"Right. And I suspect that business about Ashley's mom wanting to reconcile on her deathbed was total bullshit. Patterson, or whoever he works for, wanted Ashley found to kill her."

Mackenzie nodded. "And now that she's dead, along with the unlucky PI who found her, it's possible they have two more loose ends to tie up. Us."

I gripped the steering wheel tighter as a moment of silence underscored Mackenzie's grim words. This wasn't some movie or TV show, or even a comic book. Real hit men were trying to put Mackenzie and me in the ground.

Mackenzie spoke up first. "Our next step is obvious. We track down Raymond Patterson, or whoever he really is, then we get answers."

"You're right. That's a good place to start. And I know someone who can help."

An instant later I had Roxanna Novakova, superhacker, on my car's speakerphone. Roxanna was crazy strict about vetting people, so she'd disapprove of Mackenzie even knowing of her existence. For that reason I'd instructed Mackenzie to remain silent during the call.

"*Moje láska,*" Roxanna exclaimed affectionately in her pronounced Czech accent. "Good timing you have. My body needs your hands desperately."

Ignoring Mackenzie's wide-eyed reaction, I struck an all-business tone to discourage Roxanna from any further mention of our unusual arrangement.

"Roxanna, I'm in a tight spot. I need you to find out all you can about a lawyer who calls himself Raymond Patterson."

I gave her Patterson's office address and asked her to check everything associated with Patterson and that location—phone records, financial and real estate records, security footage. I concluded by telling her I needed the info no later than tomorrow.

Roxanna moaned. The sound had a definite sexual undertone. "*Beruško,* I'll help, of course. But for this I will need extra-long session, yes?"

Mackenzie's eyebrows shot up. I could see it took everything she had to remain silent.

"Of course, Roxanna," I said, eager to end the conversation. "Thanks. Bye." Then I killed the call before Roxanna could moan another word.

Mackenzie was on me before the call fully disconnected. "What was that?"

"I told you about Roxy. Best hacker in the world. She's on it."

"On what exactly?"

"Ha-ha. It's not what it sounds like."

"It sounds like you exchange humping for hacking."

"Even if that were true, why do you care?"

Mackenzie folded her arms across her chest. "Trust me, I don't. Thing is, I know they sometimes call PIs 'private dicks,' but you're taking it way too far."

"All right. Stop it. Look, I used to be a massage therapist, okay? That's how I met Roxy. So, you know, we exchange services. Minus the humping."

"Never?" Mackenzie cut her eyes and cocked her head.

Admittedly, her deep interest in my sex life stirred something warm inside me. Was this jealousy? I sure hoped so.

"We've never fooled around," I said, carefully watching her reaction. "Strictly massages and nothing more."

"From the sound of her moans, you must be damn good."

"If you'd like to try me out, I can make it happen."

"Excuse me?"

"We'll have some downtime at the cabin. Trust me. After what you just went through, my skills are exactly what you need."

"To be clear, we're talking about a massage, right?"

I tried to flash a smile but my face hurt too much. "What else would I be talking about?"

"Keep your eyes on the road."

"What about my hands?"

She chuckled. "You're something else. Fancy car, vacation cabin in the mountains. Your agency must be doing damn well."

"The cabin belonged to a former client who let me use it whenever I liked. I was going there so much she offered me a deal, so I bought it from her."

"What else did she let you use *whenever you liked*?"

Yup, she's definitely jealous.

"You sound a little tense," I said, glancing over at her. "I think a nice long massage is exactly what you need."

"What I need is for you to keep your eyes on the road and get us to your *love shack* in one piece."

"Funny. But I didn't hear you say no to the massage."

"Would you please just shut up and drive?"

Chapter 36

MACKENZIE

Jackson's little hideaway halfway between LA and Palm Springs was not what I had expected. As the SUV eased into the driveway, my first thought was that we were about to crash an episode of *Schitt's Creek*.

I'd stayed in crappy hotels before, but never in a place that looked as if it might collapse on itself at any moment. Piles of leaves stretched from one end of the cabin to the other. Rotting and splintered wood lined the front, and the two large windows were layered with black grime. The porch was a dangerous obstacle course of gaping holes and cracks that made it unsuitable for any activity you'd actually do on a porch.

"What?" Jackson asked, the second we stepped across the threshold.

"I didn't say anything."

"You didn't need to. Your face said it all."

I smiled to conceal my embarrassment. I didn't like that he was able to read me so well.

I'd never even heard of Idyllwild before Jackson informed me that this mountain resort community was our destination. The winding, mile-high climb to the top made it a perfect haven for two people running for their lives. Jackson seemed to know the back roads well.

"This is fine," I said, trying to be the polite daughter my parents raised me to be. "I mean . . . it's nice. Very rustic."

Jackson grunted. "Liar."

He was right. I *was* lying. The interior's condition was barely a notch above the exterior's. The room was spacious enough, but the furniture was Salvation Army chic: a worn plaid couch, a battered wooden coffee table, and a ratty recliner. The narrow kitchen was equipped with miniature appliances. A small wooden table with two chairs looked out over a backyard deck. A short hallway led to a pint-sized bathroom. No bedroom.

I covered my nose to ward off a sneeze as dust particles stung my eyes. "It's just that it doesn't exactly jibe with your persona."

"Let's not go there again."

"Go where?"

"You telling me how flashy I am. I just like nice things. I had next to nothing growing up. Now I can basically buy whatever I want. So I do."

I let the silence linger. Who was I to judge him?

For the last half of our drive, Jackson had not been his normal personable self. The stress of being hunted down by a hit man had obviously made him grumpy. Quite understandable. I was a big bundle of nerves myself. Maybe that was why I kept needling him about being flashy.

"And it's not a vacation home," Jackson snapped. "I haven't put much into fixing it up since I'm not here that often. I only kick it here when I need to escape."

"Oh, so this isn't the first time you've been on the run," I said, hoping to lighten the mood. "Who was the last person you had to hide from? A baby mama?"

"Please. Female drama ain't my style." Jackson collapsed onto the couch, forcing a small cloud of dust skyward.

I sat down gingerly on the recliner, praying nothing bit me. "How do you know we're—"

"We're safe," he said, cutting me off. "No one knows I own this place. Not a soul. Whoever's put a target on our backs can't find us here."

"Okay, okay." I glanced around. I was dying to open a door or window to air the place out. "Any food around here? I'm starving."

Jackson hopped up without responding. Four steps later, he was in the kitchen. Since he was so irritable, I kept my mouth shut as he moved about, opening and closing cabinets.

"Lunch is ready," he announced minutes later. He set two paper plates on the kitchen table and pulled out my chair.

When I walked over, I could only smile. "My favorite."

Already seated, Jackson snorted. "No need to be rude. Like I said, I don't kick it here that often. So I don't keep much food around."

"No, I'm serious. I love sardines and crackers." I raised my right hand. "If you check my kitchen cabinet, I swear you'll find at least six cans of sardines and two boxes of Ritz. I like the snack packs."

A hint of a smile touched his bruised but still beautiful lips.

"And if you have apple juice, you get major props."

This time, he gave me a full smile. He dashed over to one of the cabinets and pulled out a bottle of Mott's apple juice.

"This is so weird," I said, laughing.

Jackson filled paper cups with ice and apple juice and returned to the table. We ate slowly, without words, both of us apparently hungrier than we'd realized. There was something soothing about sharing silence with him. It was easy. Effortless.

When we were done, I put the paper plates and empty sardine

cans in the trash. After refilling my cup with juice, I rejoined Jackson at the table.

"I hope your little massage buddy is able to track Patterson down."

"She can and she will."

"Even if we're able to find him, what if he doesn't talk?"

"He will."

His declaration possessed a sense of certainty I didn't feel.

"Patterson really must've taken us for suckers," I mused. "I just wish I knew what was going on. For those guys to come at us the way they did, in broad daylight, they meant business."

Jackson nodded. "I'm figuring Ashley knew something she wasn't supposed to know. The crazy part is, they're trying to kill us and we don't know a thing."

That reality frightened me.

For the next hour or so, we used our phones to surf the internet to find out everything we could about Lance and Ashley's murders. But we didn't uncover a single clue that might tell us why they were killed. We both put alerts on our phones so we'd receive immediate updates about their deaths.

The cabin had lots of snacks, and as night approached, we munched on Doritos and M&M's and bounced around scenarios about what might be going on and what our next move should be.

Jackson got up to pour himself a gin and tonic. I passed.

"I have to ask," he said, settling back on the couch, "why'd you become a PI? Especially with your Ivy League education."

Closing my eyes, I burrowed into the recliner. "I was an investigative reporter for several years. It was fun going after dirty politicians, and I was pretty good at it. But I never liked the newsroom grind. It just made sense to put my investigative skills to work as a PI."

In truth, pissing off my mother was also a major factor in the equation. I worked overtime at rebuffing her expectations of perfection. The more she tried to rein me in, the more I bucked the norm. Maybe I'd never tried to fulfill the expectations she set for me because I knew I could never live up to them.

I yawned, not feeling much like talking anymore. "You wouldn't happen to have something I could sleep in, would you? I'd love to get out of these jeans and take a hot shower."

"You can find a T-shirt in the hallway closet. Towels are in the cabinet above the toilet. And it's probably gonna take a minute for the water to heat up."

The bathroom was barely big enough to turn around in. I was in and out of the shower in no time, feeling surprisingly refreshed.

"You sure you don't want a drink?" Jackson asked when I walked back into the main room. He was in the kitchen, his back to me, fixing his second round. "It'll relax you."

"I'm already relaxed enough." I yawned.

I eased onto the recliner and closed my eyes. I raised my arm to scratch my back and yelped in pain.

"Ow!" I winced. "I know you can't tell from looking at my face, but my back took the brunt of the beating. That goon used everything he had when he body-slammed me into the wall. I'm soooo sore."

Jackson chuckled as he walked over to me. "Sounds like you're trying to cash in on that back massage offer. Turn around. Let me help you out."

I stiffened, holding out my palm to him. "Naw, I'm good."

"Relax. I got you."

Before I could protest further, his nimble fingers were delving into pressure points along my neck and shoulders that I didn't know I had. In seconds, my body felt like a big bowl of mush in his able hands. He really *was* good at this.

"Your deltoid muscles are hella tight," Jackson said.

I lowered my head and closed my eyes again, as my body succumbed to his touch. An overwhelming sense of exhaustion began to tug at me like the pull of a powerful sedative.

I'm not sure how much time had passed, but when my eyes fluttered open, Jackson was staring down at me, smiling, drink in hand.

As I gazed up at him, a spark passed between us.

Glancing at my lap, I saw that my T-shirt had inched up my legs, revealing way too much of my thighs. My nipples were hard and visible through the thin fabric of the T-shirt.

Jackson's eyes seemed to be roaming every inch of my body, the same way his big hands had just caressed me.

I looked away and tried to will my body to stop betraying me. To stop tingling with lust. To stop wanting Jackson Jones's strong, sensual fingers touching me again.

And not just my shoulders, but every inch of my body.

Chapter 37

JACKSON

So . . . uh . . . how was the massage? You feel better?"

Mackenzie sprang forward and snatched down the bottom of the T-shirt, blocking my view of those luscious thighs. I couldn't look away and I didn't want to.

"It was . . . it was good," Mackenzie stuttered. Her eyes no longer met mine. "Thanks."

She abruptly got up and walked into the kitchen. "You have anything else to eat?"

My eyes trailed her like a helicopter spotlight tracking a getaway car. The T-shirt barely covered her ass. *Damn. I definitely should've hit that when I had the chance.*

I'd never seen Mackenzie in anything other than jeans. The girl had legs that called out to me. Toned but not muscular. Firm, yet smooth.

When she bent over to peer inside the refrigerator, I caught a much better glimpse of her ass. *Noice!*

"Okay if I drink this Pepsi?" She held up the can. "It's the only one in here."

"Have at it." I raised my glass. "I'm already imbibing my drink of choice."

She returned to the recliner. I could still see the imprint of her nipples. I might just have to frame that T-shirt.

"You okay?" Mackenzie asked.

"I'm fine," I said, suddenly realizing I was still hovering over her like an idiot. I went back to the couch.

Mackenzie's phone pinged and she picked it up from a TV tray that doubled as a side table. Her eyes squinted and horizontal lines gathered across her forehead as she read the screen.

"What's up?" I asked.

She took in a long breath. "I just got a message from Detective Mason. It appears Lance and Ashley were tortured before they were killed."

For several seconds, we both sat there stunned, quietly assessing the significance of this news.

"How?" I asked, setting my drink on the coffee table.

"He didn't say. But you know what this means, right?"

"Yep. They probably knew something, or had something, and someone was trying to force them to give it up."

Mackenzie nodded. "Exactly."

I picked up my phone and started perusing the most recent news stories about the murders. "I'm not finding anything online about them being tortured."

"The police are probably keeping that information away from the public. What do you think Ashley knew that brought all this down on her?"

I hunched my shoulders. "No idea. But that might explain why Ashley had all that high-tech equipment and why she hired Lucius to set up an offshore account. She was involved in something that made other people very nervous. But what?"

I didn't have an answer and apparently neither did Mackenzie. "Maybe a good night's sleep will help us come up with some answers."

I got up to refresh my drink.

"You're not getting drunk again, are you?" Mackenzie asked. "How many drinks did you have last night?"

I chuckled and took a sip. "*I* wasn't drunk. *You*, on the other hand, were completely wasted."

"Touché," she said, smiling. "I promise on your life, I will never drink that much again."

"*My* life? No, thanks."

I stretched my arm along the back of the couch and tried to keep my eyes on her face, not those protruding nipples.

"Last night was fun," I said.

"Yeah, it was."

I decided to test the waters. "We'll have to do it again."

Mackenzie's lips curled into another smile, this time accompanied by a sexy tilt of her head. "You should take your shower."

Instantly I felt a tug of anticipation. Was there something for me to decipher in that suggestion? Did she want me to shower so I'd be nice and clean when we . . .

Mackenzie stood up again.

Damn, I'd love to plant kisses up and down those thighs.

"I'm going to make some popcorn," she said. "Want some?"

"Sure." *But that ain't all I want.*

I made my way to the bathroom and undressed. When I saw my face in the mirror, I winced. The swelling in my jaw had gone down, but it would be a minute before the evidence of the pounding I took vanished altogether.

Gently touching my tenderized jaw, I thought about Mackenzie calling me flashy. I grew up in Compton, the birthplace of Dr. Dre and, of course, Serena and Venus Williams. During my high school years, I got into countless fights with assholes who called me and my three brothers names that were decidedly the opposite of flashy.

"Rat pack" was the taunt I hated the most. My mom raised us alone on a waitress's salary. We were often shabbily dressed, mostly well-worn hand-me-downs from cousins who also teased us. Instead of the latest Air Jordans, we'd end up with Walmart knockoffs, which we had to wear until the soles were paper-thin. Amid all the laughter and teasing, I made a silent oath to be loaded someday. To live large like Jay-Z and only have the best of everything. Well, I never struck it rich, but I do like looking the part. I make every effort to treat myself to the toys I couldn't imagine owning as a kid. Is it a crime to like nice things?

Another detriment to being the poorest teenager in town was that all the girls wanted nothing to do with me. Not just the cute ones—all of them. Well, that situation has changed, and being tastefully flashy definitely helped my game. Whether they'll admit it or not, women are drawn to shiny things. Objects that project success, health, and security. It's human nature and there's no denying it. Just like the way I heard jungle drums every time I took in Mackenzie's luscious curves.

As the warm cascade of water from the shower doused my body, I struggled to tamp down my excitement. I had to chill. Take it slow. Real slow. Mackenzie was not the kind of woman you could rush. I had to be 100 percent sure I was receiving a clear *go* signal.

I walked back into the living room shirtless, wearing only sweatpants.

Mackenzie had just pulled a bag of popcorn from the microwave when she turned around to find me standing near the couch, towel-drying my hair.

"I was looking for—" She stopped midsentence and quickly spun away from me.

I was certain her eyes had landed on my chest. *Guess all that pumping iron paid off.*

"I was looking for a couple of bowls," she mumbled. "Do you have any?"

"The cabinet to your left. Second shelf. You can have the couch," I said. "It folds out into a bed. I'll make a pallet for myself and sleep on the floor. That recliner is broken and won't go back."

"No, you can take the couch." Mackenzie divvied up the popcorn between two bowls. "I'm fine sleeping on the floor."

I stepped into the hallway and returned with two pillows and several blankets.

"You're my guest," I insisted. "What I say goes."

I removed the cushions from the couch and unfolded the bed.

"It's been a long day." Mackenzie's left hand was on her hip. "And I really don't feel like arguing. I *said* I'm sleeping on the floor."

"And *I* said you're my guest. I'm not letting you sleep on the floor."

"Why do men always have to start tripping? This macho madness is beneath you. You don't have to treat me like I'm some damsel in distress."

WTF, lady? You're really killing my buzz.

"So being nice to you is macho?" Anger slowly eased its way up my throat. "What kinda losers you used to dealing with?"

"Don't even go there. Just give me the blankets. I'll make my own pallet."

She stalked over, snatched the blankets, and laid them out in the far corner of the room.

I walked over to her. "Mackenzie, you don't have to do that."

She practically snarled at me. "Can you please just get out of my face and leave me alone?"

"Okay. Fuck it then. If you want me to treat you like a dude I will."

"You do that."

"I will."

She lowered herself to the floor and scowled up at me. "Your popcorn's on the counter."

"I don't want it."

"Neither do I."

Chapter 38

MACKENZIE

The instant I opened my eyes the next morning, a searing pain blazed down my back.

I bit my bottom lip to keep from screaming out. There was no way I would let Jackson know how much I regretted rejecting his offer to take the couch. The cabin's floor offered all the comfort of a cement slab.

I could really use another massage, but I wasn't about to risk going *there* again.

"You okay?" Jackson peered down at me. He was now sporting a tight black T-shirt, jeans, and a sexy five-o'clock shadow. "How'd you sleep?"

"Great." I struggled to sit up.

Can you please go put on a sweatshirt so I don't have to look at those sexy-ass muscles?

"So did you come up with any bright ideas about what's really going on?" Jackson asked.

I frowned. "Not a one. And you?"

"Ditto."

I glanced toward the kitchen. "Is that food I smell? Real food?"

He grinned. "Yep. I ran out to get some groceries. No telling how long we'll be on the run. We need some decent food in our systems. Let me help you up." Jackson extended his hand.

I hesitated a beat before taking it, afraid of the feelings his touch might arouse in me again. In the process of getting to my feet, the T-shirt inched up my thighs again. I pulled away from Jackson's grip and used both of my hands to snatch it back down.

I'd hated being such a bitch last night, but I had no choice. If I hadn't intentionally started an argument, I might've given in to what I was feeling. Then Jackson and I would've ended up sharing that pullout couch. In the midst of what we were up against, that would've made things complicated. Dangerously complicated.

"So you can actually cook?" I asked, following him into the kitchen.

He shrugged. "Better than most."

I perused the three pans on the stovetop.

"Turkey sausage, hash browns, and goat cheese omelets." Jackson beamed like a kid who'd just earned a gold star. "And there's coffee too."

"I'm impressed."

"You'll be even more impressed when you taste it."

I left to wash up and returned wearing my jeans and a fresh T-shirt. As hard as I tried, I couldn't stop admiring Jackson's body. Lean, muscular fitness was far more attractive to me than bulging biceps. More LL Cool J than Dwayne Johnson was my speed. Jackson was a near-perfect specimen on the LL side of the scale. I fought the urge to reach over and squeeze one of his guns.

My stomach growled as I sat down across from him. "Any news from your hacker friend?"

"Yep." Jackson set a plate—a real one, not a paper plate—in front of me, then poured my coffee.

I waited while he fixed his own plate.

"So," I asked again, "did your friend find out anything?" I took a bite of the omelet. "Oh my God! This is amazing."

"Thanks."

"No, I'm serious. This is fabulous."

A humble grin animated his face, which was healing nicely. "It's the clarified butter."

"So," I said, chewing. "Back to your little Czechoslovakian rosebud. What'd she find out?"

Jackson pursed his lips. "You might want to finish your meal first."

I put down my fork. "Stop playing around. What did she tell you?"

"There's no Raymond Patterson. His real name is Antonin Severino." He picked up a piece of sausage with two fingers. "He *is* a lawyer. But handling the affairs of rich white folks isn't his specialty."

"Jackson, please stop parsing out information and tell me what you know."

"Mr. Severino is a mob lawyer. More accurately, a mob fixer. Kinda like Michael Cohen, but much more sophisticated."

I swallowed although there was nothing in my mouth. "What else?"

"That's it. She refused to tell me more over the phone. She wants to see us in person."

"*Us?*" My brows lifted on their own. "I doubt I'm the one she wants to see."

Jackson shrugged. "She's a bit anal about her privacy and kinda flipped out when I told her I'd be bringing you along. But I calmed her down."

"Yeah, I bet you did. So where do we have to go?"

"Her place on the west side. Bel Air, to be exact."

"Of course she lives in Bel Air," I said mockingly. "You do realize people are trying to kill us, right?"

"Don't worry. I got you. Eat your breakfast."

I stared at him, even more worried than before. Reluctantly I returned to my food.

"Wow," Jackson said, minutes later. "You really wolfed that down."

"Hard not to. You could be a chef, you know that?"

"I gave it a shot, but it turned out to be yet another career that didn't work out too well for me."

I went over to the counter, grabbed the coffeepot, and refilled our cups.

"Shouldn't we know a little more about what's going on before heading back to LA?"

"We'll be all right."

"How can you say that?"

Jackson rose from his chair, walked over to the recliner, and pushed it about six feet away. He knelt and opened a trapdoor hidden in the floorboards.

He beckoned for me to come over. "Check this out."

I stood and gazed down into the hole. "Whoa."

He had a massive cache of weapons. I counted several handguns, a few assault rifles, and a couple of knives that looked like miniature swords.

"Is that a friggin' machine gun?"

"Yep." Jackson picked up a Glock and handed it to me. "You know how to use that?"

"A Glock 19 Gen4? Damn right I do."

Holding the gun filled me with a sense of security. My fingers easily curled around the cold, hard piece of steel. I released the clip to check for bullets, then slid it back into place.

He nodded approvingly. "That's my girl."

Disappearing into the hallway, he returned wearing a light-weight jacket.

He tossed a jacket to me and knelt next to the hidden compartment. I watched as he pulled out several weapons and loaded them into a duffel bag.

"Strap this one around your ankle," Jackson said, handing me a compact M&P9 Shield.

Sucking in a breath, I did as instructed.

A fearless confidence emanated from his eyes. "You ready?"

I nodded.

"Then let's do this."

Chapter 39

JACKSON

The drive from Idyllwild to Bel Air took forty minutes longer than it should have. During the 116-mile trip, Mackenzie and I never spotted a reason for the congestion. No car wrecks or road construction, which wasn't surprising. When you live in LA, you get used to the fact that sometimes the traffic gods are against you.

As I drove the 4Runner up the circular driveway to Roxanna's front door, Mackenzie gaped up at the mansion.

"She lives *here*?" she asked, making no attempt to conceal her astonishment.

"Pretty nice, huh?"

"Nice? It's amazing." Her brows tightened. "I always thought hackers lived in shitty little apartments or their mother's basement."

I laughed. "The bad ones maybe. Like I told you, Roxanna's the gold standard."

We exited the car and moved to the front door. As I rang the doorbell, Mackenzie craned her neck, eyeing several mounted security cameras.

"Somebody certainly takes her security seriously."

"Roxanna's a little paranoid. It took some work convincing her to let me bring you along. So don't take it personally if she's cold at first. Give her time to warm up to you."

"If she can tolerate you, she'll love me."

"Funny."

Just as I went to press the bell again, the front door swung open.

I was accustomed to Roxanna greeting me wearing just a clingy silk robe. To see her dressed in jeans and a T-shirt was odd. Even her hairstyle was frumpy. Instead of golden locks cascading past her shoulders, her hair was pulled back in a messy bun.

My appearance must have caught Roxanna off guard as well. She zeroed in on my bruised face and gasped. "*Moje dětátko*! What have they done to you?" She reached out and caressed my cheek.

"I'm okay. I looked a lot worse yesterday."

She winced as if she shared my pain. "Then I am glad I did not see."

With that, Roxanna hugged me and planted the gentlest kiss on both of my cheeks. I couldn't help noticing the absence of her signature perfume. I had to admit I missed the alluring fragrance.

Before Roxanna and I had a chance to separate, Mackenzie cleared her throat and said, "I'm Mackenzie Cunningham. Nice to meet you."

I shot Mackenzie a look. What the hell was she thinking? I'd made it clear that introducing her to my most important source was a sensitive matter. If Roxanna sensed even a whiff of attitude from Mackenzie, it was meeting over. Even worse, Roxanna might cut me off altogether.

My heart thudded as Roxanna released me and pivoted to square off with Mackenzie. For a long, agonizing moment, Roxanna gazed at Mackenzie, her icy Eastern European features revealing nothing.

To Mackenzie's credit, she stood there mute, flashing a respectful smile.

I was about to break the standoff with a witty crack when the unexpected happened.

Roxanna smiled and said, "It is my pleasure to meet you, Mackenzie." Then she grimaced at the lumps on Mackenzie's face. "What sort of animals treat a woman this way? Come, *sluníčka*. I know precisely what you need."

Roxanna grabbed Mackenzie's hand and tugged her into the house, abandoning me on the doorstep.

What the hell?

Roxanna called back to me, "Jackson, be a darling and lock the door."

Moments later we were in Roxanna's meticulously decorated, minimalist living room sipping chilled vodka martinis. Three olives each.

While I sat isolated in an elegant wingback chair, Roxanna and Mackenzie shared the sofa. I couldn't help noticing that despite the plush sofa's generous size, the two women sat close enough to rub elbows.

Mackenzie sipped her martini, closed her eyes, and moaned. "I drink martinis all the time, but I've never had one this delicious."

Roxanna smiled. "It is the vodka. In the world it is the best. Imported straight from Japan."

Mackenzie raised an eyebrow. "I thought Russia made the best vodka."

"Propaganda. Many believe that until they try Ukiyo."

Mackenzie took another slow, savoring sip. "Amazing. And you were right. This is exactly what I needed."

It was true. I've known for years that Roxanna's martinis were the bomb. But at that moment my drink remained untouched. I was too busy watching the two most intense women I'd ever known connect like lifelong friends.

Who are these people?

Roxanna wagged a finger at me. "I am much disappointed with you, Jackson. How you let beautiful partner be harmed in this way?"

Mackenzie playfully scowled at me. "Yeah, Jackson, how could you?"

"Hold on a minute. First of all, Mackenzie and I are not partners. And second, she can fight just as well as I can." I glared at Mackenzie. "Go on, tell her."

She nodded at Roxanna. "He's right. We're not partners and I'm definitely a better fighter than he is."

"I didn't say you were better. I said—"

"This I do not understand," Roxanna interrupted. "If not partners, then what? Lovers?"

"No!" Mackenzie and I exclaimed in unison.

"Why no?" Roxanna asked. "Jackson, you have exceptional body. And Mackenzie, you are very, very beautiful. You two would make very sexy couple. Yes?"

"No!" Mackenzie and I bellowed again.

Above a knowing smile, Roxanna's gaze ticked back and forth between me and Mackenzie. "Yes, I believe I am right. You both will see."

I looked everywhere except at Mackenzie. I didn't want to see the look on her face.

I placed my drink on the coffee table. "Okay, I think we've all had enough. Maybe we should get to why we came here."

Mackenzie put down her martini as well. "Good idea."

Roxanna shrugged, drained her glass, and stood up. "Very well. I have much to show you. Come."

I was stunned as Roxanna led us down the hall and into her study. She had never taken me into her special room. My mouth gaped open as we stepped inside. The place was equipped with enough computer screens to rival NASA. The low, constant thrum of electronics evoked an ominous feel.

As Roxanna slid behind her desk and began tapping keys, Mackenzie and I peered over her shoulder. Images populated multiple screens simultaneously.

What we saw made Mackenzie and me both gasp.

I stopped breathing. "What the fuck!"

Dozens of surveillance photos filled the screens. Photos of me. Photos of Mackenzie. Photos of the two of us together.

There were pictures of me walking into Shadows. Several shots of Mackenzie at Ashley Cross's apartment complex. They'd even captured the two of us arguing in the parking garage at Congressman Vanderpool's office.

"I downloaded these directly from Antonin Severino's servers." Roxanna's voice resonated with pride. "Quite difficult. Had to bypass much firewalls."

"They were watching our every move," I said. "Waiting for the precise moment we found Ashley."

"*Ano*," Roxanna said. "I recovered much similar images of your murdered competitor. And I am afraid I found far more disturbing images than these."

"More disturbing how?" I said.

Roxanna punched several keys, and more surveillance photos of Mackenzie and me popped onto the screens. It took me a second to understand why Roxanna considered these pictures worse than the others. The reality struck me like a Mike Tyson uppercut.

Mackenzie said it before I could, her voice a stunned whisper. "These were taken weeks before we even started working the case."

My body tensed and my breathing picked up. "Severino set us up."

"Yes," Roxanna said. "His server contained much personal information about you both. Absolute finest details. And no information about his superiors. They are careful. No paper trails. Impressive."

Mackenzie and I exchanged glances. This was bigger than either of us could have imagined.

"They certainly went to a lot of effort," Mackenzie said.

"Agree," Roxanna said. "And same with girl. Everything fake."

"You mean Ashley?" I asked.

Roxanna nodded. "No dying mother. No inheritance."

"But we both checked that hospice facility where her mother was supposed to be," I said.

"Setting up ruse like that very easy for professionals like this. Ms. Ashley moved to LA from Omaha, Nebraska, four years ago. Men, mostly bad men, take care of her."

As usual, Roxanna had kicked ass, but it struck me that she hadn't revealed the one key piece of information we needed. Information she was way too good to miss. Roxanna was obviously holding back, and that filled me with dread.

"Roxy, if you got into Severino's servers, that means you know where we can find him."

She swiveled and looked up at me, her eyes edged with concern. I couldn't remember ever seeing such a distressed look on her face.

"Better if I do not tell you. Better you and your beautiful partner to run."

"Run?" Mackenzie jumped in. "Are you serious?"

I gestured to Mackenzie to calm down, then said to Roxanna, "You know I don't run from anything. Why are you saying this?"

She gestured to the images on her computer screens. "This level of surveillance is highly organized and expensive. This is not a cheating husband case or a so-simple missing persons. Whoever Severino works for is powerful and dangerous. If I give what you ask, I worry you and Mackenzie will end up like the others. I do not want to be responsible."

"If they're as dangerous as you say," Mackenzie said, "where would we go?"

"There are places," Roxanna said, turning to Mackenzie. "I have safe houses. I can arrange everything, documents, travel. Even plenty of cash so you can live same life." Roxanna took my hand. "Jackson, please. Listen to me. Running is best. Of this I am certain."

Mackenzie shook her head. "No way. We can't be on the run for the rest of our lives. We appreciate your offer, but we can't."

I squeezed Roxanna's hand. "Roxy, she's right. We understand the danger, but we can't run."

Roxanna frowned. "And, of course, if I don't give you Severino's location, you still continue to search. Yes?"

Mackenzie and I both nodded.

Roxanna sighed, then slid an envelope out from under her keyboard. My name was written across the front with a drawing of a little heart. She handed it to me. "Be very careful. Please."

Mackenzie squeezed Roxanna's shoulder. "Thank you."

I tore open the envelope and stared at Severino's office address. The real one. Not the fake one he'd set up as part of his scheme to dupe us. I knew exactly where the building was. Just as I was about to speak, an earsplitting alarm blared.

Mackenzie's eyes expanded. "What's happening?"

"Not good." Roxanna's fingers flew across the keyboard. Instantaneously, live security camera feeds replaced the surveillance images on every screen.

On a display marked *Rear Entrance 1*, two gun-wielding masked men rushed across the expansive yard toward the back door.

"They are here!" Roxanna said.

WTF? Maybe they knew about my earlier visit and had been watching her house, figuring I'd come back.

I snatched my gun from the small of my back. "I can't believe this shit."

"We must go." Roxanna frantically tapped more keys. *Drives Purging* flashed in red letters across every screen. An instant later, the hum of computers ceased and every screen went dark.

From the rear of the house came the sound of the back door being kicked in.

"Oh, shit!" Mackenzie said, her Glock at the ready.

Roxanna reached under her desk and came out with a shotgun.

"You got another one of those?" I asked as we all moved toward the door.

"Unfortunately, I do not." Roxanna expertly cocked the weapon and raised it to a ready position. "I have safe room," she said. "Please follow."

Mackenzie and I trailed Roxanna out of the study as heavy footsteps filled the house behind us. We sprinted down the long hallway and into the living room. Still holding her gun, Roxanna threw a small painting to the ground and began tapping a keypad.

"Basement safe room," she said. "We will be secure."

We lumbered down a narrow stairwell, and just as Roxanna opened the door, we could hear movement on the stairs behind us. Roxanna and Mackenzie made it inside the safe room.

"Come! Inside!" Roxanna yelled at me, keeping the door open just a crack.

Ignoring her, I spun around and took out the two men charging down the stairs. My first bullet tore into the first man's chest, causing him to fall backward into the other guy, giving me enough time to take him out too.

When I turned around, Mackenzie was standing outside of the safe room.

"Get the fuck back inside!" I yelled at her.

"No!" she said defiantly. "If you're shooting your way out of here, I'm doing it with you."

"You sure?"

Mackenzie cocked her handgun and said to me, "Damn right."

Roxanna shouted at me from the safe room's doorway: "Jackson, this room is impenetrable. Don't be insane. Both of you come quickly!"

I threw my old friend a brave smile. "See you around, Roxy."

Roxanna shook her head. "Good luck to you." Then she slammed the door. The mechanical clang of the door bolting shut sounded like a bank vault.

Mackenzie and I charged up the staircase, not sure where the next attacker would come from.

Just as we reached the top of the stairs, I heard a noise to my left, but before I could react, Mackenzie had already opened fire. The man flailed from the multiple hits from Mac's gun before crumpling to the carpet.

We crouched down the hallway toward the front door.

"Jackson, get down!" Mackenzie shouted at me.

I dropped to the floor and found myself behind a sofa, Mackenzie right next to me.

Bullets punctured the sofa as crunching footfalls signaled that the gunmen were closing in fast.

Mackenzie pinned me with determined eyes. "On three, we kill these assholes."

I nodded.

Mackenzie whispered, "One, two, three!"

Side by side we sprang up from behind the sofa and emptied our clips. When the smoke cleared, three more men lay dead.

Chapter 40

MACKENZIE

As we sprinted toward the 4Runner, I prayed there weren't any more masked men gunning for us. I hadn't even closed my door before Jackson whipped the car around the circular driveway and onto the street like a wannabe NASCAR driver.

Leaning to my left, I peered through the back window, scanning the street behind us. As we zoomed down the wide residential street, obliterating the speed limit, I didn't spot anyone on our trail. That still did nothing to take my adrenaline level out of overdrive.

"I don't think anybody's following us," I said, turning back around to check the area in front of us.

"For now." Jackson's voice was strained.

As we took a corner way too fast, he pounded the steering wheel with his fist. "Damn! I really hate bringing Roxanna all that drama. Her place was destroyed."

"You couldn't have known. Thank God she made it to her safe room. I just hope she's okay."

Jackson made a sharp right onto Wilshire Boulevard, making the turn so suddenly I whiplashed sideways, banging my head into his shoulder. "Slow down! If the cops stop us, we'll—"

With a loud crash, the mirror on my side of the car shattered, spraying shards of glass. Before I could duck, a bullet whizzed past my head and pierced the windshield, filling the SUV with more glass.

"Shit!" Using my hand to shield my face, I dropped low in my seat. "Forget what I said about slowing down. Get us the hell out of here!"

Jackson picked up speed, zigzagging around cars, sideswiping a bus, nearly losing control of the SUV.

Inching up in my seat, I peered out of the window. Two cars back, I spotted one of our pursuers leaning out of a black Escalade. When I pointed my gun out of the window, the woman driving the Audi that separated us instantly swung out of my way, giving me a clear shot. I fired, aiming for the driver's head, but my shot missed, landing inches to the left, shattering the Escalade's windshield. That did nothing to slow the vehicle down.

I spun back around to see that Jackson was now driving on the wrong side of the street, facing oncoming traffic. "Oh my God!"

A split second before a FedEx truck hit us head-on, the 4Runner jumped the curb and leapt onto the sidewalk. Screaming pedestrians scattered like roaches.

Another shot fired from behind us took out Jackson's side mirror as we careened back into the street and made a sharp right turn.

"This is a one-way street," I yelled, glancing back to see the Escalade still on our ass.

Jackson almost smiled. "Exactly."

I was amazed that he showed no sign of distress. In fact, he actually seemed calmer now. His eyes were laser-focused on the road.

I leaned out of the window and fired again. A gush of blood spray-painted what was left of the Escalade's windshield and the passenger slumped forward. Still, the tank kept coming.

"I have an idea." I pulled out my iPhone and started tapping the screen.

"What are you doing?" Jackson's voice was still way too calm.

"Planning our escape."

As we zipped down a back alley, I fired again, determined to take out the driver. This time I hit my mark. "I got him!"

"Good job!"

The Escalade drunkenly darted from left to right before barreling into a fence.

"Pull over," I shouted as we burst out of the alley.

"*Pull over*? Are you crazy? Hell no." Jackson picked up speed.

I pointed up the street. "That's our Uber over there. So stop the car!"

"Uber?" Uncertainty filled Jackson's face. "No way. They'll track us in two seconds through your credit card."

I wanted to slug him. "I'm not stupid. I have different credit cards and different profiles for different purposes. Now, let's go."

"You expect me to just leave my truck here. My ride might be old, but it's been very, very good to me."

"Dude, you can buy another truck. We can't buy another us."

The crestfallen look on his face would've made me laugh if we weren't under such duress.

"Okay," he muttered, reaching for his duffel bag full of guns. "If we have to."

Seconds later, we jumped into the back seat of a Honda.

"LAX," I shouted at the driver. "Hurry. We're late for a flight."

Confusion glazed Jackson's face. "I thought we agreed we weren't going to run."

"We aren't," I said, lowering my voice and indicating to Jackson that our Uber driver was eavesdropping on our conversation. "We need to rent another car and that's the closest place to do it."

"Let's just go back to Terranea and pick up my Benz," Jackson said.

"Too far away," I said. "And too easy to spot. We just need to get out of town until we can figure this thing out."

. . .

As Jackson stood at the Hertz counter, I remained close by, keeping an eye on the entrance just in case another Escalade came blazing through the glass walls. We were at the off-site rental car facility, about half a mile from the airport.

When I turned around, Jackson was pulling out a credit card. The second the attendant stepped away, I whispered, "Hold up. They'll be able to track us if you use that card."

"First, you can't rent a car without one, and second, you're not the only one to have off-the-grid credit cards." He winked and waved the card at me. "I'm using one of my super-secret alter egos."

I shook my head. Sometimes he could be so corny.

Moving toward the entrance, I continued clocking everyone who walked in and out of the building, unable to shake the fear that another set of criminals was about to spring up from nowhere. Suddenly I jumped nearly three feet off the ground.

"Calm down." Jackson held up his palms. "I didn't mean to sneak up on you. Don't worry. We're good."

I lowered my head and rubbed my eyes with my thumb and index finger. "But a lot of other people aren't. There's a lot of blood on our hands."

"We didn't start any of this," Jackson said. "Everything we did was in self-defense."

"Have you ever"—I paused, surprised that I was almost choking up—"killed anyone before?"

Jackson slowly shook his head and didn't speak for several seconds. "Everything will be fine. We're both fortunate that we made it out alive."

I hugged him, enjoying the comfort of his body pressed against mine. He squeezed me back even tighter.

"Mr. Martin?" the attendant called out.

We awkwardly ended our embrace.

"So that's your super-secret alter ego?" I said. "I'm surprised you didn't invent a name with a little more pizzazz."

"Wrong move. You should know better. The goal is to blend in. Not stand out."

Before I could react to his chiding me, he turned back to the counter.

The attendant pointed to a screen. "Please initial right here that you're declining the insurance coverage."

"You're not getting the insurance?" I said. "That's a big mistake."

Jackson waved away my concern with a flick of his hand. "It's a complete rip-off. I never get the insurance."

"All right. Don't say I didn't warn you."

"Yeah, whatever."

We headed to an elevator that deposited us in an underground garage.

"We can pick anything on this row," Jackson said as he moved toward a silver BMW sedan. "How about this one?"

Of course, he'd picked a luxury car. I silently shook my head as I hopped into the passenger seat.

As I strapped on my seat belt, Jackson tossed his bag into the back seat. I closed my eyes, pressed my face into my hands, and started taking long, deep breaths. I wasn't sure how much time had passed before I realized the car wasn't moving. When I peered over at Jackson, he was just sitting there, his face full of mischief.

"What's that look all about?"

"I have an idea," he said.

"I'm listening."

He cocked his head and scratched his jaw. "How about we head over to Raymond Patterson's office or Antonin Severino's or whoever the hell he is, and make him tell us who he's working for?"

I folded my arms. The idea of torturing Severino for info did seem like the perfect payback. "First, he's probably nowhere to be found. And second, exactly what would make him do that?"

"This." He held up his gun as his lips angled into a cocky smile. "I've found it to be quite the little motivator."

"You're crazy, Jackson," I said as he started up the car and backed out of the stall.

Jackson's smile broadened devilishly. "Don't you think it's about time for us to get a little crazy?"

Chapter 41

JACKSON

The critical piece of information Roxanna had uncovered was a simple downtown Los Angeles address: 2150 Grand Avenue. That's where the man formerly known to us as Raymond Patterson worked out of an office on the fourteenth floor. His real office. Not the phony one he'd set up to dupe me and Mackenzie.

As I drove the rental car toward that address, all I could think about was getting my hands on that asshole. I'd already planned out everything in my head. First make him talk, then make him pay. I was going to commemorate the trashing of Roxanna's house with a twenty-one-fist salute.

For the record, I was angry, not stupid. I didn't plan to kill Severino. Just make him wish I had.

"You okay?" Mackenzie asked.

I wasn't sure whether it was my prolonged silence or the way my hands white-knuckled the steering wheel that prompted her inquiry.

"Nope," I answered honestly. "I'm not okay. But I will be as soon as I get my hands on that phony lawyer."

The closer we got to his office, the more I began to perk up. My lips curved into a smile as I imagined introducing my fists to Severino's face.

Miraculously, I found a metered parking spot directly in front of the building. Unlike the soot-stained art deco buildings of yesteryear that languished in its shadow, Severino's office tower was a shiny behemoth of glass and steel boldly piercing LA's smog-filled sky. An architectural marvel that, in my opinion, seemed like a ballsy choice for a city famous for occasionally getting the shakes. Sure, almost certainly the skyscraper had been designed to withstand earthquakes, kinda like the *Titanic* was designed to be unsinkable. Only time would tell. Anyway, today our benefactor Severino had a far more pressing problem. A DoorDash delivery of a juicy knuckle sandwich.

Armed and ready, Mackenzie and I hopped out of the BMW. I was already halfway up the marble steps leading to the lobby when I noticed that my partner-on-the-run wasn't behind me. Mackenzie was checking the parking meter.

"You have any change?"

Seriously?

"Would you come on," I yelled back.

"Hold on. You want a ticket?"

What I wanted was to hear the bridge of Severino's nose crack. ASAP.

"I don't care about that. C'mon."

Mackenzie shrugged and started toward the steps. "Fine. Your name's on that rental car agreement, not mine. If you get a ticket, don't—"

Crash!

Seemingly from nowhere, something plummeted from the sky and crashed onto the BMW's trunk before rolling into the street.

Mackenzie and I rushed over, along with a fast-growing throng of shocked passersby. A man on a bike took out his phone and started snapping pictures.

A body lay twisted in the gutter, blood pooling from his head like a ruby-red oil spill. I recognized him instantly.

204 PAMELA SAMUELS YOUNG & DWAYNE ALEXANDER SMITH

Raymond Patterson, aka Antonin Severino.

Mackenzie's face constricted in horror. By contrast, I was pissed off. Now we'd never get the answers we wanted.

As more and more people rushed over, I could already hear sirens in the distance. A definite testament to the old adage *location, location, location.* You never got that kind of split-second response from cops in the 'hood.

Mackenzie and I didn't need to speak. We were already on the same page. She snatched open the passenger door while I rounded the back of car.

The BMW's trunk was caved in and splattered with blood, but the car was otherwise in good shape.

As I started the engine, the crowd pelted us with a chorus of shouts.

"Hey! You can't leave."

"Somebody take a picture of his license plate!"

"Did they have something to do with it?"

We were a couple miles away before either of us spoke.

"Can you believe that?" Mackenzie said.

"Yeah, I can. And you know what it means, right?"

She looked at me. "We're next?"

I nodded.

"So what are we going to do?"

"We're going to come up with a plan," I said.

"What kind of plan?"

"I'm not sure yet. But there's one thing I do know."

"What's that?"

"I should've listened to you about that damn insurance."

Mackenzie didn't say a word. She didn't have to. Her smirk said it all.

Chapter 42

MACKENZIE

By the time we made it back to Jackson's cabin, we were both physically and mentally drained. Before we got there, Jackson ordered takeout from Fratello's, which he claimed had the best pizza and pasta on the mountain.

We reclined in lounge chairs on the cabin's back deck, enjoying the tasty food, the fresh air, and most of all the tranquility. Being hunted by killers gave you a greater appreciation for simple things, like chilling in the woods and watching the sun go down.

After stuffing ourselves with pepperoni pizza and fettucine alfredo, we could barely move. It was dark out now, and the only light came from a small firepit. Jackson took the empty containers inside and returned with his signature gin and tonic, extending a glass to me as well.

"No, thanks. I want to keep a clear head. You remember what happened the last time I had a drink, right?"

Jackson smiled seductively. "Yeah, you definitely need to lay off the liquor."

I laughed softly, but still refused to take the drink.

"You need to chill out," he pushed. "Your adrenaline level is probably still pumping just as fast as mine. I made yours light, mostly tonic. If it's too strong, I'll go back inside and bring you a Pepsi."

I took the drink, intending to take a quick swallow and hand the glass right back to him. I took a small sip. He was right. I could barely taste the alcohol.

"Is it okay?"

I nodded.

Jackson settled back into the chair next to me. Anyone watching us would assume we were vacationers, escaping from city life for a moment in the slow lane. The flames from the firepit felt comfortingly warm.

When his phone rang, Jackson picked it up from the small side table separating us, glanced at the screen, and set it back down.

Seconds later, his phone pinged with a text. Again, he glanced at the screen and ignored it.

"You better answer her call," I said. "She obviously misses you."

"You're right. She does."

A twinge of jealousy filled my chest, but I shoved it down.

The phone pinged again. Jackson ignored it.

"I guess you like the stalker type, huh?"

"Why do you care what I like?" His lips angled into a grin. "Sounds like you're jealous."

"Not at all. I'm just taking notes on how you treat your women."

"Why would you need to take notes on that? You planning to date me?"

"You wish."

"Look," Jackson said, "it's my cousin Nadine. She's also my assistant. She hasn't heard from me since the break-in and she's worried."

I sat up in my chair. "So call her back and let her know you're okay."

"I can't do that," he said, his tone somber.

"Why not?"

"Because whoever is looking for us could also be watching her. . I can't risk putting her in any danger. When this madness is over, she'll be the first person I call."

I fell back into the chair. Would we actually survive this *madness*, as Jackson called it? More than anything else, his refusal to take his cousin's calls underlined the gravity of our situation. That made me wonder how my mother was faring. Despite the brave face she put on, it had to be scary not knowing whether she had breast cancer. I needed to be there for her. As dysfunctional as my family was, it was still *my* family and the thought of never seeing them again created a heavy ache deep in my heart.

"So what now?" I finally asked.

"Hell if I know. But I can definitely say whoever's calling the shots is getting desperate. The way they came after us, guns blazing, was right out of a friggin' 007 movie. And to dump Severino's body like that in broad daylight tells me these people are serious. And they are either so arrogant or so highly connected that they aren't afraid of making a spectacle."

"This is nuts," I said. "We're a threat, yet we don't know a damn thing about what's going on. It's going to be impossible for us to get out of this mess when we don't even know why we have targets on our backs."

Jackson sipped his drink. "I'd say we've been doing a pretty good job of defending ourselves so far."

"Yeah, but how long can we stay on the run like this? After our high-speed shootout down Wilshire Boulevard and the way we ran off leaving Severino's body in the street, the cops are no doubt looking for us too. They'll easily trace your SUV back to you. And eventually that rental car will be tied to you too, even though you used a fake identity."

"Maybe," Jackson said. "But they won't be able to track us here. There's absolutely nothing that ties me to this place. The purchase wasn't made in my name."

I moved to the end of my chair and held my hands over the fire. "Do you really think we can outrun these people?"

Instead of answering my question, Jackson posed one to me. "If you had a job to do and the stick you were using to get it done wasn't big enough, what would you do?"

I didn't like his question, but I knew the answer. "Get a bigger stick."

"Exactly."

"If you're trying to scare me, it's working."

"I'm not trying to scare you. I'm trying to prepare you. And there's nothing like fear to keep you on your toes."

"I've experienced enough fear over the past few days to last me a lifetime," I said. "No need for another dose."

Jackson hopped up and started pacing the length of the deck. "Like Roxanna said, these guys are good, CIA-level good. We have to be as good and as bold as they are. Maybe even bolder. I have an idea." He stopped and leaned back against the railing. "A rather kick-ass one."

I felt myself grow tense as I braced for Jackson's next jump shot from center court. Admittedly, his brazenness was a bit of a turn-on. I just wished I could experience that part of him without our lives being on the line. I drained my glass.

"Hand me your glass, Jackson," I said.

His forehead creased. "Why?"

"Because I need to be a lot more relaxed than I am right now before hearing your *kick-ass* idea."

Jackson smiled, then picked up his glass from a side table and handed it to me.

I took a big gulp. "Okay. I'm listening."

"We need to break into Severino's office and take a look around. Maybe we can find something helpful. No one would expect us to do that."

"Of course they wouldn't. Because it's insane."

He shrugged. "It is what it is."

I emptied Jackson's glass and tried to decide if I should push back. As far as I was concerned, going anywhere near LA was only asking for trouble. Deadly trouble. Jackson obviously wasn't thinking straight. But I didn't have the energy for a debate right now. Perhaps by morning I could reason with him.

"Can we at least wait until tomorrow night before going back into the city? I need a good eight hours of sleep to replenish my brain cells. And maybe by morning more of this swelling will be gone."

Jackson touched his jaw. "You're almost as good as new. Can't say the same about my battered face."

I smiled. "Don't worry. You're still a pretty boy, bruises and all."

We spent the next few minutes enjoying the sounds of the birds and crickets, lost in our own thoughts.

"Jackson?" I decided to level with him.

He turned to face me. "Yeah?"

"Are you sure we're really safe here?"

It was rare for me to show this degree of vulnerability. I wasn't sure whether my willingness to do so now was a reflection of my fear or my growing trust in Jackson.

"Yes, Mackenzie. Completely safe. I'm not going to let anything happen to you. I promise."

The unabashed assurance in his voice almost made me believe him. As I felt myself drowsing off, the same thought kept resurfacing in my mind, no matter how many times I tried to dismiss it.

If we were going to make it out of this ordeal alive, I was going to have to learn to trust him.

Chapter 43

JACKSON

I gently nudged Mackenzie's shoulder. "Hey, wake up. The temperature's going to drop another twenty degrees tonight. Let's go back inside."

She drowsily gazed up at me. "Okay if I shower first?"

"No prob."

While Mackenzie showered, I sat on the couch, panicked as hell that I wouldn't be able to get us out of this mess alive as I'd just promised her I would. I wanted to keep her safe. I had to.

I'd apparently dozed off because when I opened my eyes, Mackenzie was standing in front of me dressed in one of my T-shirts.

"Your turn," she said.

Once again, my elevator eyes gravitated to her smooth thighs and then back up to her breasts. I definitely had to find her a T-shirt made of thicker fabric. I could see the dark outlines of her areolas. I averted my eyes and hopped up off the couch. Resisting her was going to be a whole lot harder than it had been last time.

When I finished my shower and returned to the room, all I could do was laugh.

Mackenzie had unfolded the couch and was sprawled across

the bed, buried under a pile of blankets. She'd fixed a pallet on the floor. Presumably for me.

"What's the deal? Last time you insisted on sleeping on the floor. If I recall correctly, you said I was treating you like some damsel in distress."

"Did I say that?" She tried not to smile, but couldn't help herself. "I don't remember. Anyway, good night." She rolled over on her side. "Can you hit the lights?"

I shook my head. *Women.*

As soon as I lay down, extreme exhaustion lulled me into a heavy slumber. I had no idea how long I'd been asleep when Mackenzie's frantic cries rocked the room.

"Noooooo!"

I jolted awake and dashed over to the couch. She cried out as her body thrashed from side to side as if warding off an invisible assailant.

"Mackenzie," I yelled, turning on the light. "Wake up. You're dreaming. Wake up."

She suddenly sprang upright, her chest heaving, her T-shirt matted to her chest, wet with perspiration. It took another few seconds before she got her bearings.

"Are you okay?"

She took a few calming breaths, then nodded. "Sorry to wake you up. Bad dream. Or more like a nightmare. So much blood." Her voice quivered. "It was horrible."

"All the blood and violence we saw today can mess with your head. I hate that you had to relive that."

I wanted to sit down next to her and take her into my arms, but I knew she would reject the overture.

She stared up at me with pained eyes. "It wasn't just that. It was you . . . I dreamed that somebody threw *you* off the roof of a building."

A chill stung my skin, but I couldn't let Mackenzie see that. I tried to keep things light.

"Hey, I don't mind if you dream about me, but keep it dirty. Okay?"

"It's not funny! You were lying there in the street, your bones sticking through your skin, your guts hanging out. Blood was everywhere and I couldn't do anything to help you. All I could do was watch you die." She buried her face in her hands.

Without thinking, I went with my gut. I plopped down on the flimsy bed, scooped her into my arms, and pulled her into a tight hug. To my surprise, she let me, brushing her face against my bare chest, her tears wetting my skin.

"I was so scared!"

I didn't know what to say, so I settled for the old standby. "It's okay. It's okay. Look at me."

She sniffled, then raised her head and peered into my eyes.

"You're fine now, okay?"

The moment lingered longer than either of us expected. We were so close that I could feel her heartbeat reverberate through my body. I was certain she could feel mine because it was suddenly pounding hard enough to explode from my chest.

Then it happened. I leaned forward, grabbing her face in my hands, and kissed her deeply, passionately, hungrily. The kind of kiss you see in movies and swear it's over the top.

Seconds later, we awkwardly separated, our eyes unwilling to meet, unable to acknowledge what had just occurred.

Then I heard myself say, "Uh . . . sorry about that."

Mackenzie's eyes locked on mine. "I'm not."

Before I could respond, she leaned in, touching her lips to mine, this time with heightened urgency. We stretched out on the bed, our tongues jockeying for control as we kissed and groped each other. Her fingers roamed my chest as I pulled her T-shirt over her head. She bucked forward, allowing me to caress her perfect breasts.

Mackenzie untied the string of my sweats, pushing them farther down my legs. Her right hand gently stroked me through my boxers while her mouth alternated between sucking my nipples and biting my chest.

She rolled herself on top of me as I kissed every inch of her face and cupped her ass with both hands. As we frenetically pressed and ground against each other, the thin layers of underwear separating us did nothing to lessen the intensity. Ripples of pleasure ignited every sensor in my body as I anticipated the approaching connection. We were two potent magnets, unable to fight the powerful pull of gravity.

Then I froze. My body and my brain were waging an intense tug-of-war. One yearned for pleasure. The other demanded practicality. This simply wasn't the right time for us to connect.

I gently lifted her off me, pulled up my sweats, and stood up.

Mackenzie blinked. "What? What's wrong?"

"Nothing. I mean . . . we can't do this. We *shouldn't* do this."

My words seemed to hit her like a gut punch. A frown settled across her face as she searched the jumble of blankets looking for her T-shirt and squirmed back into it without saying a word.

"Mackenzie, look, we can't—"

"It's okay. I get it."

She rolled over, turning her back to me and pulling the blankets over her head.

"Mac, please. Just listen."

"Jackson, I'm fine." Her voice sounded small and wounded. "Just go back to sleep."

• • •

The next morning, I woke up wishing I were still in bed with Mackenzie. I tried to rehearse in my head what I was going to say to smooth things over with her. I knew from experience that once we took the plunge, there'd be no going back. I'd made that mistake way too many times. Relying on my little head rather than the big one.

Mackenzie was probably the most incredible woman I'd ever met. No matter how much I desired her, it didn't make sense to sacrifice the possibility of a lifelong friendship for one night of pleasure.

"Hey, Mac? You awake?"

No response.

Okay, so she was going to give me the silent treatment. *Great.*

It wasn't until I stood up that I realized Mackenzie wasn't there. She'd bunched up the blankets, making it look like she was still in bed.

What the fuck?

I peered through the window. The porch was empty and the rental car was still parked out front. I checked the bathroom, then stepped out onto the deck, bristling at the cold.

No Mackenzie.

She probably just went for a walk. Relax.

My pulse started to climb, but not faster than my anger. Or my fear. Mackenzie had no business being in the woods by herself. Even a seasoned outdoorsman could get lost or worse in unfamiliar wilderness.

I descended the stairs of the deck to the grassy area below, my eyes scanning the expansive woods. "Mackenzie?" I yelled. "Are you out there?"

My own voice echoed back to me.

I dashed back inside, grabbed my phone, and called Mackenzie's number. My call went straight to voicemail.

I ran back outside, charging down the deck stairs and into the woods.

"Mackenzie!" I shouted at the top of my lungs.

Where the fuck are you?

Chapter 44

MACKENZIE

Mackenzie!"

When I heard Jackson shouting my name, my mind instantly leapt to the worst-case scenario. *Oh my God! They found us!*

"Mackenzie!"

I took off in the direction of Jackson's voice at breakneck speed.

Seconds later, I spotted him not far from the deck. Why in the hell was he outside in the freezing cold without a jacket, not to mention a shirt?

I charged up to him, almost bowling him down as I gasped for air. "What's the matter? Did something happen?"

Jackson snatched me by the shoulders. "Where have you been? Don't disappear like that again. Ever!"

"I didn't disappear," I said, pulling away. "I just went for a walk."

I'd only left the cabin minutes earlier. I needed to clear my head after our erotic debacle.

"Next time, just let me know you're leaving," he said, still shaking.

"I didn't want to wake you. You were—"

"Just wake me next time, okay?" he sighed, finally beginning to calm down.

217

It said a lot that he'd dashed out of the cabin without even grabbing a jacket, desperate to find me. The same way he tore across town after hearing me being attacked on the phone.

I smiled. "Aw, you were worried."

His face scrunched up. "Of course I was."

"After last night, I didn't think you cared one way or the other."

Jackson exhaled a thick puff of fog. "Don't be ridiculous. If I didn't care about you, last night would've ended differently."

I pursed my lips. "Oh, okay. I get it. You only screw women you *don't* care about. But the ones you actually care about, you like to get them all hot and bothered and then shut it down."

"That's not it at all and I'm surprised you're not smart enough to understand that."

"Oh, so now I'm *not smart*? Okay."

He opened his mouth to speak, but no words came out. Instead, he threw up his hands and started marching back toward the cabin. "Whatever."

"So you're just going to walk away?" I called after him.

"Yep. It's way too cold out here for this nonsense."

He had almost reached the stairs of the deck when I called out to him again.

"I'm actually glad you stopped us from . . ." I struggled for the right words. ". . . from, you know."

Jackson stopped walking but didn't turn around.

"I said I'm sorry. Now accept my apology or I'll—"

He finally turned back to face me. Now he was smiling, his arms locked across his chest, enhancing his beautiful pecs.

Damn. I'll probably never get the chance to lick them again.

"Or you'll what?" he challenged me.

"I don't know. Shoot you or something."

We both couldn't help laughing.

He started walking back over to me. "Is this the way you act with all men or just with me?"

"Exactly what *way* would you be referring to?"

"Like a major hard-ass."

I pressed a finger to my chin and looked skyward. "Now that I think about it, this behavior is pretty much reserved for you."

"Lucky me," he said, chuckling.

We both stood there awkwardly, the body heat from the night before threatening to erupt again despite the near-freezing temperature.

"I like you a lot, Mackenzie Cunningham, but the time isn't right. It *has* to be right."

I nodded.

After another few moments of uncomfortable silence, Jackson's face brightened. "There's something I want to show you, but it's cold as fuck out here. Let me go grab a jacket."

I pointed to his feet. "And a pair of shoes too."

Jackson was in and out of the cabin in seconds. "Follow me."

We ambled along a path, then veered off into deeper brush. He swiped branches out of the way as we went. When we stopped a few minutes later, he pointed to a colorful patch of flowers, so vibrant it looked as if a rainbow had parked itself in the middle of the woods.

"Wow! Those are beautiful. What kind of flowers are they?"

Jackson shrugged. "I have no idea."

I slipped my phone out of my pocket and snapped a picture before we turned back toward the cabin. "I'm going to look them up. Maybe they're—"

As we neared the clearing, I felt myself being yanked backward. Next thing I knew, Jackson had pinned me against a tree, so close I could feel his chest rising and falling with every breath.

"Did you hear that?" he whispered.

"Hear what?" I whispered back.

My pulse raced as I strained to hear what Jackson had heard.

"Somebody's driving onto my property," he said.

"Do you have dog ears or something? I don't hear a thing. Maybe it's a deer or some other animal. Why don't we—"

"Shhh." He placed a finger to his lips. "Come this way and walk very lightly."

He released me and took us in another direction, to a spot that gave us a view of both the front and back of the cabin.

We stopped several yards away and hid behind a tree trunk almost as wide as a car bumper.

A Range Rover pulled to a stop and three armed men dressed in camouflage and black masks spilled out. Toting guns almost as big as they were, they wasted no time kicking in the front door and storming inside. Even from a distance, we could hear glass breaking and wood splintering as they rampaged through the cabin.

In a matter of seconds, the men flooded back outside, guns at the ready, and started visually scanning the area. Jackson and I ducked back behind the tree.

"Find them!" one of them ordered. "They have to be here somewhere!"

The men took off in different directions, one of them heading straight toward us.

Jackson and I looked at each other, our eyes communicating without words.

Then we ran for our lives.

Chapter 45

JACKSON

Mackenzie and I sprinted through the woods, away from our invaded cabin, dodging trees and vaulting over rocks. We heard the footfalls and shouts of the gunmen, but neither of us dared to glance back. We just kept running. No destination. No sense of location. Just pounding forward with the single goal of putting distance between us and our pursuers.

I'm not sure how much time passed before somehow, despite the fear pounding in my chest and blaring in my ears, I noticed the silence.

"Wait," I hissed to Mackenzie. "Hold up."

We both hit the brakes. As we gasped for air, we listened. The shouts and footsteps were gone. All we could hear were the serene sounds of nature.

After narrowly evading death, the music of life seemed especially soothing.

Mackenzie bent forward, still struggling to catch her breath. "I think we're good."

I nodded, my chest heaving from the workout. "They're probably already headed back down the mountain. They can't risk exposing themselves, even out here."

We were in a dense thicket of trees and brush. No paths, recognizable landmarks, or visible clearings.

"I don't get it," Mackenzie said.

"Get what?"

"How in the hell did they find us?"

"I wish I knew."

"Wait," Mac said. "Please tell me you paid cash at the pizza place."

I shrugged. "Naw, I used my—"

"Super-secret alter ego credit card?" she asked, her tone more than critical.

When the realization hit me, my stomach dropped. That was very likely how they'd found us. That card was supposed to be untraceable. But Roxanna had said these guys were good.

I sighed, then boldly faced her and waited for the inevitable verbal dropkick to land.

Instead she just stared back with a puzzled look. "Why are you looking at me like that?"

I scratched my jaw and turned away. "Go ahead. Let me have it."

"Let you have what?" Mac asked.

"Hold on. You mean you're not going to get on my case for breaking my promise?"

"What are you talking about?"

"I promised that you'd be safe at my cabin. I screwed up. I'm sorry."

Mackenzie locked her arms across her chest. "I'm a big girl. We're in this together." She went quiet for a beat. "But you're right, this is all your fault."

"What? See, I knew it. I knew you'd—"

It wasn't until she flashed a devilish smile that I realized she was joking.

"You're too easy." Mackenzie chuckled.

"Having fun, are you?" I couldn't believe the scale of the mess I'd gotten us into.

"Do I need to remind you we're lost in the middle of nowhere?"

The smile vanished from her face. "Lost? What do you mean, lost? You live here."

"No. I *occasionally* spend a few days at the cabin. And when I do, I don't wander deep into the woods."

Mackenzie scanned the surrounding landscape. "Are you telling me you don't know where we are?"

"Calm down." I pointed into the distance. "I'm almost sure if we go that way, we'll hit a road."

"*Almost sure*? That's it?"

Ignoring her, I pulled my phone from the pocket of my sweatpants to see if I could pinpoint our location.

"It's dead," I said with a frown. "Please tell me you have yours with you."

Mackenzie retrieved her phone from the pocket of her jacket, then groaned. "I've got juice, but I can't get a signal."

"Which means my *almost sure* is the best we've got."

With that, I started walking. "You coming?"

Mackenzie groaned again, but followed me.

My hunch was right. After about a two-mile hike, we emerged from the woods onto a two-lane mountain road that had a decent flow of traffic. We tried to wave down a car or truck, but time after time a driver would slow down, then speed off once he got a closer look at us. I'm not one to frivolously play the race card, but I'm also not oblivious to reality. It took close to an hour before a trucker with Arizona license plates finally picked us up.

The nice but overly talkative Latino trucker dropped us off in downtown Los Angeles near Union Station. We then took a Metro Rail train to a friend's condo about a mile away. She traveled quite a bit and had given me the code to her door so I could keep an eye on the place.

Mackenzie questioned the wisdom of this move, but other than a hotel, we didn't have many other options. Besides, we needed a new ride. I stored my '68 Shelby Mustang beneath a custom double-layered tarp in the building's underground garage. I didn't love the idea of using a classic car on a case, but it was safer than trying to book another rental.

"Nice place," Mackenzie said as she entered the condo, riveted to the twenty-foot-high picture window. She ogled the Italian leather couch, marble coffee table, and high-tech entertainment center, all the while nodding approvingly.

"This place has hints of you written all over it. I'd bet good money that you lived here with your *friend*"—she raised her hand to make air quotes—"at some point in the past, right?"

Damn, how'd she figure that out so fast? "Something like that."

"You sure she's not going to mind me being here?"

"She's out of the country."

"Since you have keys to the place and store your car here, sounds like this is an ongoing situation."

"Not exactly. *Intermittent* might be a better word. We have a very clear understanding. No strings."

"You're such a dog."

"Excuse me?"

"You have a woman in your life, yet you're constantly hitting on me."

"I don't have a woman in my life. It's not that kind of relationship. Some women don't want or need to have a man on lockdown. And I'm not *constantly* hitting on you."

"You're right," she said. "Not constantly. Intermittently."

I couldn't help but laugh.

Before I could invite Mackenzie to make herself at home, she kicked off her shoes and flopped down on the couch.

Our plan was to wait until nightfall to break into Severino's office. Until then, we'd just lie low and pray our pursuers didn't track us here.

I joined Mackenzie on the couch. Not close enough for things to get touchy, and not so far away that it felt awkward. And for a while we just sat there. Savoring the quiet and the absence of thugs trying to kill us.

Mackenzie finally spoke. "You ever break into a place before?"

"No. You?"

"Nope. But I've studied how to pick locks on YouTube," she bragged.

"Me too," I said. "I even bought a set of lockpicks."

"Wow!" Mackenzie said, grinning.

"From lockpickworld.com," we said in unison.

I smiled. "We totally got this."

Mackenzie raised her hand for a fist bump, and I enthusiastically bumped back.

Chapter 46

MACKENZIE

I still say all this bullshit is completely unnecessary," Jackson griped as we parked his Mustang in an alley behind the loading dock of Severino's office building. It was close to ten and the area was completely dark.

Jackson had been complaining for the last fifteen minutes and I was half a second away from my breaking point. In order to finagle our way into the building, we'd come up with a plan to pose as elevator repairmen. At my insistence, we'd picked up some matching gray mechanics' coveralls at a costume store on Washington Boulevard. I thought they were the perfect disguise for our little B&E. Jackson disagreed. Strongly.

"But you look so cute in your little onesie," I teased. "And don't worry, nobody you know is going to see you."

"Better not. I know my baby's offended." He patted the Mustang's dashboard affectionately. "I haven't taken her for a ride in weeks and when I finally do, I'm dressed like this?"

I rolled my eyes. "As soon as we get to the bottom of this madness, you can return to your thousand-dollar suits."

"Thousand-dollar?" Jackson frowned. "I'd never wear a suit that cheap."

I laughed. "You're such a prima donna."

Since fleeing the cabin, we'd done a great deal of laughing. I got the sense that Jackson was working overtime to keep my spirits high so I wouldn't have time to think about the fact that somebody wanted us dead.

He checked his watch. "You ready?"

Nodding, I scanned the neighboring office buildings, searching for cameras, which was nearly impossible to do in the dark. These days, it was hard for anyone to commit a crime without being picked up on somebody's camera. Building surveillance systems were as common as insulated windows, especially in a newer buildings like the one housing Severino's office. But we couldn't be concerned about that right now. Our lives were on the line.

As I opened the passenger door, Jackson was already popping the trunk and grabbing his tool bag, which was mostly stuffed with balled-up newspapers.

My heart started to pound as we ascended the loading dock ramp. We must've set off motion sensors because the area suddenly lit up like Times Square. At the same moment, a truck pulled up and reversed toward the loading dock, and a heavyset guy holding an iPad barreled through the back door of the receiving area. He barely gave us a glance, more concerned about guiding the truck as it backed up to the dock.

Is it really going to be this easy to get inside?

We continued walking toward the back door and, miraculously, nobody stopped us. As we entered the building, Jackson and I kept our gazes straight ahead, our mouths shut. I punched the button of the freight elevator and it opened almost instantly.

We stepped inside, and just as I was about to exhale, someone called out to us.

It was the roly-poly guy with the iPad. "Where you guys headed?"

Jackson stuck out his hand, preventing the elevator door from closing. "There's a problem with the main elevator bank stopping and starting," he said, leaning his head out. Jackson's delivery was so calm even I believed him. "We're here to take a look."

The guy abruptly looked away. "Hey, don't load that stuff over there," he shouted at the truck driver. He turned back to us with a perverted grin. "Lucky you. I deal with truck drivers all day while you get to pal around with a hottie."

Jackson winked. "Please don't ever say that in front of my wife."

The guy smirked and walked away.

"He acted like I wasn't even standing here," I said, the second the elevator doors closed. "Men are such pigs."

Jackson sighed. "So true."

I punched the button for the fourteenth floor and held my breath again.

We stepped off the elevator into a small foyer, then opened a set of double glass doors that were fortunately unlocked. Inside the actual office space, the outer walls were lined with offices, while rectangular cubicles filled the center area. We started perusing the nameplates on the office doors.

"Let's go this way," Jackson whispered.

"No, this way." I pointed east. "It has to be one of the offices that faces Grand. They couldn't have thrown his body onto the street from the other side of the building."

Jackson shrugged his consent.

We walked past six offices before spotting Severino's. Turns out, it was an easy find. The door was crisscrossed with yellow crime scene tape.

Jackson wasted no time pulling out an object that resembled a metal toothpick with a handle. He slid it into the center of the lock.

"You should try the door first," I said, peeling off the tape. "It might be open."

"No way it's open," Jackson said, turning the knob to show me how right he was. It clicked open, and I brushed past him inside Severino's office.

"Damn. I really wanted to impress you with my lock-picking skills."

We closed the door behind us and turned on our flashlights. The office was spacious and aggressively efficient. The decor stylish, yet somehow cold. One thing for certain, it did not look like a murder scene. Nothing was disturbed. I shined my flashlight all around the room. The office had large, sliding glass doors that led out onto a balcony. The balcony from which somebody had tossed Severino to his death.

I made my way to a file cabinet in the corner, which was locked.

"Hey, Mr. Locksmith, show off your skills on that," I said, moving on to Severino's elegant oak desk.

Jackson fiddled with the file cabinet while I rummaged through the desk drawers. None of them were locked. The first one held pens, markers, and other supplies. I found a large jar of Twizzlers in one; another was empty. There wasn't a single document in or even on the desk.

"Got it!" Jackson said excitedly, as he opened a drawer and started pulling folders from the file cabinet. He opened a folder and used his flashlight to scan the pages.

I continued rummaging through the desk, desperate to find anything with Ashley Cross's name on it. I took a stab at trying to sign on to Severino's desktop computer, but guessing his password was like trying to guess how many nose hairs he had.

"This is a complete waste of time," I muttered. "We're not going to find anything in here."

"Will you please stop your bitching and just keep looking?"

I grudgingly went back to Severino's desk, pulled out the middle drawer again, and reached farther back to make sure I hadn't missed anything.

"Whoaaa."

"What?" Jackson whispered.

"I found a thumb drive," I said, holding it up.

"That could be anything," Jackson said dismissively. "Severino wouldn't just leave something incriminating in his unlocked desk."

"Maybe. Too bad we don't have a computer to look at it."

"Who said we don't?" Jackson pulled a thin laptop from his tool bag and handed it to me. It barely weighed a pound.

"Where'd you get that?" I asked, turning it on and sticking in the drive.

"Borrowed it from my friend's place. Had a feeling we might need it."

In seconds, images of Ashley Cross appeared on the laptop screen. Images of Ashley Cross having sex with Lucius. The same videos Roxanna had managed to download from Ashley's cloud account.

"Whoaaa," I said again. "So Severino has a connection to Lucius? Really?"

Jackson scratched his head. "Maybe he was—"

The sound of footsteps coming down the hallway immobilized us. As they got closer, I dashed underneath the desk while Jackson splayed his body against the wall behind the door.

The door swung open and a flash of light engulfed the room. "Hey! Anybody in here?" a voice called out.

From underneath the desk, I could see the guard's flashlight circling the room. My panicked breathing sounded like a foghorn in my ears.

"There's nobody in here," said another voice. "This is the tenth office we checked. Everybody knows Marty hits the bottle. He didn't see any elevator repairmen. As lazy as he is, I'm surprised he even called us."

"Yeah, okay. Just let me check behind the door."

Before he could, Jackson shoved the door forward, slamming the guy's face against the doorframe, sending his flashlight rolling across the room.

"Owww! What the fuck?" The guard fell to his knees and grabbed his now bloody nose. His scaredy-cat partner took off running down the hallway.

"Let's go!" Jackson yelled, jumping over the cowering guard.

In our race to get out, Jackson and I practically got stuck in the doorway. We charged at top speed down the corridor.

"The stairwell is over there," I said, pointing to the far corner of the building.

We powered through the stairwell door and hurtled down the stairs. As we rounded the first landing, a door burst open above us.

"Here they are!" It was scaredy-cat, now back with reinforcements. The two rent-a-cops racing to his aid appeared more formidable.

"Stop!" one of them shouted. "Stop now!"

"Jump!" Jackson yelled at me, then leapt the entire flight of stairs to the lower landing.

I did the same, and somehow didn't break a leg.

"Come on!" Jackson urged. Side by side, we continued pounding down the steps. With every floor we conquered, we could hear footsteps behind us. But from the sound of the guards' breathing, one of them would have a heart attack before they caught up with us.

"This way," Jackson yelled, after opening the heavy stairwell door onto the first floor.

"No," I said, already moving in the opposite direction. "The loading dock's over here."

He hesitated, then followed me. When we pushed through the door onto the loading dock, no one was in sight. We raced our way to the Mustang, and before I could close my door, Jackson was screeching off.

"We could've been arrested for burglary. But at least we found that thumb drive."

Jackson didn't respond. Several seconds ticked by before he finally turned to look at me, his face plastered with that sexy playboy grin.

"And that's not all," he said, whipping out a piece of paper from his coveralls with a magician's flourish.

"What's that?" I asked.

"Severino's home address."

Chapter 47

JACKSON

Turns out Severino had the Kardashians for neighbors. Well, kind of. His Spanish-style mansion was located in Calabasas, less than a mile from the estate of America's favorite reality TV family. I didn't mention this bit of trivia to Mackenzie because then I'd have to confess that *The Kardashians* was a guilty pleasure of mine. No way I was giving Mac that kind of ammunition.

We parked across the street from Severino's house and killed the engine. The house was completely dark and appeared unoccupied, which was what we'd hoped for since the mob lawyer wasn't married. And, oh yeah, he was dead too.

Still, Mackenzie and I sat there staring out at Severino's behemoth of a house, deciding it was best to wait and watch for a bit.

During the drive over we'd pit-stopped at a gas station and dumped the coveralls. It was a relief to look like me again.

"I was wrong," I said to Mackenzie.

She turned to look at me. "Of course you were. You're always wrong. What was it this time?"

"The whole elevator repairman costume ploy. I gave you shit

about it, but turns out it worked pretty well. Also, thanks for not saying *I told you so*."

Mackenzie smiled. "I told you so."

"Funny."

"Now it's your turn," I said.

Mac's smile vanished.

"My turn?"

"Where're my props for getting Severino's address and having that laptop handy?"

Mackenzie chuckled. "Seriously?"

I lowered my head and faked a pout. "No *good job*? No pat on the back? Nothing? I feel neglected."

Mackenzie's brows furrowed. "I really can't tell if you're joking or not. So, just in case . . ." She leaned forward, so close our lips almost touched. "Good job," she whispered.

For the record, I *was* kidding, but, *man*, that near-kiss had me going. The warmth of her body, her soft scent, made me want to pull her into my arms and kiss her properly.

"Better?"

Mackenzie's voice snapped me out of my reverie.

"Uh, yeah."

She checked her watch. "We've been here more than twenty minutes. Zero movement. Zero lights. I think we're good."

"Okay. Let's do it."

We climbed out of the Mustang and hurried across the circular driveway to the front door. There were only two other estates on the block, both dark as well and too far away to present a real threat of us being spotted. I hoped.

As I pulled out my lock-picking tools, Mackenzie stopped me. Again.

"Try the door first, remember?"

"People may leave their offices open, but not their homes." To prove my point, I twisted the knob, but it didn't turn. "See? Now, watch the master."

I went to insert the lockpicks again, but Mackenzie grabbed my arm. "Wait. There's an alarm." She pointed to a red sticker on a nearby window.

WARNING! THESE PREMISES PROTECTED BY A MONITORED ALARM SYSTEM.

"Yeah, I saw that. Could be just a decoy sticker. Could be the real thing. We'll soon find out."

"And if it's the real thing?"

"You wouldn't believe how many people neglect to set their alarms before leaving home."

"And what if they have a silent alarm?"

"That only happens in the movies. People want alarms that make enough noise to wake up the neighbors." I held up my lock-picks. "May I proceed?"

Mackenzie waved to the keyhole with the flourish of a game-show hostess.

I inserted the picks, quickly getting a feel for the tumblers and the correct amount of tension. With a click, the lock succumbed. Taking hold of the doorknob, I glanced at Mackenzie with a hefty dose of bravado. "Here goes nothing."

I turned the knob and pushed open the door.

We waited. Only the soothing sound of silence.

A moment later, we stood in Severino's impressive living room. To avoid making our presence known, we left the lights off. Moonlight through tall windows would have to do.

Severino might have been a piece of garbage, but, like Lance, he had good taste in interior decorators. The home was stunning. Custom furnishings. Huge art pieces. Finishes of the highest quality. We'd just walked into a home worthy of an *Architectural Digest* spread.

"Who says crime doesn't pay?" Mackenzie muttered as she soaked in the luxury. "Now I hate him even more."

We found Severino's study at the end of a long hallway lined with framed photographs of hallways. Nice touch. Made me wish my place had a long hallway so I could steal the idea.

In the study, Severino's mahogany desk looked like a museum piece.

Mackenzie and I weren't all that careful as we conducted our search of Severino's study. If a vase or painting crashed to the floor, oh well. Was this behavior petty? Hell no. That asshole had tried to kill us.

In the end, we didn't find one shred of anything that might lead us to whoever was pulling Severino's strings. We were about to leave the study and head for the bedroom when Mackenzie pointed to a framed photograph on the wall. "Check this out."

In the photo, Severino stood smiling alongside three other people.

The first shocker was seeing Ashley Cross in that photograph. She wore a pretty blue dress and a bright smile. She looked so full of life. But we already knew there was a connection between Ashley and Severino. This simply confirmed it.

The real stunner was the couple standing next to them.

Why in the hell was Severino pictured with Congressman Martin Vanderpool and his wife, Abigail?

Chapter 48

MACKENZIE

I planted myself next to Jackson on a sectional sofa the size of a tanker truck in Severino's great room. The shock of finding Ashley pictured with Severino and the Vanderpools had hurled us into silence, our bodies and minds apparently overtaxed by this entire murderous ordeal.

I was about to say something when Jackson got up and walked over to a shiny, mahogany-glazed bar that stretched from one end of the great room to the other. Stocked with a boatload of pricey booze, the bar looked as if it had been transplanted from a high-end hotel.

"What are you doing?"

"Exactly what you think I'm doing. Pouring myself a scotch."

Jackson turned his back to me as he took his time surveying Severino's extensive collection of alcohol.

"I've never seen so many brands of scotch in one place." His voice gushed with a childlike excitement.

Our search of the rest of Severino's house had come up empty and I was anxious to leave. It was one thing to break into somebody's house, but another to hang out like we were renting an Airbnb.

"We need to get the hell out of here and dig up some new leads."

"What we need is a break. And anyway, it's not like Severino's about to walk through the door. He's dead. Remember? And he apparently lived alone."

"The police are going to search his home at some point. We shouldn't be here when they show up."

"Chillax. We'll bounce as soon as I have a drink."

"Are you nuts? Alcohol is the last thing we need right now."

He glared at me over his shoulder. "It may not be what *you* need, but a drink is exactly what *I* need. I think better when my mind is relaxed."

I sank deeper into the couch and pressed the back of my head against the cushy pillow.

"Fine. Then fix me a drink too."

I closed my eyes, sucked in a deep breath, and slowly let it escape. I was hoping some deep-breathing exercises would soothe my shattered nerves.

"And for the record," I said, "scotch isn't my drink of choice. If you were half the suave playboy you think you are, you would've remembered that from the last time you got me drunk."

"First, *I* didn't get you drunk. Second, how do you know I didn't remember? Here."

When I opened my eyes, Jackson was standing over me, arm extended, glass in hand. As my eyes landed on the green-tinted liquid, a big smile consumed every inch of his handsome face.

"Apple martini, right? Lucky for you Severino just happened to have some green apple liqueur to mix with the vodka in the bar's refrigerator."

I tried to resist, but I couldn't help smiling back.

"So how many points do I get for that?" Jackson asked.

"A couple," I said, taking the drink.

"Is that all?" He took a sip of his scotch and stood there. "You know, you really need to work on your attitude. If you lost just a tad bit of your edge, you might be . . ." His words trailed off.

"I might be what?" *Fuckable*, I almost said.

Jackson didn't respond to my question. He just stood there, staring at me like he wanted to slurp me down too. He finally joined me on the couch.

I said, "While you lubricate your mind, is it okay if we at least discuss the case?"

"But you haven't touched your drink. At least take one sip."

I did as he asked . . . and winced. It was strong.

"Too strong?"

"A little, but it's good." I wasn't lying. Despite Jackson's heavy hand, the drink was delicious. I took another sip, then set my glass down on the oddly shaped steel and glass coffee table in front of us. "Can we talk shop now?"

"If you insist." Jackson leaned back, crossed his legs, took a sip of scotch, then said, "Shoot."

"I was thinking, since Ashley was living such an extravagant life-style with no evidence of a real job, I'd say she probably had a sugar daddy."

"Or two," Jackson added.

"But I suspect she earned her real living by blackmailing wealthy and powerful men, men like Vanderpool. That would explain all that expensive video equipment in her apartment. She definitely didn't have a problem documenting her trysts on camera. We've seen the video of her and Lucius. And we know that Severino had seen the video of her and Lucius. But this time, her plan backfired and she ended up dead."

Jackson nodded in agreement. "Vanderpool had a lot to lose if Ashley exposed him. He's a powerful, wealthy, right-wing politician who's a stone's throw from the White House. Everybody thinks he eats and drinks the Bible, but the truth is, he's not just cheating on his ever faithful wife, he's getting freaky with a black woman half his age. Severino was no doubt his fixer. The guy he hired to get rid of the evidence."

"Except they couldn't find the video she'd made," I added. "That's why they killed Lance and Ashley."

"And that would also explain why they're after us," Jackson said. "That's why they tore apart the cabin. They must think we have it."

"That all adds up," I said.

"Told you I think better when I'm relaxed. Apparently you do too."

Jackson raised his glass, ready to underscore the point by clinking glasses—but when I picked up my glass and reached out, he snatched his glass back.

"Wait," he said. "Something doesn't fit. If Severino was Vanderpool's fixer, why would Vanderpool kill him?"

"Maybe the congressman decided he couldn't have *any* loose ends, not even his right-hand man," I said. "Vanderpool has spent the last decade building his political power base. He couldn't afford to have a Michael Cohen out there who knows where all the bodies are buried. Literally. Anyone who could threaten his bid for the White House had to be eliminated. Anyone."

"But why hire three PIs just to kill them?" Jackson mused. "That doesn't make sense."

"Perhaps that wasn't the original plan and things just got out of hand. They wanted that video. Not us."

"Okay," Jackson said. "And?"

I took another sip of my drink as an idea slowly began to take shape.

"We know that Ashley and Lance were tortured, right? Assuming the killers were after the video, I can't see Ashley enduring the pain. She would've spilled her guts."

"True," Jackson said.

"What if she turned the video over to Lance and he tried to do a little blackmailing of his own?"

"Yeah, Lance was sleazy enough to backstab a client like that. But I can't see a blowhard like him holding up under the pressure of torture any better than Ashley."

"The guy was so out of shape, he probably died of a heart attack before they could get anything out of him."

"So what are you saying? Lance had the video, but died before he could tell them where it was? That's a really big leap."

"Not that big, since Lance was tortured and killed and Severino's goons are still searching for the video. It makes sense."

"Kind of." Jackson set his drink down and took a few moments to think. "Okay, if Lance did have the video, where is it?"

"Knowing Lance, he would've kept it close, somewhere at his home or office," I said, my mental gears turning.

I suddenly shot to my feet. "I think I know where to find the video!" I was practically jumping up and down.

"What, all of a sudden you're psychic or something? How could you possibly know that?"

"Remember when we were in Lance's office? I saw a wall safe behind his desk."

"A wall safe, huh? That's interesting."

"Damn right it is. And I'd bet anything there's a flash drive in that safe, like the one that contained the Lucius video. That would be the perfect place to put it. With all his goons protecting the strip club, Lance probably felt secure stashing it there."

"Hmmmmm."

Despite Jackson's expression of doubt, I could tell from the hesitancy in his voice that he was slowly coming around to my way of thinking. Suddenly he nodded.

"I do like the way your brain works, little lady."

I flinched. "Please don't call me that again. Ever."

Jackson laughed. "No, seriously, I think you might be on to something. You think Crystal will let us take a peek?"

"We'll just convince her that if the evidence is in there, she should give it to us so we can turn it over to the police. By doing that, she'd be avenging her boss's death."

Jackson pressed three fingers to his temple. "Crystal was Lance's confidant. He probably told her everything. If she knows Lance had irrefutable evidence that Ashley and the family-values congressman were getting busy, she could very well be the next dead body that crosses our path."

The realization that Jackson might be right sent a terrifying chill through me. I wasn't sure I could handle another dead body falling from the sky.

I sat back down and massaged the back of my neck. The stress, the booze, the sleep deprivation, the mental exhaustion were all taking their toll.

Jackson walked over to a stereo near the bar and turned on a relaxing jazz station. "Let's just take a quick power nap and then head over to Lance's place."

I was too tired to protest. We took opposite ends of the couch and quickly fell asleep.

I have no idea how long I was out, but I woke up blinking against sunlight that streamed into the room. Only when I tried to lift my head to glance at my watch did I notice that I was nuzzled against Jackson's chest, and he had his arms around me.

What the hell?

He was fast asleep. Breathing evenly. The slow heaves of his chest like a gently rolling wave. Admittedly, being wrapped in Jackson's embrace felt nice. Soothing. But the last thing I wanted was for him to wake up and find us snuggling. As I tried to slowly peel his arms from around my body, he moaned and snapped awake.

Still clutching me tight, he blinked at me groggily. "What are you doing?"

"Me? You're the one hugging me like a big teddy bear."

"True. But you don't seem to mind." He smiled. "Hey, did we sleep like this?"

"It's almost seven," I said, glancing at my watch. "We should—"

A tiny woman wearing a maid's uniform entered the living room and immediately started waving a broom and shouting at us. "Get out! I call *policía*! Get out! Out!"

Jackson and I scrambled to grab our stuff and bolted.

Chapter 49

JACKSON

Mackenzie and I tore out of Severino's house, grateful that we'd been discovered by Severino's housekeeper and not the police.

"You think she called the cops?" Mackenzie asked as my Mustang sped along Highway 101, headed in the direction of the Lucky Lancelot.

I shrugged. "Naw. That woman doesn't want to be involved with the police any more than we do."

Mackenzie glared over at me from the passenger's seat. "Why do you keep staring at me?"

"How can I be staring at you? I'm driving."

"You keep looking over here. Like there's something on your mind."

There was something on my mind, all right. That we'd been all warm and cozy on the sofa. I could get used to that.

"See! You just did it again. Stop being weird."

"Did you sleep well?" I asked. "I know I did."

"Shut up."

I laughed and returned my focus to the road.

Mackenzie's phone, which was sitting on the center console, rang with Snoop Dogg's "Who Am I?" as the ringtone.

I glanced at the screen. "Who's Winston and why does he get a special ringtone?"

She smiled big. "So you're the jealous type, huh?"

The phone continued to ring. Mac didn't pick up.

"So who is he?" I pushed.

"None of your business."

"Of course it's my business. We just slept together."

"Ha-ha."

Once the phone stopped ringing, she listened to the voicemail message.

"Put it on speaker," I said. "I wanna know what kind of dudes you deal with."

She laughed. "You're so annoying."

"Come on, was that your dude or not?"

Mackenzie rolled her eyes, then grudgingly replayed the message on speakerphone.

"Hey, sis. You know I'm pissed at you, right? You left us hanging for dinner Saturday night. The guy I wanted to introduce you to was really disappointed he didn't get a chance to meet you. Call a brotha so we can schedule another date. I'm not letting you off the hook."

"*Call a brotha*? Your parents didn't have enough money to send him to Princeton too?"

She laughed. "Actually, he's a Harvard grad *and* an orthopedic surgeon. He just gets off on talking like he's from the 'hood."

"No shit? So if we hadn't been on the run, would you have shown up for your blind date?"

"Probably not. My brother and his wife are always trying to set me up."

"Sounds like they're just looking out for you."

"I can look out for myself."

"By groping men while they sleep?"

"Just drive."

We made a stop at a McDonald's and scarfed down coffee and Sausage McMuffins. We had some time to waste, so I we stopped at CVS and picked up a throwaway phone so I could check in on Nicky.

"How you doing, baby?"

"Okay, Daddy."

"Have you been practicing for your second shot at the belt test?"

"Yep. Every day. I'm going to nail it for sure this time."

"I have no doubt you will. And afterward we're going out for Starbucks and ice cream and pizza."

Nicole giggled. "Mom will never go for that. Plus we'd get crazy sick."

"You, maybe."

Nicole and I chatted and laughed a little longer. When I finally hung up, Mackenzie gazed at me with a strange look.

"You okay?"

"Nope," she said. "I guess now I'm the jealous one."

"Jealous? Of what?"

"Your relationship with your daughter. My parents never had time to take me and my brother out for ice cream or pizza. That was left to our nanny. They had too many court appearances, banquets, and award dinners to attend."

I didn't know what to say, so I didn't say anything.

"So were ice cream and pizza big parts of your childhood?" Mac asked.

"Not even. My mom never had extra money for treats like that. She worked her butt off to make sure the lights stayed on. I didn't want my daughter growing up like that."

"No father in the picture for you?"

"Nope."

I appreciated Mackenzie for picking up on my discomfort and not digging any deeper.

"I hope we can get these thugs off our backs and wrap this case up soon," I said. "There's no way I can miss Nicky's next belt test."

"I'm ready to put all this behind me too. I'm not sure when my mother's biopsy is, but I really need to be there."

We arrived at the Lucky Lancelot a little before nine. The lot was empty and the strip club was closed, which was no surprise considering the time of day. But we were banking on someone showing up soon since the club opened in a couple of hours for the lunchtime crowd.

So we parked and waited. Ten minutes later, a well-used blue pickup truck wheeled into the lot.

As we jumped out of my Mustang and hurried across the lot, I instantly recognized the female bartender who was unlocking the club's front door.

"Do you remember us?" Mackenzie asked. "We were here a few days ago to meet with Lance."

The bartender responded with a bored nod. "Sure. Kind of. Anyway, if you haven't heard, Lance is dead, so—"

"I know," Mackenzie interrupted. "We're actually investigating a case related to his death, and—"

"Investigating?" Her gaze went from me to Mackenzie and back again. "You two are cops?"

"No," I jumped in. "Private investigators."

"No shit," she said, looking us up and down. Her suspicious glare implied that we weren't dressed the part. "Like on TV?"

"Yep." Mackenzie smiled, then held up a twenty-dollar bill. "We just want to ask you a few questions."

The bartender turned up her nose. "Seems to me the PIs on TV do a lot better than that."

Mackenzie pulled out another twenty. The bartender hunched a shoulder, plucked the bills from her hand, then pushed open the front door. "Come on in."

"Before we talk, we'd really like to take a quick look around Lance's office. Can you help us?"

"No way, José," she said, flicking on the lights. "I like this job. The tips are great."

I took out a fifty.

"I said no," she repeated, barely glancing at the bill.

A voice to our rear—an irate voice—interrupted our bribe fest.

"How dare you come here at a time like this."

It was a puffy-eyed Crystal. She was dressed in all black, black pants, black turtleneck, even black lipstick and nail polish. "Everybody here is grieving."

Based on the bartender's demeanor, I took exception to the word *everybody*.

"We're sorry for your loss," Mackenzie said, "but we really need to search Lance's office. We think there could be evidence in there that might tell us why he was killed."

"There's no evidence in his office. I already removed his files and everything from his safe."

"Where is it?" I asked.

"None of your business."

"Lance is dead, and we think his killer was looking for something in his possession," I pressed. "It would be safer for you to turn everything over to us. Or at least let us take a look at it. Having that in your possession now makes you a target."

A flash of fear widened her eyes.

"Where did you take the stuff?" Mackenzie asked.

"It's at my place," she whispered.

"You'd be smart to let us have it," Mackenzie said. "Don't put yourself between dangerous people and what they want."

Crystal bit one of her black nails, clearly uncertain about what she should do.

"I have a couple of things I need to take care of around here," she finally said. "My place isn't far. Why don't you meet me there in about an hour?"

Chapter 50

MACKENZIE

To pass the time until our meeting with Crystal, Jackson and I grabbed sandwiches and chips at a nearby Subway. I collected my sandwich and soda and was on my way back to his car when Jackson stopped me.

"Uh, sorry, but I don't allow people to eat in my car."

I didn't have the energy to respond to his narcissism, so I said nothing. I simply did a U-turn and took a seat at a small metal table outside the fast-food restaurant.

Crystal's unassuming single-story house was on a tree-lined street of similarly modest homes. Every lawn in sight was perfectly trimmed, a sure sign of a finicky homeowners' association. I was relieved when I saw Crystal's white Tesla Model 3 parked in the driveway. I'd noticed the car as we were leaving the Lucky Lancelot parking lot. The license plate had Crystal written all over it: FOXY007.

Frankly, I was more than relieved to see her car. I'd wanted to stay parked outside the Lucky Lancelot to make sure Crystal didn't stiff us and disappear. But Jackson said he didn't get that kind of vibe from her. Turned out he was right.

Jackson knocked on Crystal's front door. A bracket for a video doorbell was mounted to the doorframe, but there was no sign of the actual device.

We waited. And waited some more. Crystal didn't answer.

My gut went into overdrive. Something wasn't right.

Jackson started pounding on the door while I moved to the nearest window and tried to peek inside. Through a sliver in the curtains, I managed a glimpse of the living room. That was enough to see that something was indeed very wrong.

"Jackson, get over here."

I stepped back so he could take a look.

Jackson peered through the curtain. "What the hell? We're going in."

We both pulled out our guns, rushed back to the front door, and tried the knob.

The door swung open with ease. Not a good sign.

Crystal's place had been ransacked. Couches and chairs were turned over. Artwork slashed. Glass broken.

Somebody had reached the same conclusion that we did. That Crystal was in possession of that video.

"Where is she?" I asked, fearing the worst.

Our footsteps crunched on broken glass as we crossed the living room and started down the long hall. After peering into the bathroom and a small guest bedroom, both similarly trashed, we continued down the hall toward the closed door of what looked to be the master bedroom.

Jackson reached for the doorknob, but suddenly froze and glanced over his shoulder at me. "I have a bad feeling." Then he pushed the bedroom door open.

Like the rest of the house, the master bedroom was in shambles. Everything strewn about, as if a tornado had bounced around the room. Despite the mess, Jackson and I spotted it at the same time.

On the carpeted floor, a limp woman's hand peeked out from behind the corner of the bed. The black nail polish left no doubt.

"Crystal!" I heard myself cry out as Jackson and I rushed in and rounded the bed.

In a narrow space between the queen-sized bed and a curtained window, Crystal Douglass lay on the floor in a tangle of blood-stained sheets. A bullet hole in her head.

Jackson and I gasped simultaneously.

"Oh my God," I murmured.

Jackson dropped to one knee and checked Crystal's pulse. "She's gone."

"We need to get out of here," I said. "Right now."

"Wait," Jackson said, standing back up. "Maybe they didn't find the video."

I looked at him like he was insane. "Seriously? You want to search this place with a dead body on the floor?"

Before Jackson could respond, another voice answered.

A husky voice behind us. "Drop your guns. Now!"

Chapter 51

JACKSON

Mackenzie and I traded *oh shit* glances.

"I said now!" the voice boomed.

We had no choice but to drop our guns on the floor beside Crystal's corpse.

"Good. Now raise your fucking hands and turn. Slowly."

We did as instructed and found ourselves facing two white goons who stood just inside the bedroom doorway. Both wore shitty suits and were pointing big guns. They strode into the bedroom and stood shoulder to shoulder on the opposite side of the bed, directly across from us. Keeping the bed between us was a smart move on their part, telling me instantly I was dealing with pros.

I recognized the tall one. He was none other than the corrupt gold shield who'd attacked me at my town house. And from the way Mackenzie stared at the shorter one, it was a safe bet that he was the asshole who'd tried to kill her.

Both of their sneering mugs were made uglier by cuts and ripe bruises, courtesy of my and Mac's fists. No doubt these two jokers were about to kill us.

Never let 'em see you sweat is one of the codes I live by, so I stared down the two fuckheads as if they were pointing pencils instead of high-powered Glocks.

When I glanced over at Mackenzie, I was impressed to see panic-free eyes and tightly balled fists. *That's my girl.*

"You fellas find what you were looking for?"

Blindsided by my casual tone, they exchanged puzzled glances before Big Man answered. "As a matter of fact, we did." Wearing a snide smirk, he held up a red thumb drive. "I guess this is what you were searching for too, huh? Well, you're too late. Sorry."

He raised his gun.

"Do you know what's on it?'"

He paused and gave it some thought. Just like I expected him to. My plan was simple: the more I kept them talking, the more time Mackenzie and I had to save our asses.

"You don't, do you?" I pushed.

"Don't know and don't give a fuck," he finally barked back.

The short one chimed in: "Our marching orders were to find it, no matter what. And, oh yeah, to get rid of you two."

"Who hired you?" Mackenzie demanded. She'd picked up on my ruse and knew how to keep the ball in play.

Big Man laughed. "Do I look stupid to you?"

"Actually, you do," I said, then I turned to Mackenzie. "Don't these two look like they were kicked in the head at birth?" When I uttered the word *kicked*, I added a tad more emphasis, and surreptitiously dropped my eyes to the queen-sized bed that stood between us and our captors. All I could do was pray that Mac understood the message I was sending.

"You're right," Mackenzie said, her eyes back on our assailants. "They have to be the two dumbest-looking clowns I've ever seen."

Glaring murderously, the tall one snarled, "This conversation is over." Then both men began to raise their guns.

"Now!" I shouted.

Mackenzie and I simultaneously kicked the side of the bed with all our might.

The bed scraped across the floor and slammed into the knees of the gunmen. Both of their guns discharged, but missed, as they slammed face-first onto the bed.

Working in perfect sync, Mackenzie and I hoisted the mattress with the startled men still on it, and shoved it forward. Both men slammed backward into a dresser with a queen-sized mattress pressed to their faces.

Blind gunfire pierced the mattress as it began to fall back toward the bed frame.

As blasted feathers and foam rubber filled the air, Mac and I scooped up our guns from the floor.

When the mattress slammed back onto the box spring, the dirty cops fired where they last saw us standing. Big mistake.

Mac and I were still crouched low, aiming at those fuckers as if we were at a firing range.

I emptied my gun into the tall one and Mac emptied hers into the short one.

Kind of poetic.

The two cops, both riddled with gunshots, tumbled onto the mattress and slept forever.

"Oh my God," Mackenzie said breathlessly.

We both stood up. Panting. Staring at each other with wide eyes.

"Good plan," she finally said.

"Glad you got it."

"I wasn't sure," Mackenzie said, holstering her gun, "but the way you said *kicked*, it sure sounded like a plan."

"I know, right?"

I had a weird feeling in my stomach. Obviously I was relieved that we'd survived, but two other people hadn't. We'd just killed them. There was a wild look on Mac's face that told me she was close to crumbling.

"We have to hurry," I said.

The neighbors would've heard the gunfire. The average police response time in Los Angeles County was seven minutes. That gave Mackenzie and me about three minutes to find that thumb drive and bounce.

Assuming the drive would be on the mattress, we rolled the two dead cops out of the way.

It wasn't there.

We dropped to our knees and searched the floor around the bed.

Suddenly Mackenzie cried out, "Oh, no!"

I hurried over to her. "What?"

She held out her hand. "One of them must've stepped on it."

Resting in her palm were fragments of red plastic and broken microcircuitry.

Chapter 52

MACKENZIE

Approaching sirens wailed as we sped away from Crystal Douglass's neighborhood in Jackson's Mustang. Only when we jumped onto the 405 and sirens were replaced by the drone of traffic did my pulse truly begin to settle down.

Considering that Jackson and I had just gunned down two men, it wasn't surprising that I was very much on edge. I'd wanted to wait for the police to arrive and make sure they got the story straight. Jackson and I had acted in self-defense. It was them or us, plain and simple. Jackson, on the other hand, because of his law enforcement background, saw it differently. A cop killing, he explained, even the killing of dirty cops, was a nuclear event. We'd be entangled in probes, interrogations, and paperwork for months or longer. Also, without video evidence of Vanderpool's sexual involvement with Ashley, there was no guarantee the LAPD or the DA would take our story seriously. And neither of them, Jackson reminded me, were fans of PIs infringing upon their turf. Self-defense or not, we could both still end up facing murder charges. Jackson had managed to convince me that our best bet was to nail Vanderpool, then let the inevitable federal investigation of the scandal shield us from falling through any legal cracks.

There was just one problem with Jackson's reasoning. Tiny

pieces of electronics that used to be a red thumb drive were now in a small plastic bag inside Jackson's pocket. The evidence we needed to nail Vanderpool and clear our names had been completely destroyed.

Jackson saw this differently as well, and he had a plan. A long shot, for sure, but I had to hand it to the brother, there was zero quit in him.

For a moment I quietly watched him drive. His jaw set. His forearms bulging as he worked the steering wheel. Narrowed, determined eyes. Mr. Jackson Jones had never looked more attractive to me than he did at that very moment.

Finally I said, "You really think there's a chance the video can be recovered?"

Never taking his eyes from the road, Jackson nodded. "If Roxanna can't do it herself, she'll know someone who can."

Thirty minutes later, instead of Bel Air, we were cruising along what had to be the richest street in Brentwood, and that's saying something. Jackson wheeled his Mustang into the cobblestone driveway of maybe the biggest mansion on the block. This was where Roxanna had retreated after her Bel Air palace was invaded.

"She calls this a safe house?" I said, as Jackson pulled to a stop outside the front door.

He shrugged. "Hey, the lady lives well."

Roxanna, sporting a pink jumpsuit for some reason, greeted us at the door like a worried mother. She actually patted Jackson's cheeks. "*Moje láska*, you alive. So good. So good." Then she kissed me on the cheek. "I much worried about you two!"

"We were worried about you too," I said, moving in for a hug. "What happened after we left?"

"More thugs come. Tried to get into my safe room, but it very secure. I call for my Czech friends. They come quick and the thugs run away. My friends bring me here."

"I'm so sorry we brought all this down on you," Jackson said.

"No worry. Roxanna is big girl."

He hesitated. "We need your help again. With this."

Jackson handed Roxanna the plastic baggie containing the smashed thumb drive.

She took one look at it and said, "Why you give me garbage?"

"There's a video on that drive of Ashley sleeping with Congressman Vanderpool. I was hoping you could recover it."

Roxanna raised an eyebrow. "I work with computers, yes. Not witchcraft."

"Could you at least try? This is very important. It could break the case for us. Please."

Roxanna smiled and patted Jackson's cheek again. "Anything for my *milacid*. Of course, will try. Come, come."

We waited in Roxanna's plush, all-white living room, sipping chilled vodka, while she slipped off down the hallway. Both of us were too nervous to exchange more than a few words. Twenty minutes later Roxanna returned carrying the pieces of the smashed drive in a small plastic tray.

"Sorry. Won't work. Too bad for you Ms. Ashley never put video with congressman on the cloud. Then I could get them easy. But this—" She handed Jackson the tray of tiny parts. "This only the FBI could fix. Maybe."

Jackson winced as if he had just been punched.

I said to Roxanna, "So what you're saying is, it's impossible to recover the video."

"For the FBI, maybe no. For Roxanna, much impossible."

I turned to Jackson. "Okay, I guess we have no choice but to go to the police. It might get sticky, but once the FBI—"

Jackson pounded his fist into his palm. "No. There has to be another way."

"Don't you have a contact at the FBI?" I asked him.

Jackson ignored my question and turned to Roxanna. "You have, like, a thousand connections. You don't know anyone who could help us?"

Roxanna's eyes grew serious. "No one who would help Americans. Sorry."

Jackson punched his palm again. "Damn it."

I reached over and grabbed his arm. "Jackson, listen. We can—"

"No, you listen," he snapped. "We go to the police, we go to jail. Got it?" With that, he groaned and buried his face in his hands.

"Look," I persisted, "nobody wanted to see the look on Vanderpool's face when we showed up with that video more than me, but without that video we're out of options."

Jackson's head shot up, eyes wide with sudden inspiration. "That's it."

"What's it?"

A knowing smile appeared on his face and his eyes went even wider. "I know how to get Vanderpool. I have the perfect plan."

I'd never seen Jackson this elated. He almost looked high. I couldn't be sure if he'd snapped or had truly hit on something.

"Okay. Would you like to share?"

Showing no sign of having heard me, he turned to Roxanna. "Turns out your particular skills are going to help us after all."

Roxanna's brow tightened. "How?"

"Yeah, how?" I demanded. "What's this perfect plan of yours?"

"Actually," Jackson replied with a chuckle, "you already know it."

"Jackson, if you don't spit it out right now, I swear I'm going to choke you."

"Don't you get it? The plan hasn't changed at all. We're going to show Vanderpool our video evidence."

There was no longer any doubt. Jackson Jones had finally lost his mind.

Chapter 53

JACKSON

Mackenzie was sitting in the passenger seat of my Mustang, fussing my ear off. But she had no idea how skilled I was at blocking out unwanted noise.

"What you're about to do is nuts."

"I disagree. And I'm doing it. So please just stop your bitchin'."

She locked her arms across her chest, a move that I hoped meant she was giving up the fight.

Ever since I'd told her where we were going, she had done nothing but complain. During the entire ride, she'd been like an annoying Chihuahua tugging at the hem of my pant leg, refusing to let go.

As I pulled into the underground parking garage and turned off the engine, she started up again.

"Jackson, I'm telling you, this is a bad move. We need to go to the feds with everything we know and let them handle things."

I was already climbing out of the car, hell-bent on what I was about to do.

"If you're not down with this, stay your ass in the car. I'll handle it by myself."

"You're such an arrogant prick," she muttered, trudging behind me as I headed toward the garage elevator.

"There you go again. You just can't seem to get my *prick* out of your head, can you?"

I stepped into the elevator car and pressed the button for the third floor. Mackenzie didn't follow me in. Instead, she stood just outside, glaring at me, as if her stare could will me into changing my mind. As the elevator doors began to close, she dashed inside.

"Jackson—"

I held up my right index finger as if I were scolding a child. "Enough. There's nothing you can say to convince me not to do this, so put a lid on it." Then I couldn't resist adding, "Black women never know when to give it a fuckin' rest."

Mac's hands reflexively gripped her waist. "Who do you think you're talking to? You—"

The elevator doors sprang open, dumping us squarely in front of the massive REELECT REPRESENTATIVE MARTIN VANDER- POOL FOR US CONGRESS sign.

I stalked up to the reception desk before Mackenzie could get revved up again. There was a different young woman manning the desk this time, but just as perky and professional as her pre- decessor.

"I'd like to speak to the congressman," I told her.

"*We'd* like to speak to the congressman," Mackenzie corrected me, then planted her forearms on the granite countertop.

The woman flashed us a practiced smile. "Do you have an ap- pointment?"

"Nope," I said. "But I'm sure he'll want to see me."

"See *us*," Mackenzie interrupted again. "Mackenzie Cunning- ham and Jackson Jones. We're private investigators. We met with the Vanderpools a few days ago. Like he said, the congressman will *definitely* want to see us."

The woman apparently detected the tension between us. How

could she not? Her smile faded as her eyes darted from me to Mackenzie, then back to me. Instead of picking up the phone, she slowly rose from her seat. "Just give me a second. I'll go see if the congressman is available."

As she disappeared down the hallway, I turned to face my companion. "Two seconds ago, you were complaining about me coming here. Now you're all up in my Kool-Aid acting like this was your idea. Make up your friggin' mind."

"I'm just trying to make sure you don't screw everything up."

I shook my head. "I was actually enjoying this little caper with you. I finally got you to let your hair down, but then you had to go mess things up by morphing back into the uptight babe who claimed I stole her booth."

"You're such an—"

"Asshole," I said, finishing her sentence. "Yeah, I know. You need to come up with a better go-to word."

Before she could fire back, the receptionist reappeared. "I'm sorry, but the congressman isn't available. If you'd like to make an appointment, his schedule is fairly open next month."

"What about Mrs. Vanderpool?" I asked. "See if she's available."

"She's out of the office." The girl puffed out her B-cups, trying hard to appear assertive, though clearly uncomfortable in that role. "So you'll have to leave."

"We're not leaving," I said. "Go back there and tell the congressman we have an important message for him from Ashley Cross. The dead Ashley Cross. And tell him we have it on video."

The girl's cheeks glowed red.

Mackenzie shook her head as the receptionist dashed back down the hallway. "You're making a big mistake," she whispered.

"We shall see. I'm betting on Vanderpool being the kind of guy who'll cower and sing like a bird when he's cornered."

"And if he doesn't, you'll have played your entire hand. The police or the FBI should be handling this. Not us."

Seconds later, two men—two very large white men in dark suits—lumbered toward us.

"Secret Service?" Mackenzie asked in a low voice.

"Nope. Suits are way too cheap. And congressmen don't get Secret Service protection. He's not president yet. And if I have anything to say about it, he never will be."

Could they be the dudes who'd tried to hunt us down at the cabin? I was beginning to think Mackenzie might be right. Maybe this *was* a mistake.

The taller of the two men stepped forward. "Please follow me."

Instead of being taken to the congressman's office, we were led down a hallway I hadn't noticed during my last visit and into a small conference room a good distance away from the main part of the office. Eight chairs were scattered around an oblong oak table. Other than a landline phone perched on a pedestal in the corner, there was nothing else in the room. There were no windows, nothing on the dark-gray walls, and no other exits.

"Have a seat," goon number one said. "The congressman will be with you shortly." He walked out, joining his buddy in the hall, and closed the door behind him.

Mackenzie glanced around. "This room is soundproof."

I took a few seconds to conduct my own inspection. She was right. So Congressman Vanderpool had his very own situation room. I pulled out a chair and took a seat. Mac walked around the table and sat down opposite me.

"You have your gun on you, right?" Mackenzie asked.

Of course I had my gun on me. But I refrained from hitting her with a surly comeback because I'd picked up on the genuine anxiety in her voice. It was the same anxiety blazing a trail across my chest.

"Yup," I said. "What about you?"

She nodded.

"You got bullets in yours?" I quipped.

I waited for a smart-alecky reply that didn't come. She just smiled at me, a response that told me she recognized the seriousness of our situation.

At times, this chick could get under my skin like an ugly, painful rash. But when the going got tough, she knew how to set the bullshit aside and handle her business. I really dug that about her.

A good fifteen minutes passed without anyone coming into the room. Fifteen minutes without a word between us.

"I pride myself on my intuition," Mackenzie finally said. "And right now, it's telling me that something not so good is about to go down."

I agreed with her, but couldn't bring myself to tell her that. Being confined in this cramped, soundproof room only heightened the uncertainty of our situation.

We both flinched at the sound of the door opening.

The congressman stepped inside, his face etched with fury. "Please wait outside," he told his two boys in black.

"What now?" he demanded once the door was closed. "You really frightened my receptionist. Why are you here again?"

I took a quick glance at Mackenzie. Despite her disagreement about my renegade move to come here, her eyes told me that she was with me. So I got right to the point and proceeded to back the congressman into a very tight corner.

"We know all about your affair with Ashley Cross," I said.

"And we also have proof of it," Mackenzie chimed in. "On video."

The congressman's face flashed confusion. "That's ridiculous. I wasn't having an affair with Ashley or anyone else. Adulterous activity is not what I stand for. Is this some kind of extortion ploy?"

I had expected surprise. Or fear. Or guilt. But his expression was pure bewilderment.

"We didn't come here for money," I said. "We just wanted you to know that we know you killed her. You're going down for murdering Ashley, as well as Lance Brooks and your henchman Antonin Severino. Lance's coworker Crystal Douglass too."

The congressman's face contorted as if he'd just smelled something foul. "Are you out of your mind? I didn't kill that girl or anyone else."

"Maybe not personally," I continued. "But you had them killed." I pointed toward the door. "Were the guys out there the ones who did it for you?"

"This is insane. Is this some kind of joke?"

"We know Ashley was blackmailing you," Mackenzie joined in, rising from her seat.

Following her lead, I stood up as well and angled a shoulder against the wall.

"Blackmailing me? Nobody was blackmailing me. What in the hell are you talking about?"

This guy had some serious acting chops. He really looked as if he was telling the truth.

The door flew open and Mrs. Vanderpool rushed inside, closing the door behind her. "What's going on? Why are you two back here accosting my husband?"

The congressman turned to his wife. "Abigail, they're accusing me of having an affair with Ashley, but I swear I didn't. And they're trying to pin her murder on me too." He was almost in tears. "Three other murders too."

Mrs. Vanderpool gasped. "This is outrageous." She turned to the congressman. "Honey, you don't need to be involved in this nonsense. I'll handle this. Why don't you go back to your office."

The congressman hesitated, then stalked out of the room.

"He can deny it all he wants," I bluffed, "but we have your husband on video."

Abigail Vanderpool didn't blink. "No, you don't. I know my husband. There's no way he was involved with Ashley. He's a good Christian man. He would never dishonor his marriage vows. And to accuse him of killing her and three other people is preposterous."

"Okay then, take a look at this." I pulled out my cell phone and tapped the screen.

Mrs. Vanderpool silently watched the video of the congressman and Ashley in bed without blinking, as if she was examining every frame. When her eyes turned back to me, they were stone cold.

"Do you think I'm stupid?" she said. "My husband never lies. If he says he wasn't sleeping with Ashley Cross, then he wasn't. I know where he is every second of the day. There's no way he had an affair with her."

I chuckled. "Then how do you explain this video?"

Now she was the one laughing. "That's obviously one of those deep-fake things. My husband has a very large birthmark on his right hip. The man in that video does not. So this little scheme you cooked up to blackmail the next president of the United States isn't going to work."

Now it was Mac and me who were thrown off-kilter. A baffled gaze ricocheted between us as my mouth fell open, exposing my astonishment.

When I'd asked Roxanna to take one of the videos of Lucius and Ashley and use deep-fake technology to substitute Martin Vanderpool, I'd been convinced it would work. I had fully expected the video to get us a confession out of the congressman.

Mac looked at me. *I told you this trip was a mistake* was written all over her face.

But if Ashley wasn't sleeping with the congressman, what was on that video everybody was searching for? Why were Ashley and Lance dead? And why were their killers hunting us down?

"Okay, I admit it. The video's a fake," I said, improvising a new play on the spot. "We're saving the real one. It's the one your goons rampaged through Crystal Douglass's house looking for, killing her in the process."

Mrs. Vanderpool flinched, then composed herself.

I took her reaction as a tell. I was on to something.

"The other video is real and it's under safekeeping," I continued.

Again, I saw just a flicker of something in her eyes. Was it fear? Or maybe that was just wishful thinking on my part.

"I don't believe a word you're telling me. If you had anything, you'd produce it," she challenged me.

Mrs. Vanderpool had just given herself away. *If you had anything, you'd produce it.* If she and the congressman really had nothing to hide, she would've said as much. I needed to keep my foot on the gas.

Before I could think up another tactic, Mac stepped in and pressed the pedal to the floor.

"And by the way, we know it was *your* antics, not your husband's, that you were trying to cover up," she said. "But don't worry. We'll keep your little secret. For now."

This time I was sure that flash in Mrs. Vanderpool's eyes was panic.

"We'll give you some time to think about all this," I said. "But you *will* be hearing from us. And from the police too. There's no way you'll ever convince us that you and your husband weren't behind the murders of Ashley and Lance, not to mention Severino and Crystal. And once the FBI sees that video, your husband's bid for reelection—and for the presidency—will be over."

Suddenly Mrs. Vanderpool closed her eyes and lowered her head. When she looked up again, her whole body seemed to slump in defeat.

"That stupid little bitch ruined everything!" she hissed. "Ashley wasn't blackmailing my husband, she was blackmailing me. I was the one she was sleeping with."

Chapter 54

Before Jackson and I could react to Mrs. Vanderpool's startling admission, the door sprang open and the congressman charged into the room. His hands were balled into tight fists and a thick vein throbbed at his temple.

"What did you just say?" he shouted at his wife.

Mrs. Vanderpool was nearly catatonic. "I . . . I . . . Martin, dear . . . you need to wait in the other room."

"Did you forget that I can hear everything going on in here from my office? Are you telling me you were having . . . *sex* . . . with Ashley? How can that be?" he said, seemingly baffled by the idea of two women engaging in a sexual relationship.

She reached for his forearm, but he snatched it away.

"Martin, please. Just calm down," Mrs. Vanderpool pleaded. "Ashley meant nothing to me. The stupid little girl was in love with me. When I refused to run away with her, she vowed to expose our affair."

"So you're . . . you're a lesbian?"

"Of course not. But I do like to experiment. And Ashley was a very beautiful woman. In the beginning, she saw me as a mother figure. Then things just got out of hand."

"Do you realize what you've done? Everything I've worked for is over," he moaned, nearly in tears. He was no longer a poised politician, but a devastated old man.

Mrs. Vanderpool glared at her husband. "Everything *you* worked for? *I* made you who you are. You'd be nothing without me."

"Well, I'll definitely be nothing now. Do know how my supporters will react when they find out? I can't believe you betrayed me like this," he whimpered. "You betrayed our children. You betrayed God."

"I can fix this, Martin," she said, tugging his arm and refusing to let go. "No one else has to know."

I glanced over at Jackson. He was no longer casually leaning against the wall.

"So *you* had Ashley killed?" the congressman asked. "And those others too? Because Ashley was blackmailing you?"

"I spent the last twenty years of my life preparing us for the White House," she insisted. "You think I was going to let some naive little girl put that all at risk? She was stupid enough to believe I'd give up being first lady to be with her. But I told you I can fix this and I will."

She snatched the door open and the two Secret Service wannabes lumbered into the room, guns drawn.

Mrs. Vanderpool pointed at me and Jackson. "Pat them down."

"Hands where I can see 'em," one of the men ordered, his weapon pointed at us. "And stand over there next to her," he ordered Jackson.

Once Jackson was by my side, the other man took our guns and placed them on the far end of the table, far out of our reach.

"Abigail, what are you doing?" The congressman's face was twisted in horror.

"Shut up, you idiot," she yelled. "I'm saving your ass. Just as I always do. Take their phones too," she ordered her henchman.

The man slid both of our phones across the table toward Mrs. Vanderpool. She checked them and saw that mine had been recording everything that had just happened.

"Smart girl." She glared at me as she deleted the file. "But not smarter than me."

I watched as she took the additional step of deleting the recording from the trash bin too.

Jackson and I were both speechless. Neither of us could've predicted that Mrs. Vanderpool, not her husband, was the mastermind behind this chaos.

"Where's the flash drive?" She stepped up to Jackson, staring him down.

"Back at my office," Jackson lied. "In my safe."

"I don't believe you. That flash drive is a valuable piece of evidence," she mused. "If you do have it, you probably wouldn't let it out of your sight. So maybe you have it with you now. Or maybe it's in your car."

She started patting Jackson down herself, checking all of his pockets back and front. She walked over to me and did the same. Nothing. She was about to turn away, when a sly smile crawled across her face.

At that instant, I wanted to throw up, but struggled to maintain a blank expression. "If I were you," she said tauntingly to me, "I know exactly where I'd hide something that valuable."

She snatched up my shirt, reached into my bra, and pulled out the small plastic bag holding the disassembled thumb drive.

"Found it!" she said with sheer glee. She threw it to the floor and started stomping it with her heel. When that didn't do the job, she placed it on the table and grabbed the telephone receiver from the pedestal. I watched in horror as she pounded the remnants of the drive into smithereens.

Mrs. Vanderpool exhaled as she turned back to her goons, who still had their guns aimed squarely at us. "Shoot them," she ordered.

"Abigail, no!" the congressman cried. "You can't do this. You can't kill anybody else."

"Shut up!" she screamed.

The congressman turned to us. "I'm so sorry. I didn't know. I swear I didn't."

"You're so weak!" Mrs. Vanderpool shrieked, a deranged look in her eyes. "We'll name a national park after them when you're president. Now shoot them!"

Out of nowhere, Jackson started yelling at me. "You're so damn hardheaded. I told you to leave that thumb drive in the car. I can't believe you were stupid enough to keep it in your fuckin' bra."

What? Why is Jackson . . .

It took me just a second to understand what Jackson was doing. Taking his cue, I grabbed the ball and ran with it.

"I'm not the stupid one! And don't yell at me!"

"You deserve to be yelled at. Your stupidity is about to get us killed. If you hadn't been carrying that drive, we wouldn't be about to die. There's no way they'd kill us without finding it first."

"If you'd listened to me," I fired back, "we wouldn't even be here in the first place!"

I pushed him hard in the chest with both palms and he went gliding across the table like a human bowling ball, hurtling into the taller goon, causing his gun to clatter to the floor.

At the same moment, I ducked underneath the table and scrambled to grab the feet of the other gunman. He lost his balance and fell backward, banging his head against the wall. As he wobbled about, dazed from the blow, his gun fell to the floor and I had just enough time to kick it away, out of reach of both of us.

"No, no, no!" the congressman cried out. "This is not God's will."

"Shut up!" Mrs. Vanderpool screamed. "You're all incompetent idiots!"

I was still under the table, trying to get to my feet, when a gun blast rocked the room, momentarily freezing me in place.

"Oh my God! Jackson!"

I scrambled to my feet, relieved to see Jackson standing over the man he'd just shot. The other goon appeared to be unconscious from the blow he'd suffered when his head collided with the wall. Blood pooled in a slowly expanding circle around his head.

Mrs. Vanderpool dashed for the door, but Jackson got there first, blocking her path.

"You're not going anywhere," he said, brandishing his gun at her.

I planted my palms on the table for support and tried to catch my breath.

Then I felt something icy cold pressed against my temple. My heart rate instantly climbed ten notches.

"Put that gun down," said a voice coming from behind me, but directed across the room at Jackson. "Or I'll blow her brains out."

Chapter 55

JACKSON

The congressman had hooked his arm tightly around Mackenzie's neck in a perfect wrestler's stranglehold. He was holding the gun that belonged to the dead man just steps away. His hand was shaking so badly, I feared the gun pressed to Mac's head might go off simply from the force of his tremors.

"I'm not playing around," he said, sobbing now. "Put that gun on the floor!"

I saw nothing but terror in Mackenzie's eyes. Every muscle in my body longed to run to her. To save her. To hold her.

Instead, I followed orders. I leaned forward and gently set the gun on the table. Far enough away from me to satisfy him, but not so far away that I couldn't reach it and blow his fucking brains out if the opportunity presented itself. And that was exactly what I intended to do.

"It's about time you got some balls!" his wife congratulated him. "Now shoot them!"

The congressman gazed longingly at his wife as tears streamed down his face. "Abigail, we can't do this."

"Yes, we can," she said tenderly. "They're trying to take the presidency away from us, my love."

The congressman looked at me, then back at his wife.

"Honey, listen to me," she continued. "We can fix this. I just destroyed the evidence of my affair with Ashley. These two are the last loose ends."

"Why'd you even involve us in this?" I said to Mrs. Vanderpool, hoping to distract them both and buy myself some time to figure out how to free Mackenzie.

The woman actually smiled. "I wanted Ashley found immediately, so I needed as many eyes searching for her as possible. But I considered all three of you expendable. Middle-grade PIs nobody would make a stink over if you just happened to die in a car accident or suffer what looked like a heart attack. But you had to go and mess up the plan."

"Why were we expendable?" I asked. "Because we're black?"

Mrs. Vanderpool didn't respond. She just smiled. "Unfortunately for you, Lance got greedy and tried to blackmail me once he found out about my affair with Ashley. Then you fools started nosing around. You spoiled everything."

"So what now?" I taunted her. "You're actually going to kill us with your office staff right outside that door?"

Mrs. Vanderpool didn't miss a beat. "This room is soundproof, remember? Nobody outside has a clue about what's going on in here."

"But the congressman heard everything from his office. How do you know one of your other staff members isn't listening right now?"

"Martin and I are the only ones with access to the listening devices. Once everybody leaves the office tonight, we'll get rid of your bodies." She turned to her husband with pleading eyes. "We've won. And we can still win the White House."

The congressman, still holding Mackenzie, wearily shook his head. "No, honey, it's over. Just go. Get out of the country. Save yourself."

Her face flashed with anger. "You're such a fool! We worked too hard for this to throw it all away."

"You're the one being foolish!" His tone was harsh. Forceful. "Just go!"

Still Mrs. Vanderpool hesitated. She glowered at me and Mackenzie, as if we were to blame for her predicament. Then, with a howl, she finally rushed out of the room.

I could see that the congressman had loosened his grip around Mackenzie's neck, but the gun was still firmly pressed against her temple. I prayed she didn't try any heroics of her own before I could figure something out.

My eyes met Mackenzie's and I tried to silently signal to her.

Just relax, I conveyed with my eyes. *Don't make a move.*

I was just glad Mackenzie couldn't see what I saw. A quivering, unstable man who was at the end of a very short rope. If she even coughed, that gun might go off.

"Let her go, Congressman," I said gently. "Nobody else needs to die."

"I'm so sorry," Vanderpool wept. "I never wanted any of this to happen."

"I know that," I said. "You didn't do anything wrong. Your wife is responsible for all of this. And that's exactly what we'll tell the police. Now, let my partner go."

I saw the hint of a smile on Mac's lips.

Partner. Where in the hell had that come from? We both locked eyes.

"You have to believe me," I said, taking an imperceptible step closer to the gun I'd just set on the table. "Everything's going to be all right."

"No, it's not," the congressman blubbered.

In what seemed like a fraction of a second, Congressman Martin Vanderpool shoved Mackenzie away, pressed the gun to his own temple, and pulled the trigger.

Chapter 56

MACKENZIE

Jackson and I spent the next four hours in an interrogation room at FBI headquarters in downtown Los Angeles, sharing everything we'd learned about Ashley Cross, Lance Brooks, Antonin Severino, Crystal Douglass, and the Vanderpools. By the time we walked out of there, we were physically exhausted and mentally spent.

We trudged to the elevators as if boulders were weighing down our bodies. I barely had the strength to press the button.

I pulled out my phone as we stepped inside.

"Who're you calling?" Jackson asked.

"Uber."

"I can take you home."

"Nah, that's okay."

Jackson shrugged.

The elevator doors opened and we slogged our way to the front of the building.

"It's weird," he said. "I poured all of my energy into bringing down Vanderpool, when he actually was the saint he professed to be. A saint with a sinner for a wife."

That was certainly an understatement. Mrs. Vanderpool had

been arrested by federal marshals at a private airfield only an hour after she rushed out of the office. She'd been about to board a chartered plane to the Maldives, which doesn't have an extradition treaty with the United States. Under questioning by the FBI, she'd made a full confession. Instead of spending four years in the White House, she'd end up spending the rest of her days in a federal prison.

"Well, so long, *partner*," I said.

Jackson looked down at his feet. "So you picked up on that, huh?"

"Yep. Must've been a Freudian slip."

"Probably so." He snapped his fingers. "I forgot to give you your props on that smart move."

I frowned. "What smart move?"

"Picking up on the fact that it was Mrs. Vanderpool who had something to hide."

I daintily cocked my head. "Yeah, that *was* kind of smart of me, wasn't it? I didn't know she was sleeping with Ashley, but after what Marva Dawson told us, I figured she was knee-deep in whatever was going on."

He grinned. "I can wait with you until your Uber gets here."

"You don't have to do that."

"I know I don't," Jackson insisted. "But I want to."

The cool night air felt good. We both went mute until Jackson broke the silence. "You know, it really wasn't so bad working with you."

I nodded. "Yep. Wasn't that terrible at all."

More awkward silence.

"Since you saved my life and I saved yours," he said, "I think we should at least treat each other to lunch."

I smiled. "How about dinner instead?"

Jackson grinned. "For sure."

In fact, why don't I cook you dinner? Tonight. At my place. Naked.

I was tired as hell, but not too tired to have naughty thoughts about this sexy-ass sleuth.

My phone dinged.

"My Uber's here," I said, floating toward a silver Prius that was just pulling up. "Thanks for everything, Jackson."

I climbed inside, shut the door, and refused to look back for fear that the magnetic force tugging at my heart might yank me out of the car into his arms.

Chapter 57

JACKSON

Don't you ever disappear on me like that again," Nadine scolded me. "You have no idea how worried I was about you. I was just about to file a missing person's report."

"Aw, cuz, I had no idea you cared that much."

This was my first time back at work in almost a week. Before heading into my office, I'd stopped at Nadine's cubicle to flip through the mail.

"Anything important come in?" I asked. "A new client? A check? A winning lottery ticket?"

She chuckled. "Nope. Just bills."

Continuing to my office, I opened the door and stopped in my tracks. I'd put the vandalism out of my mind.

I glanced back over my shoulder at Nadine. Yeah, she cared all right. But not enough to clean up my office.

"Uh, Nadine," I called out to her, "my office looks exactly like it did the last time I was here."

"Yeah, and?" she said.

"You couldn't clean it up? It's not like you had anything else to do while I was gone."

"That's a crime scene in there," she said, trying to keep a straight face. "For all I knew, the police were still investigating. Perhaps if you hadn't just disappeared on me with no communication *whatsoever,* I might've had an inkling that it was okay to clean it up."

I stepped inside, the remnants of the tornado conjured by Lance Brooks causing my anger to spike. But I quickly shut it down. He *was* an asshole, but he was also a dead asshole. I, on the other hand, was alive.

Hopscotching through the debris, I made my way to the chair behind my desk. My biggest regret about this catastrophe was the condition of my beloved Ernesto Basile desk. The Italian model had set me back almost five grand. It had been viciously slashed. Most of my stuff could be repaired or replaced, but my desk was a total loss.

Sitting down, I turned toward the window and spent the next few minutes watching the traffic below on Century City Boulevard.

I wondered what Mackenzie was doing right now. Probably the same thing I was. Sitting in a trashed office dreading the thought of having to clean it up.

Picking up the phone, I started to dial her number, but hung up before the first ring. I didn't want to seem too thirsty. That wasn't a good look on a dude. Mac was the one who'd offered to take me to dinner instead of lunch. I'd wait for her to call.

Hopefully, that would happen sooner rather than later.

Chapter 58

MACKENZIE

I still can't believe that crazy case you were involved in," my father said. "But I'm really proud of you."

"Thanks, Dad."

I'd just arrived at my parents' home. We were gathering to celebrate my mother's negative biopsy. There was a personal chef in the kitchen putting the finishing touches on our meal. My mother rarely cooked and ordering takeout was beneath her. Since her breast cancer scare, she'd become a committed vegan, which meant we also had to embrace meatless meals.

My dear brother had yet to show. And if he didn't appear soon, I was going to kill him. Whenever I was in my mother's presence, I needed both of my defensive linemen blocking for me.

"The whole thing sounded pretty dangerous to me," my mother said. "I'm glad I didn't know about it until after the fact. I would've been worried to death."

She was standing in the kitchen retrieving dishes from her special china cabinet.

The news that she was going to be okay was more than a relief. It made me reflect on our relationship. Maybe she wasn't totally to blame for the distance between us. I was certainly a closed book. Perhaps it was time for me to meet her halfway.

I walked up behind her and kissed her on the cheek. "I'm glad you're okay, Mom. I really am."

I couldn't remember the last time I'd kissed my mother. It was probably in high school, before I became a total renegade. Her raised eyebrows told me the gesture surprised her as much as it did me.

"Thank you, sweetie." It would've been great to give her a hug too, but she gave me no indication that she would welcome such a gesture.

Just then, Winston and Alexis walked through the door. The three of us exchanged hugs.

"Hey, Wonder Woman. You're making me pretty famous down at the hospital. I don't know many dudes who have a sister who packs a gun *and* brings down presidential candidates."

I wasn't so thrilled about bringing down Vanderpool. I disagreed with his politics, but he wasn't a villain. He was exactly who he'd presented himself to be. His only mistake was marrying a woman even hungrier for power than he was.

We settled into dinner, and the conversation was surprisingly comfortable. It felt like we were an actual family.

As hard as I tried, I couldn't stop thinking about Jackson. All night, my mind kept drifting off to something funny he'd said. His smile. His lips. His touch.

I really hoped we would reconnect for dinner. But I wasn't about to make the first move. And why in the world had I suggested dinner when he'd only proposed lunch?

A straightforward, businesslike lunch would've been much more appropriate. I didn't need to be sitting across from him in some dimly lit restaurant, torturing myself. There's no way I could get involved with a guy like that. He was too arrogant. Too much of a know-it-all. And too damn fine. It would be a total disaster.

What I needed to do was stop wasting my time swooning over him and concentrate on getting some clients through the door.

After dinner, we gathered in the media room to watch a new documentary on the civil rights movement that my parents had helped fund. After about twenty minutes, I wandered off to my father's office.

"You okay?" Winston asked, sticking his head inside.

"Yep," I said.

"You don't seem okay."

Sometimes I hated that my brother knew me so well.

"I just wanted to check out Dad's desk. Mine got trashed in the break-in, so I have to buy a new one."

"You definitely don't need a monstrosity like that."

"True. Something this big would never even fit in my office."

He stepped up to the desk and ran his fingers across it. "I'm worried about you, sis."

"Well, don't be. I'm doing great."

"You're such a liar. You're a mess, girl."

"Thanks a lot," I said. "Remind me to call you the next time I need my spirits lifted."

"You just look so sad. And lonely." Winston didn't give me a chance to deny it. "Is it the dude you were on that case with?"

Damn. Is it that obvious?

"I'm just exhausted from the case. As you know, the woman we were trying to find ended up dead. Murdered. I've been thinking a lot about her lately."

"I'm sure you did everything you could to find her."

"I did."

"Okay then, stop beating yourself up. I still want you to meet that friend of Alexis's. I checked him out. He's a good dude. And when's the last time you had a booty call?"

"Winston!"

"Stop trying to act all prudish. And it's not like you have to marry the guy. Some commitment-free smashing would do you good."

"If you don't stop, I'm going back in with Mom and Dad."

"Okay," he said, following me through the door. "I'm just saying."

I rolled my eyes. If he only knew how long it had been. Maybe Winston was right. I should just throw caution to the wind. Call Jackson. Fuck him. And keep it moving.

Later, when I got home, I picked up the phone to call Jackson, but my fingers refused to dial his number.

The truth was, I couldn't handle a one-night stand. Not with him. The physical attraction between us was way too intense. I'd never be satisfied with just a taste. I'd want more and he'd turn into an addiction, a dangerous one. An addiction that would probably break my heart.

The best thing for me to do was to put Jackson Jones out of my head.

Or at least try.

Chapter 59

JACKSON

As I watched Sensei Linton hand Nicole her orange belt, I brushed tears from my eyes and I didn't care who saw me.

"Here you go." Robin handed me a Kleenex, then used another one to wipe away her own tears.

"I did it! I did it," Nicole yelled as she ran across the dojo toward us. As usual, Robin got the first hug, then Nicole pivoted into my arms. I didn't mind always being second because my hugs lasted longer.

"Okay," Nicole said. "Now we can go get Starbucks, pizza, and ice cream, just like Daddy promised."

"Excuse me," Robin said, leveling narrowed eyes at me. "Please tell me you didn't promise her that?"

"What's wrong?" I replied, maintaining my cool. "That's a perfectly fine three-course meal."

Robin frowned and shook her head.

"Come on, Mom," Nicole cajoled. "It'll be fun. Please."

Robin's mouth took on an indecisive curl. I couldn't believe she was actually considering it.

"Better look out," I said to Robin. "Our little girl is now a deadly orange belt. Say no and she might kick your butt."

Robin laughed, then shook her head in defeat. "Fine, but you're paying this time."

This time? I always pay. There she goes again.

Nicole and I traded a victorious high-five, then set off to what I was sure would be another wonderful joint-parenting experience.

• • •

Later that afternoon, I stepped into a furniture store on Melrose Avenue after spotting a desk in the window that literally gave me chills. It was a sleek Italian model that would set me back more than eight grand.

As much as I wanted to replace my Ernesto Basile with an equally elegant desk, my bank account wasn't having it. Still, I couldn't stop staring at it.

"Dang, you have expensive taste."

I whirled around to find Mackenzie standing in front of me. Without even an instant of hesitation, I reached out and pulled her into a snug embrace. She held on to me just as tight.

Damn, she feels good.

"Are you desk shopping too?" I asked when we finally let go of each other.

"Yep, thanks to Lance," she griped. "But I'm on the other side of the store. Where the desks don't cost as much as cars."

"I'm just window-shopping," I said wistfully. "Business definitely isn't good enough for me to drop this much cash on a piece of furniture."

Mackenzie nodded. "Ditto that."

That uncomfortable silence that always seemed to appear from nowhere put a halt to our easy conversation yet again.

"I've missed being on the run with you," I said, surprised at myself for being so candid. "We made a pretty good team."

"Yes, we did."

"At least when you weren't complaining," I joked.

"I wouldn't have had to complain if you'd just placed your ego on the shelf and relied on my superior knowledge."

We both laughed, followed by another burst of silence.

I was still kicking myself for not insisting on taking her home after our meeting with the FBI. Since that night it was as if a piece of me was missing. The only joy I'd experienced since being with Mackenzie every day was watching Nicky nail her belt test. I wanted the two of them to meet, I realized.

"Well, I guess I better get back to the poor people's side of the store," Mackenzie said.

I wasn't going to let her get away this time. I couldn't remember how many times I'd lain in bed the last few weeks thinking about her, reliving our time in the cabin. Replaying how it would've felt had we acted on our feelings.

"How about I come with you?"

"Why? You think I can't pick out a desk by myself?"

"See, there you go, complaining about nothing. Maybe I just like your company."

She smiled. "Okay, fine. Maybe I like yours too."

"Really?" I said.

"Yeah. A little."

"If you like my company, why haven't you called to schedule our dinner?"

Mackenzie cocked her head. "I was going to call you. It's only been three weeks. Stop acting so desperate."

"You're something else," I said, grinning. "You really are."

"That would be true."

I followed her to the other side of the store. The desks were nice, but none of them were made by known designers.

"You like this one?" She pointed at a garish Swedish model that was only a step or two above Ikea furniture.

"Actually, not so much." I ran my fingers across the one next to it, a vintage golden oak desk, sturdy as hell, but still petite and stylish. "I think this one's more your style."

"And how would you know my style?"

I shrugged. "I don't know. It just seems like you. Do you like it?"

She nodded. "Actually, that one was my second choice."

We laughed, then I abruptly stopped.

"What's the matter?" Mackenzie had apparently noticed the smile evaporate from my face.

For a long, long beat, I didn't say a word. This moment was so perfect, I didn't want to say something that would mess it up.

As we approached the exit, I stepped in front of her and opened the door, bracing for some salty remark about her being able to open her own door.

But it didn't come. She just smiled at me. A smile that made me feel more than hopeful about our future.

I followed her through the door into the crisp evening air and walked with her to her Jeep, which was parked on the street.

I couldn't let her walk away again.

"I want to ask you something," I said, stuffing my hands into my pockets. "But I'm a little nervous about how you'll react."

Mackenzie frowned. "No, Jackson, I will not marry you."

That made us both laugh.

I steeled my nerves and plowed ahead. "I have a crazy idea."

"So what else is new?" She folded her arms and leaned back against her Jeep. Then she softened and smiled. "I'm listening."

"How would you feel about us becoming a team?"

Mackenzie smiled, but didn't speak. She took so long to respond, in fact, that my heart fell to my feet. She seemed to be trying to come up with a nice way to reject my offer.

"Why don't we discuss it over dinner," she finally said. "To-night."

I let myself breathe again.

"Sounds like a plan."

Acknowledgments

To those friends who read the early drafts of this book, Darlene Hayes, Arlene Walker, Karen Williams, Zoe Zeigler, Suzanne Miller, and Robert Brody, thanks for encouraging us and giving us your honest feedback.

To Peter Borland, our editor at Atria Books, thanks for your insight into our characters and your enthusiasm about this book. Your expert literary guidance helped us produce a better product. And a big thank-you to the rest of our Atria team, specifically Libby McGuire, Holly Rice, Zakiya Jamal, Paige Lytle, and Sean deLone. We appreciate your work in taking care of all the behind-the-scenes tasks that helped bring this book to life.

And last, but certainly not least, our agent Lucy Carson, who read the manuscript for *Sounds Like a Plan* and was just as excited as we were about seeing it in print. Thanks for making it happen. We really appreciate your motivating spirit.

Jackson Jones and Mackenzie Cunningham
will return in

SOUNDS LIKE TROUBLE

Coming from Atria Books in July 2025
Turn the page for a sneak peek.

Chapter 1

JACKSON

Despite the two armed thugs looming over me, it was a beautiful sunny morning in Venice Beach, California.

I was seated on the patio of a hip beachfront coffee shop called Drip Drop. The tiny café was part of the carnival-like collage of souvenir shops, fast-food joints, weed dispensaries, psychic parlors, and artist stalls that lined the Venice boardwalk. My loft was just a block away, so on those mornings when I felt like giving my Keurig a rest, I'd throw on some sweatpants and wander down for a freshly brewed cup of vanilla nut roast.

Prior to the arrival of my two surly visitors, I was sipping my coffee, watching the daily parade of local oddballs on the boardwalk, and strategizing about how to convince my new business partner, Mackenzie Cunningham, to double the furniture budget for our office.

A little over a week ago, Mac and I had received the keys to our new office. The 650-square-foot storefront space, located in downtown Culver City, was move-in ready. Unfortunately, Mac and I weren't ready to move in. In fact, currently the only things occupying our new place were a couple of cheap folding chairs and stacks of file storage boxes. The problem was, we couldn't agree on how to decorate the place. Mackenzie was all about function. A clean and professional look was good enough. I disagreed totally. Just as important as looking professional was looking successful. When clients crossed our threshold, I wanted them to believe we were killing it and didn't need their business. For almost a week now, she and I had visited dozens of office furniture stores in search of a happy medium with zero success. So, today I was determined to have it out with Mac. Somehow convince her to see things my way. At least, that was my plan until my two visitors dropped into the Drip Drop.

"Sorry to bother you. Are you Jackson Jones?"

Admittedly, that opener threw me. When I first spotted the two African American men approaching me in designer suits with hip-level gun bulges, I instantly pegged them as professional lawbreakers . . . aka gangsters. Detectives can't afford Tom Ford and Hugo Boss. What I didn't expect was polite gangsters. Either way, I knew these brothers were trouble, so I went for a Hail Mary.

"Nope," I said, shaking my head and focusing on my coffee. "Sorry."

The two men didn't budge or take their eyes off me.

I figured the dude who spoke first was the one in charge. He had a perfectly cropped beard and better shoes than his pal, and I was pretty sure his hands were manicured. And although he was the younger of the two—I guessed early thirties—there was an aloof certainty in his eyes, like someone who deemed himself untouchable.

"Mr. Jones," he said, "let's forego the games." His voice was even-toned and measured with an educated ring. He sounded more like a lawyer than a criminal. "My name is Prentice Willis. My father is Cedric Willis. I'm here on his behalf regarding an urgent matter."

I was mid-sip when Prentice brandished his father's name, and I damn near did a spit take. Cedric Willis was infamous. Known on the streets as Big Ced, head of the most powerful criminal organization in LA. Big Ced's crew didn't really have a name, but whispers called them the black mafia. Even the old-school Italian mob, which had slipped a rung or two over the decades, didn't screw with Big Ced's operation. His big black fist had a grip on everything, from traditional rackets like drugs, gambling, and sex trafficking to cutting-edge misdeeds like cyber scams and ransomware attacks. Over the last decade or so, Cedric Willis had launched many legit businesses in an effort to go corporate and rehabilitate his image, but everyone knew that Willis Worldwide was just a facade for a sophisticated and very dangerous criminal empire.

I couldn't imagine what *urgent matter* had caused Big Ced to seek me out, but the very idea put a knot in my gut. Trying hard to maintain my cool, I said to Prentice, "I don't believe I've ever met your father."

"You haven't. Not yet. That's why I'm here. He'd like a meeting at his office."

"About what?"

"All I'm allowed to say is what I've already said . . . it's an urgent matter."

"Oh, I see. He's looking to hire a private investigator."

"Correct."

I sighed under my breath and eased back in my chair. I didn't want anything to do with public enemy number one and now I saw a way out. I frowned and said to Prentice, "Unfortunately, right now I'm moving into a new office, so I'm kind of on a break. If it's urgent like you say, you might want to find someone else. Sorry."

I'm not sure Godfather Junior heard a word I said, because he didn't miss a beat. "Mr. Jones, if you know who my father is, and I'm certain you do, then you know on what scale he operates. This could be an enormous opportunity for you."

"Right, I get that, but—" I hit the pause button because of the way Prentice's sidekick eyeballed me. Not only was he older, but he was also bigger. An ex–football player was my bet. Seeing his jaw tighten and his hands ball into fists instantly told me they hadn't come out to Venice Beach to hear Jackson Jones say no.

"You know what?" I said, changing my tone. "Let's set a time for the meeting tomorrow. I'm guessing Big Ced—sorry, Mr. Willis—likes to sleep in so, I don't know, how about eleven a.m.?"

"He's expecting you now."

I blinked. "Now? You want me to drive there now?"

"No. I have a car waiting around the corner. It's better if you ride with us."

Time stopped briefly as I absorbed his words. Then I couldn't help myself. I shook my head and laughed.

The two men traded looks, then Prentice said, "Something funny?"

"Yeah. I thought bogart shit like this only happened in movies."

Prentice, to his credit, wasn't offended. Instead, he chuckled. "Look, my father just wants to talk. Nothing more. You'll be perfectly safe. You have my word."

I don't know why I would believe the word of a gangster, but the dude sounded legit. Also, to be honest, I was damn curious about this whole *urgent matter* business. Lastly, Prentice wasn't kidding about his old man. Cedric Willis wasn't called Big Ced because he was fat or muscular. No, he earned that nickname because everything Big Ced did, legal or illegal, he did, well . . . big. Maybe this would turn out to be a straight-up PI gig with a Big Ced–sized payday. Maybe this truly was an *enormous opportunity*.

"Okay, I'm in," I said, reaching for my iPhone. "Just let me call my partner so she can meet us there."

"There's no need to call Ms. Cunningham," he said. "That's being handled."

I almost laughed at his reference to Mac as *Ms. Cunningham.* He obviously didn't know my fiery little cohort the way I did.

"Um. When you say *being handled*, do you mean like the way you two ran up on me? Just so you know, she isn't as easygoing as I am. I mean, she might even—"

Prentice held up a definitely manicured hand. "We're wasting time. My father hates to be kept waiting."

"Sure." I left a tip on the table, then exited the patio and followed them.

For an instant I considered taking off down the boardwalk, but then I remembered that I was no longer working alone. I now had a partner to worry about . . . and count on. And she had to be able to count on me. Even if I gave these jokers the slip, there was no way to be certain what would happen to Mackenzie.

So, yes, I willingly followed two armed criminals to their car.

There's a popular T-shirt many vendors sell on the Venice boardwalk that warns: *Venice Beach, Where Art Meets Crime.*

Yeah, no shit.

Chapter 2

MACKENZIE

Standing at the base of the steepest hill at Kenneth Hahn Park, I was about to embark on my fifth and final sprint. The panoramic view of LA awaiting me at the top of the hill was well worth the grueling workout.

This secluded haven, a favorite of true fitness fanatics, was an ideal spot to get a rigorous workout without having to dart around dog walkers and baby strollers.

The park was also my go-to spot for releasing any pent-up frustration. And after a week of dealing with Jackson Jones, my agitation meter was inching into the red zone.

While I was still excited about our joint venture, I was exhausted from our epic battles over everything from office decor to billing rates to the name of our new firm. After a stalemate over whose name would go first, we finally settled on Safe and Sound Investigations. A tad mundane, yet charming in its own right.

I stretched my arms high above my head, took a deep breath, then blasted up the hill like an Olympic sprinter. By the time I reached the top, my lungs were on fire. I bent forward, gripping my thighs for support as I gasped for air.

As I rose to my full height of just over five feet, a man leaning against a shiny silver Cadillac Escalade several yards away set off some serious red flags. He was not here for a workout. He was casually dressed in a sport coat over a black T-shirt, but there was nothing casual about his hulking demeanor.

I zeroed in on his white leather tennis shoes, clearly crafted for style rather than function. The emblem on the side looked familiar, but even under duress, I couldn't tell you if the brand was Armani or Adidas. Of course, my snob of a partner would've instantly recognized them and bragged that he had two pairs still in their original shoeboxes sitting in a closet three times the size of my bathroom.

As I kept my focus on the WWE-wannabe, the SUV's passenger door opened and a woman emerged. She rounded the car and headed straight for me. Dressed in a black tailored leather blazer, her hair pulled back in a ponytail, she was probably in her midforties, but could pass for much younger.

I took a step back, letting her know I didn't appreciate people getting in my personal space.

"Can I help you?" I asked.

"My name is Jada." She smiled and extended her hand like she wanted to be my friend.

When I left her hanging, she continued, the smile still in place.

"Ms. Cunningham, my boss would like to hire you for a job," she said.

"I'm off today. Have your boss, whoever he is, call my assistant and set up a meeting."

Before continuing my stroll, I mentally ran through a few Krav Maga moves just in case the pair was looking for trouble. I also surveyed the area. The nearby picnic tables were empty. A handful of walkers were headed toward the bowl-shaped, circular walking path. If something was about to go down, at least there would be witnesses.

"Mackenzie, please wait. My boss is Cedric Willis. He needs to talk to you. Today. Now. We're here to take you to his office. He sent me to make you feel more comfortable."

That stopped me cold. Cedric Willis was what you'd call a respectable criminal. For decades, his network of underworld, political, and financial connections had shielded him from any repercussions from his myriad of illegal activities. But despite his scary reputation, that didn't give him the right to summon me to his office like I was one of his underlings.

"Tell your boss I appreciate the gesture," I said with a chuckle, "but I don't accept rides from strangers. Male or female."

For the first time, Jada dropped her smiley face. "Cedric Willis never accepts no for an answer."

Her tone was menacing now. Still, I remained unfazed.

"Exactly what kind of job does Mr. Willis want to hire me for?"

"I'm not at liberty to say. But after the meeting, we'll bring you back here," she said, reverting to friendship mode. "I promise."

"Give me the address. I'll drive myself."

I had no intention of going to meet Willis. Let him make an appointment and come to my office like most clients. His intimidation tactics were a major turnoff.

"That won't work," she said. "I've been instructed to take you to him."

My eyes crisscrossed the immediate area. The walkers I'd seen earlier were gone. If Jada instructed the wrestler dude to force me into their car, they might just get away with it. I patted the cell phone in the side pocket of my leggings, wishing it was my .38.

I purposely slowed my breathing and forced myself to think rationally. Snatching women off the street was not Big Ced's MO. It was highly unlikely that they were going to take me to some abandoned warehouse and work me over.

Jada apparently sensed that I was coming around.

"This is on the up-and-up," she assured me. "Your physical safety is not at risk."

"So where is this meeting supposed to take place?" I asked as I committed the Escalade's license plate to memory.

"Mr. Willis's office downtown. On Fifth Street."

Strangely, a bit of excitement began to bubble up in my chest. If a mogul like Willis wanted to hire me, the job would probably come with a big paycheck. I'd worked for some seedy people in the past, granted not on his scale. As long as a gig wouldn't land me in jail or a graveyard, I was usually game. A smile eased across my face. I was going to love showing Jackson up by landing our first big case.

"I'll go with you," I said, pulling my phone from my pocket. "But I have to let my partner know where I'll be."

Just in case he needs to play superhero and rescue me. Jackson would love that.

"No need," Jada replied. "Mr. Jones is already en route."

Whoa. I wasn't sure if that little tidbit was reason for relief or concern.

Jada walked over to the Escalade and swung open the front

passenger door. "You can ride shotgun." She flashed me another faux smile.

Ignoring her, I reached for the handle of the back door.

"I'll go with you," I said, climbing inside, "but I prefer the view from back here."

The story continues in SOUNDS LIKE TROUBLE
by Pamela Samuels Young and Dwayne Alexander Smith,
coming in July 2025